TWISTED FATE

THE FATE & FLAME DUET
BOOK ONE

LIZ HAMBLETON

EDITED BY
BETH HUDSON INK

COVER DESIGN BY
K.B. BARRETT DESIGNS

LIZHAMBLETONBOOKSLLC

CONTENTS

~For McNevin~
We know best friends are soulmates, and you my redheaded happy little Libra, are mine.

CONTENT WARNING

Before you read...

The Fate & Flame duet contains mature subject matter that may not be for everyone. If you are uncomfortable reading detailed, explicit, on-page romance, this book is not for you.

There are mentions of kidnapping, medical torment, and therapy. Although not described in great detail, there is mention of others taking their life or undergoing trauma.

Please be mindful when you read.

THE BOND

It was spontaneous, the discovery of the bond. One couple first
and then a dozen, all of them granted youth and health
because they touched the skin of their one true person. Their
love for each other was immediate but true, and once
bondmates found each other, they were never apart.

As the world watched in awe, two groups formed amongst its inhabitants.

Searchers and Settlers.

Searchers spent their lives looking for their bonded, and since the only way to find their fated partner was by skin-to-skin contact, everyone within reach was a candidate. It became the norm, people brushing against your body everywhere you went, but the bond was rare, and very few were granted the spark of its existence.

Settlers opted for a traditional life, finding a partner and settling down to enjoy their family. Wedding bands were replaced by tattoos, symbolizing the permanency of their choice in the face of a world obsessed with bonding.

Years went on and the business of the bond became the most lucrative enterprise. As greed often does, it bred sinister endeavors. The Genome Theory fronted as a research facility, capturing and holding lost youths, using them for torturous scientific research in desperation to find the key to the bond.

After years of going undiscovered, a competitor, NeXus, uncovered the kidnappings and infiltrated Genome's operation, rescuing hundreds of children who had undergone years of abuse.

To this day, no one knows why bondmates exist or how they find one another.

CHAPTER 1

MONTHS HELD CAPTIVE - 26

He's not the usual man that makes the rounds.

Not even close.

A nervous-looking employee with skeletal limbs and discerning eyes comes by here every day, but that's not who stands before me.

This one is broad and tall, with a muscled chest wider than the doorframe. He's so large, he blocks the light from the world outside. The sudden shift out of darkness blinds me most days, but as he ducks and turns sideways to step through my doorway, only a small halo of white crests over his head and around his body. It disappears when he's fully inside, standing straight, his head almost touching the ceiling.

They never come inside this soon.

My latest procedure was only yesterday, and I panic,

worried they'll drag me back to that white room full of needles and machines. It's not fair to go through all of that, only to face their torture again so soon.

Will this ever stop?

Solid thuds from his boots sound against the steel floor, a subtle growl emitting from his chest when he gets closer.

Oh, fuck.

I've done everything they asked, and I never complain or fight back. He's angry, and I search my memory for a reason. There is nothing but hazy recollections of waking up and going to sleep in my room.

No more, please.

I'd rather die.

I try to sit up and fail. My weakened state from whatever drug pumps into my veins makes every movement nearly impossible. The unbearable throbbing in my head when I'm finally upright almost causes me to cry out in pain, but that will only make matters worse.

They don't want reminders of our suffering.

Biting back any sound, I press myself against the wall. My gown opens at the back, leaving nothing but bare skin that turns to ice when it hits the cold metal. Someone turns on the lights, and I'm blinded, throwing my hands over my face to shield my eyes.

"Turn them off," a voice booms, the same one that growled moments earlier. It's so thick and deep that I press my palms against my face, afraid of what I might see if I lower them.

"Sorry, Seb," another man says with the click of the switch.

"Leave," the deep voice orders, and someone skitters away, shoes squeaking in their rush.

More footsteps.

Softer this time.

Cries pour in from the hallway, growing louder as someone

passes my room. A girl is sobbing, unable to control herself while a woman's voice speaks softly to her, muttering words I can't decipher.

I can't make sense of what I'm hearing. This place stays silent or we all suffer the consequences. My heart thuds from confusion and fear, and I curl my legs up to my chest, trembling so hard I feel my bones shake.

He's in front of me. I feel his presence only inches away, so close that his warm breath glides against my frigid fingertips, sending goosebumps across my skin. The tubes in my arms burn and sting being pinched from my awkward position, but I'm too afraid to move — to breathe.

"Hello there," the voice says, an unexpected greeting from the hulking man.

I don't respond, my teeth chattering and clicking in my ears.

A gentle hand touches my kneecap, and I jolt, yelping from the contact. Every time someone reaches for me, pain follows, and I doubt a man who growls will treat me any differently.

"Did you find another one?" a woman calls from the hallway.

The boots stomp away from me, and then the door slams. The bang is so loud that it echoes throughout the room, making the metal bed I sit upon vibrate. Darkness creeps in through my shaking fingertips, the room void of light.

"Fuck," the voice grunts.

Seconds tick by as a cold sweat mists my forehead, my stomach twisted in knots.

I wait, preparing myself for the worst.

"I didn't mean to slam the door. I don't want to…" His words trail off, and I hear him take in a shuddered breath before he continues. "This must be scary. I can't imagine. I'm sorry."

His words make little sense, saying things I never hear in this place.

I didn't mean to.

I don't want to.

I'm sorry.

He's on the other side of the room, his voice distant but deep, awakening something inside me. A click sounds, and light from the lamp in the room's corner shines softly through my fingertips. I clamp them shut as tightly as I can, tucking my limbs tighter against my body.

I'm a frightened animal, helpless to endure more tests... more suffering.

A lab rat.

"I won't hurt you," he promises. "Not ever."

More nonsensical words catch in his throat as his footsteps make their way back in my direction.

What he says, or maybe it's the way he says it, sends a spark of something into my heart.

A sense of hope.

I don't speak, not because I don't want to. It's that I can't make the words escape my lips, my body so frozen by fear. I'm too scared to let myself believe this person could be kind, so I stay locked in this position, unable to move or reply.

His smell wafts towards me, a woodsy scent I inhale and let into my lungs. It's the smell of outside, a place I haven't seen in years.

Will he take me... outside?

Another touch to my leg, but I don't recoil this time, allowing the warmth of his embrace to linger on my skin. My hands lower just enough to peek through, and I look down at the large fingers that curl over my bare knee, his thumb sliding back and forth across my flesh.

When I flick my eyes up, I confirm my suspicions. He doesn't belong here. There's no lab coat or badge and his eyes...

He looks at me.

They never do that.

His eyes stare into mine for endless seconds, refusing to pull away. Looking at him, that growl from earlier feels misplaced, as if it was meant for someone else.

There's no disdain from this man, and I would know. I've come to memorize the eyes of those filled with hate, or worse, indifference. There's an emptiness beyond the irises that separates what they witness from what they choose to see. When they look down at a sickly child, they only see a job. When I lay on their table, they convince themselves they're merely examining a test subject.

This man sees... me.

Another cry comes from the other side of my door, but he doesn't break his gaze. It's a boy this time, his soft wails telling me he's younger than most. I might be the oldest at sixteen.

Or am I seventeen? I've lost count.

"Mitchell, will you take this one?" a woman's voice calls from outside my room.

What's happening? Where are they taking us?

We carry on, simply looking at each other, and I notice his chest rise as he takes in a heavy breath. Those dark eyes search mine as he reaches his free hand out to my cheek, fingertips grazing my sallow skin.

I lean into it, surprising myself when I do. I want to cry, but I'm unable to find the strength. Instead, I just breathe, trying to swallow the smell of the woods into my soul, remembering how it felt to walk on the grass and touch the bark of a tree.

Hope sparks in my heart, flickering to life and setting fire to my senses.

Could this be the end?

A smile forms on my dry and cracked lips, and he does the same. It's tender and careful, letting me know there's still sorrow behind his expression. I wonder what he sees that brings him such sadness mixed with relief, but I close my eyes tightly with the realization.

It's been years since I've seen my reflection.

I don't think even I would recognize the gaunt body that sits before him.

"I'm Sebastian," he says.

I relax my limbs, letting my legs drop, and his touch moves to my thigh. My shaking hand reaches for his, and he stretches thick, warm fingers around it. It's such an odd sensation to be held with care. I almost forgot how magical it feels, how much strength it provides.

He swallows hard, the smell of the earth strengthening as he leans closer before speaking again.

"I've got you."

CHAPTER 2

THIRTEEN YEARS LATER

"Welcome to evolutionary biogenetics. I'm Professor Emry Crowe, and the drop deadline is next Friday."

My voice echoes through the room as far as the microphone will carry. Most students use headphones for the lectures and don't look up as I stand at the front of a full classroom. They don't think I see them staring down at their devices, distracting themselves with anything else, but they're eighteen, and their stealth is lacking.

It's going to be another long year.

My pants itch and the room is hot, full of everyone's curiosity and longing. My fingernails scratch down my thighs while my head drops, letting my hair fall over my shoulders.

Students shuffle in their seats, making the metal chairs squeak and moan.

I hate this part.

"Get up," I call out. A few people stand, unsure on their feet, followed by a few more. I motion my hands upward and nod my head, impatience filling my tone. "Up. Up."

They all stand, swaying in a wave before me. A sea of souls, all rocking in rhythm, and all wanting the same thing.

"I'm sure there was enough poking and prodding before I got here, but some of you snuck in through the side doors. Late." My eyes cast to a group of young men with tousled hair and dirty clothes I surmise they wore to bed the night before. "But if you don't get it out of your system now, you'll be distracted with it the entire class. And as I said, the drop date is next Friday."

Everyone perks up, ready for their chance to run eager hands over every classmate. They're young and don't know what a journey searchers put themselves through.

I roll my sleeves up, displaying my tattoo, and several students squint in curiosity at the last name, Crowe, written in scripts across my wrist.

The name I've chosen with my husband dances in their vision, and I wonder if I'm the first married person some of them have met. They know we mark ourselves with the ink, identifying our choice, but the way they look at me, I might as well have two heads.

I'm an oddity to them and to most everyone I meet. A married woman teaching the science of evolution and what brought us to this world of searcher versus settler. Some might say it's a choice, but it feels like an argument, maybe even a battle — each side desperately trying to prove their point.

There is no point.

Searchers are the vast majority, especially in this class-room. If media and politics carry on the way they have been, that will never change.

I don't give them the opportunity to ask me questions, especially not ones they won't like the answer to. "Each row has sixty-seven seats and there are sixteen rows. Row one, walk through, touch everyone, get back to your seats, and sit down. Then row two, go through everyone standing up. Hurry. We don't want to waste time because as I said, the drop date is when?"

"Next Friday!" They call out in unison.

"Very good, now—"

I don't finish my sentence before they're rushing through the people, hands running over bare skin, gleams of hope in their eyes. I huff out a breath and tap my foot, impatiently waiting for this show to be over. It's an efficient system, and one I've done every year except my first.

That first year, I managed four classes in frustration before another professor informed me I had missed a critical step. Every student thinks of finding their bondmate first, and their education comes second. Perhaps second is sex and some recreational drugs, followed by school third. Now that I think about it, food might be in the top three because all these kids do is eat and fuck and hope they find a bond.

One thing never changes year after year. The top priority is always, and will always be, the bond. The precious fucking bond that one in a million finds. Those are mathematical facts. There are under one hundred thousand attending this university, and my mind spins with the percentage of opportunity for a bonding.

It's fucking low.

There are less than sixty thousand bondmates in a world of fifteen billion people.

I think about all of this, watching these young minds scatter through the rows, their hope fading with every step. It's depressing when you think about the light in their eyes dimming as they reach the end. For so many of them, this university is the largest grouping of people they've ever encountered. They came here, wanting to find their person, and some believed they would.

The last student takes her seat with a thud, crossing her legs and bobbing her foot in frustration.

"Anyone want to drop now?" I ask, bringing my hands to my front in prayer and tilting my head. "No hard feelings."

I give them a full minute, counting the seconds in silence to myself. Two students get up, their chairs scratching the floor as they kick them back, and the door hisses shut behind them.

I clap my hands together and step forward. "Like I was saying. Welcome to evolutionary biogenetics. I'm Professor Emry Crowe, and the drop deadline is next Friday."

Alison rests her chin on her hand, smiling as I complain about my morning. The lunchroom is louder than normal, everyone carrying on about the start of the school year.

"You think you're in the right field?" she chuckles. "You seem to loathe the youth of today. I can see your skin crawling from across this table."

"Someone has to make sure they aren't inept." I take a bite of my sandwich, chewing like an animal. There's an edge to me today, and I'm taking it out on my turkey and rye. "So," I try to choke down my food and continue my rant. Alison slides a glass of water in my direction, and I take a few swallows. "Anyone bond today?"

She shakes her head. "Not even me."

I glance down at the messages on my phone.

SEBASTIAN

I love you. I hope you're having a great first
day of classes.

EMRY

Only lost two so far, but the day is young.

SEBASTIAN

Give em hell.

Hearing from Sebastian eases my tension, reminding me he'll be waiting at home, probably starting dinner when my last class finishes.

I smile at Alison and bite my bottom lip, deciding to give my attempt at matchmaking another shot. "Sebastian's brother has decided to—"

"Be a settler?" Alison interrupts.

I wipe my mouth with the back of my hand, letting the term roll off my back. It's not that I find it an insult. The words searcher and settler are common tongue, but it's her sullen tone when the word rolls off her lips. I imagine she sees the entire world in a long-distance race and the settlers stopped running, too tired to continue, but she perseveres.

"Choose a life partner," I argue. "He's decided to settle down, and I'd like to have you over for dinner to meet him."

Alison stacks things on her tray, wadding up the garbage with extra aggression. "I'm busy. There's a reception I'm getting ready for."

"I didn't even tell you the night!" I'm not finished eating, but I stack my tray, ready to chase her out of the cafeteria. "They all end up being duds — fizzers. When was the last time someone actually bonded at one of those things?"

"Just last week in Canada," Alison snips, rising from her seat with me on her heels.

"I read about that, and it was a driver taking someone home from the reception," I argue. "You're mathematically more likely to get bitten by a shark on land."

"That is not true. I believe in fate. I believe it will happen."

"Do you believe in homemade pasta?" I quip.

She groans and picks up her pace, ready to throw her lunch tray and run.

"Would you please consider dinner?" I beg. "You could spend time with me and Sebastian. His brother's just more friendly company."

Alison slows and lets me catch up to her. She knows I won't relent, and this way is less dramatic. The last time we argued on campus, we both received letters in our email and slid under our doors about how we were disturbing the student body.

If there was ever a place to have a debate, it would be a university, but not when it comes to this, the biggest money-maker in the world. The largest sponsors for this school run some of the all-nighters Alison spends every spare moment attending.

"Does he want to be a co-parent?" she asks.

"No, Alison," I lament. "He wants to find a partner, not make a baby that he only sees fifty percent of the time." There's me judging her, letting my words drip with disgust, and I hate myself for that. I don't like it when it's done to me, and I swallow hard, trying to reset my thoughts.

Not every co-parent treats their children like a paycheck, but the ones that do make me hate the entire system. They agree to create life, but then give all their time and energy to finding a bonded. Alison wouldn't do that, and I need to shake my pre-conceived notions about co-parenting and give her some grace.

She chucks her garbage and slams the tray onto the rack, crossing her arms when she spins around to face me. "Please drop this. If you have a good suggestion for a co-parent, I'm all ears. There will be some at the next few events I'm going to, and I plan to hold some interviews."

I let my shoulders drop and nod my head. "Sure. Okay."

I'm not one to give up easily, and I notice the flash of shock in her eyes when I concede. I rub my chest, hoping to erase the discomfort I feel there. There's a voice in my head telling me to keep pushing her, force her to see my side of things, but my heart aches at the thought of losing another friend. It's her life, and I need to let her live it.

"Does he look like Seb?" Alison asks, a coy smile stretching across her lips.

"What? You mean his brother?" I ask. "Yes, they look alike. I'll... I'll ask him about the co-parenting."

Alison beams a smile at me and comes up on her toes before she turns and hooks her arm into mine. We stroll out of the cafeteria, surviving another difficult conversation that I fear we left unresolved.

"How many kids left your class after they touched every-one?" she asks. We step out into the hallway to the smell of coffee. This place always smells of caffeine, and I can't help but partake when it's within reach.

"Two or three," I answer. "What about you?"

"Fourteen." She widens her eyes, and I shake my head. "But I don't know how many were truly mine." During the first few weeks of school, students come to the larger lecture halls even when they don't have the class, hopeful they'll find their person.

"We'll weed out who really wants to be here," I continue. "Big money maker, you know, overcrowding the school when nearly a thousand drop after they don't bond."

"Yes," Alison sighs, walking toward the smell of coffee. "We all know."

I bump her shoulder into mine. "I had to get one last comment in."

She smiles, grabs two cups, and hands me one. "When's dinner? There better be good wine," she says.

My heart flutters, and I beam at her, my eyes wide with excitement. It's just dinner, but who knows what the future holds for any of us.

"I've made salads," Sebastian calls out from the kitchen. "Sorry, I'm boring today. We had drills, and they took forever and I just..." He trails off, walking into the entryway with a dish towel in his hand.

"You don't have to feed me all the time, you know?" I say with a grin. "I'm an adult, and I can take care of myself."

Sebastian lowers his eyebrows and saunters in my direction, wrapping his arms around my waist and lifting me to his lips. He's taller than me by a good foot, more without shoes, and I just slipped mine off.

I'm so light in his arms, but what isn't to Sebastian? He's over six and a half feet tall and covered in brutish muscle from head to toe. The looks of the man are domineering, frightening to some, which bodes well for his job. But there's a softness to him that's only for me, his wife.

The way his muscles relax and those dark eyes soften when he sees me has melted my heart every day since I threatened to leave college if he didn't go on a date with me.

It might have been an empty threat, but I was out of options.

Men asked me out all the time, and I dated, but none of them measured up. Sebastian and I had been friends since I was sixteen, but I always wanted more. I'm glad we waited, but years of dealing with sub-par men was enough to tell me that Sebastian is the catch of a lifetime.

He's my protector and caretaker, and coming home to him every day is a joy I wish Alison would allow herself.

"I like to feed you." He trails kisses down my neck.

I kick my feet before he puts me down, letting my chest glide down his in slow motion. My nipples harden, and I blush, biting my lip and giggling. I can't believe how lucky I am to be with Sebastian. Everything I've suffered feels so far away when we're together.

"But tomorrow it's risotto," he promises. "With that wine from the vineyard where we got married."

"Pulling out all the stops on a Wednesday," I giggle.

"On our anniversary," he corrects.

I'm still on my toes as I look up at him with curious eyes. I relax, letting my heels drop and tsk at him. "Did you hit your head in drills, sir? Our anniversary is months away."

Sebastian tosses the towel over his shoulder, cups my face in his hands, and runs a thumb over my cheek. "You don't like this anniversary, but I do," he confesses.

The ache in my heart returns when I understand his meaning, and I rub my chest, the spot growing sore when the heel of my hand digs into the skin.

"Seb, it's not that I'm not happy about the day we met—"

"I know, and I'm sorry," he interrupts, tracing his fingertips down my neck. "If you don't want to celebrate, we don't have to, but that day changed everything for me — for us."

I nod and force my hand away from my throbbing chest.

"No, I want to have the dinner. I also love that wine, and I hope you have a bottle just for me."

"You have every right to get properly smashed tomorrow," Sebastian says. He brings his lips to mine and kisses me once more, his hand wrapping behind my neck, holding me there for a moment after our lips separate. "As long as I reap the benefits when you're tipsy enough."

"Always." I smile and smack my lips against his. "Now, where's this pathetic salad? I'm starving."

He's set the kitchen table even though it's just us two, and I take a seat, pulling the napkin into my lap. Like always, he'll serve us both, making sure he meets my needs before he takes his seat. I'm so spoiled, and I've grown accustomed to a life where I'm adored at every turn. Goosebumps cover my skin when I think about how he'll adore me later, ravaging my body in all the right ways, making me cry out his name and add more scratches to our wood headboard.

Seb fills my plate and gives me a kiss on the head. "Your mother called," he murmurs into my hair. My good mood deflates that instant.

"Why did she call you and not me?" I ask, even when I know the answer. Sebastian is nicer to my mother, and that's because he doesn't know her as well as I do. Grudges aren't something I like to carry. They're heavy and burdensome, keeping people in the past when we should look to the future.

I make an exception for my mother.

She's a searcher since her legs could carry her, and even when she decided to co-parent, she dragged me from reception to reception, hoping to find her bonded. That was... until it all went to shit.

To this day, I struggle to believe her side of the story, but I can't hold on to that anger. I may never know the truth, but trusting her is the path I've chosen... after many years of therapy.

She resurfaces more often now that I've married Sebastian. He's an excellent buffer for us, and she's intrigued by a man that works so closely with the government's geneticists.

That's all she knows, and that's all anyone knows except me. His work is classified, but jokes on her because my husband is the muscle of the operation, not the brain. He's smart about the things he cares about. Cooking and me, mostly, but he doesn't care about what scientific breakthroughs they make regarding the bond. Neither of us mind with any of that.

He's no closer to the answer than she is, and I wonder if telling her that would make her go away. I won't do that, even though I like to tease myself with the idea. She's my mother, and everything I went through doesn't change the fact that as much as I struggle with our relationship, I'm not ready to let it go.

"She wants to have dinner," he says. "She sent some wine over and asked when would be a good time."

"Not anytime soon," I huff. "School just started, and I just can't deal with her incessant questions. She's bound to ask for money, too." He fills my glass with a heavy pour, and pulls his chair closer to mine, resting a hand on my thigh and kissing my shoulder. Heat flushes where his lips meet my skin, softening my resolve a fraction.

"People change," he says, dark eyes softening in that way that makes me melt. "Every day."

I pick up my wineglass and bring it to my lips, inhaling the scent before I take a long sip and set it back down. All the commonalities Sebastian and I share keep us connected stronger than I imagine a bond ever would, but this moment exemplifies the key difference between us.

Sebastian carries hope in all things, and I'm grateful. It saved my life and brought us together, but that inherent optimism shields him from truths he doesn't want to admit.

"No one changes, Seb," I tell him, trailing a finger down the side of his jaw, watching the disappointment spread across his face. "Especially not searchers that have been in the game as long as her."

CHAPTER 3

THEO

"I understand it's my first week, but you hired me for a reason. Why waste time and money letting me... acclimate?" I barely bite out the word this old man uses instead of saying what he really wants, which is for me to see things his way. His company is close to ruin, and the board wants me to pick up the pieces that are left and make two cents with them. All the while, this man is telling me to take time to... acclimate.

This isn't a fucking desert. I'm not trekking up Mt. Everest.

"You can't make these assumptions without knowing the ins and outs of our day-to-day activities," he tells me.

I pull at the neck of my shirt, sitting in this suit while he wears joggers and slippers to our meeting. It's a sign of arrogance he doesn't have the right to carry. He's bleeding cash each minute, and a good portion of that goes to me. He pays my retainer daily and for good reason. You never know when the well will dry up.

"I'm reporting my findings in real-time," I say. "There's no time to waste."

He points a bony finger at me. "In your opinion."

"In my well-educated and experienced assessment, which your board of directors evaluated prior to contracting me — yes."

Fuck, this guy is grating on my last damn nerve. I'm here for two months if he can generate enough output to keep me that long. If he would take one of my fifteen suggestions, his profits would increase, or he'd at least see some profit. Their books have been in the red for three years.

I stand to take off my jacket, because if he can't even wear shoes, I don't know why I'm forced to dress like a puppet. "The revenue you could earn if you used your transports for just four events would put you in the black in six months."

"That's not what we're about, son."

His use of *son* makes me cringe from the inside out, and I curl my fingers around the top of the chair I'm leaning against.

"Principles aside—"

He laughs, cutting off my point. "Principles are all we have."

"Well, you certainly don't have money," I bite out.

He pulls his shirtsleeves up, showing his faded tattoo. He must have been one of the first from the looks of the drawing. I've been to a hundred cities in my career and all of them carry a firm divide. They might think they're inclusive of everyone's life decisions, but the landscape is clearer when you're an outsider. I see things as they are without the smog of history getting in the way.

He won't see my side when he's glaring at my bare arm. The only reason he doesn't show indignant hate toward me is because of my age. I'm still young enough to see things his way, and based on the number of hours I pull in this office, he doesn't think I'm a searcher. In his mind, a searcher would be taking every chance they could in a new town, rubbing literal elbows with anyone and everyone.

Everyone I meet needs to label me, put me in a box so they feel comfortable about where I belong. No one gets that chance because I'm out of town before any real conversations start. Being just Theo isn't enough. They need to know my motivations, but that still won't help anyone understand me.

I'm neither a searcher nor a settler, and I'm certainly not a man that needs to explain myself.

Still, I need a new approach.

"You pride yourself on being a company that believes in matrimony and the natural order of things." I take in a deep breath, feeling the tightness in my chest, running my hand across my breastbone and letting my heart find its rhythm while the old man leans back in his chair. "You believe in the family unit. Most of your workers have chosen a life partner and have children. They've chosen to... age and retire."

He nods but says nothing, a frown forming on his face because he knows I'm about to make a point he can't refute. The thud of my heart evens and calms, sending the flow of blood back in a rush.

Ignoring the wave of dizziness, I continue. "My projections have never been wrong, and they aren't this time. You own hundreds of buses, and the number one need is searcher transportation to and from reception events. If you don't take my advice and use your fleet of vehicles to make money, you'll need to cut over three hundred employees. Five months and you close the doors. That's a lot of families that will struggle. Families that can't care for each other or retire. Families who have children that might be a searcher in need of safe transportation. Like your own, perhaps?"

I'm cutting deep with that comment and it's a risk, but my

bonus is huge if I turn this place around. This man's daughter may be on the outs with him because she's a searcher, but he sends her money every month. I do my research, and I've seen the logs.

I turn to leave him with that thought, loosening my tie as I step outside.

He'll see things my way.

They always do.

I roll up my sleeves before I head out into the city. It's the common thing to do, a sign of politeness when you give people ample access to touch your skin. A bare arm is easy to brush, but long sleeves mean they have to reach for the back of your hand.

They'll touch you regardless, but it's considered rude to cover yourself from head to toe.

Even though I've done this a thousand times before, the action makes my skin prickle with discomfort. I'm opposite most people in that way, and it's helped me succeed in business. My distaste for human interaction keeps me working longer and harder, leveling up faster than anyone else.

While others go out, relief flooding their veins when the workday is done, mine fill with dread. In an office or meeting, I have control. Always ten steps ahead, I manage the room and everyone inside, using my wit and skills to command respect.

No one respects you outside those walls. They slide by, touching you without permission, scratching and poking at your skin no matter who you were fifteen minutes before.

The billionaire gets no different treatment than the homeless person, and no one cares because they're all after the same thing.

The bond.

I'm after things of value, and a million-to-one lottery ticket is worth absolutely zero. That's what the bond is because the whole charade is math, not science. There's a higher chance of actually winning the ticketed lottery. People bring home barrels of cash from that every day, and when was the last bond?

I check my phone as I walk out the door, still rolling up one sleeve with a grimace that wrinkles my face. I'm after the latest stock prices, but it's no surprise who leads the pack again. Adherence Corporation and all its subsidiaries continue to rise, and one of those companies will hold an event here this month.

They need transports, and this company needs cash flow. I stop on a street corner and prop myself against a wall, letting the heat from the sun burn my arms, and dial Robin's number.

Fuck that old man. The board can handle his temper tantrum.

"Robin." Her voice echoes down the line. She's no-nonsense, and I love that about her. Most of his board has their head on straight, but hers is at a perfect ninety-degree angle every minute of the day. I bet she sleeps sitting up, she's so stiff.

A billboard blinks in my line of sight as someone curves their walk to touch my arm. I release my fist from my pocket and let it hang as they swoop by and graze the back of my hand.

Your life mate is waiting. Are you looking?

I stare at the bright letters and clear my throat. "Adherence is holding a string of receptions in the coming weeks."

The line is silent. I haven't asked a question, so Robin has nothing to say. The simplicity of our interaction makes me smile, and the billboard blinks again.

Fulfillment is companionship.

"Your company needs to transport searchers at these events or you're bankrupt." I'm to the point, and I know she respects my candor. "I've done the research, and over ninety percent of this town is searchers. They'll find the money for an event like this."

"Did he agree?" she asks.

Another blink of the billboard and another graze of my hand by a couple, this time with a child. Co-parents, I surmise.

Give your children the edge and test.

"Of course not," I admit. "There's nothing else lined up within two hours of this city for months. It's this or death."

"I understand," she grits out. "I'll... handle him."

She might kill him.

I end the call with that morbid thought. We all die anyway, even bondmates eventually. Well, I think they will. None have died yet, but the research shows their age regressing and then slowing at a pace that would last hundreds of years.

The billboard blinks again. This time it's the beaming face of a young politician and quotes with his promises to find the key to the bond. This is probably the first time in human history where there's very little pushback about an increase in taxes. Every penny goes to unlocking this bond. I chuckle, remembering our current president's slogan.

Fate is our future, but let's figure it out.

We haven't yet, and he won't make it another term.

A row of young girls passes by me, touching my arm for a beat too long. I give them a narrowed gaze, and they rush off. Not because they're embarrassed, but because I'm not the one.

Ninety-two percent, I think to myself. That's the statistics in this city of searchers, and I bet that number is low. People employed by settler companies, like the one I'm currently contracted with, don't believe their answers to the census are anonymous and they lie.

I run my hand down my face, which grows warm from the sun, and start walking. If Robin doesn't deal with the old man, I'm out of this place in a few weeks, anyway.

My stomach growls, and I crane my neck, looking for a place to grab a bite to eat. It's been a long week, and all I've had is takeout brought into their office as I *acclimate*. It's not the last working day of the month, so some things will be open over the weekend, but the options will be sparse. I'll need to stock up just in case.

Unbearable heat barrels down on me, and I consider taking my shirt off, but no one else is bare-chested. Some towns could double as a nudist colony, stripping as many clothes as possible to increase their chances of grazing that one person.

I don't partake, but on a day like today, where sweat trickles down my back from a light walk, I would consider stripping.

Crowds circle at crosswalks, the blinking lights set to three minutes at a time, giving everyone ample opportunity to check each other like dogs. I scoff at the sight and step into a shop that's about to close its doors. They have sandwiches in the window, and they will keep in the hotel refrigerator if I order in something else.

A woman welcomes me inside by grabbing my hand. It takes everything in me not to yank it back, but I clench my jaw and force a smile instead. A group of young men find me in the aisle and all clasp a hand around my forearm before they continue shopping.

Grabbing a few sandwiches without looking at what they

are, I toss some cash on the register — too much cash — and head for the door.

"Wait," the woman calls out.

"I paid you more than enough," I say. "Keep the rest."

"My daughter's walking down from upstairs," she explains.

She doesn't need to say anymore. I'm from out of town, and she wants her to touch me. My feet stop despite my desire to run from the shop, and I take in a long breath.

"Sure," I say as I turn around and face her without flicking her off. A small victory considering the week I've had, but I remind myself that everyone is a potential connection to my next job.

My reputation is important to me, not just in business, but in life. There's nothing to be gained by being rude, so I grit my teeth and tap my foot, waiting for this mystery woman to appear.

"I know it's ridiculous," she admits.

Something ill-mannered would fly out of my mouth if I open it, so instead I cock my head in surprise, raising my eyebrows in question. The woman's wrists are bare, so if she's not a settler, she must have co-parented.

She's not too much older than me, pretty, and definitely a full-time mother, not someone who cashes a check and suffers through their fifty percent of the split. There's something about her that's maternal and friendly. I could be wrong, of course, but reading people is a large part of my work, and I know I'm good at it.

"She's eighteen, but as long as she's under my roof, I won't allow her to go to those reception parties," she huffs. "I want her to know I support her life choices, though."

"Making the new guy in town wait so she can try him out is a good way to do that." The words fly out, but they're followed by her laughter. I like this woman. She's honest and upfront, and thankfully, difficult to offend.

"I appreciate it," she says with a smile. "Do you have children?"

I shake my head no.

She raises her hands to her hips and steps closer. "It's not all it's cracked up to be in the teenage years, I'll admit, but it's the closest thing to... the bond I imagine."

I've heard that before, but I don't understand the sentiment. They describe biological children as the closest thing to a bondmate, but the problem is, the kids can't wait to leave their parents. It seems... illogical to put oneself through purposeful torture.

A young redhead bounces through a back door and rushes to my side, wrapping her thin fingers around my arm. She frowns when there's nothing but her cold skin on my thick muscles.

"Have a good weekend," I tell her. She releases her grip and storms off without a word, and I understand a bit about the teenager issues the woman was referencing.

She chokes out a stuttered, "Well, th-thank you, and here." She grabs a few packages of soup, puts them in a bag, and hands them to me. "These pair perfectly. Trust me."

I stand there with one hand on the door, another damn billboard beaming light into the shop.

What you crave is with the one of your choosing.

My conscience gets the better of me. "Ma'am."

"Moira," she introduces herself, holding out a hand.

I take it and step close enough to whisper a warning. "I'm Theo, and listen, I wouldn't let her go to the Adherence receptions until she's older. They can get... rowdy."

I stare into her eyes for a moment, our hands still gripped together. Her pupils dilate, and her mouth drops slightly with a small gasp. We've all heard the rumors, but there's something about my tone that tells her I *know*.

"But there's another company, Matchmade, that holds mobile classes for universities. Is she going to school?"

Moira nods her head. "She just started at the local college."

"Look them up. She can spend a semester traveling with some classes, and there are chaperones — lots of security. It's no more expensive than Adherence, and she'd still be going to school."

"Oh, wow," Moira gasps. "I'd never heard of it."

I release her hand and shoot her a smile. "I was a consultant for Link this year, and this company is a new branch of it. They took government grants for this idea, and it's already a big hit. It helps lessen the runaways—" I stop short, realizing I may be upsetting the mother of a young girl who is eager to find her match. Some of them are too eager, and they pay the price.

Moira agrees, and I exhale in relief, grateful she's not upset. "There have been so many. My neighbors' twin boys just ran off on a cross-country search. They were all set to go to school, and poof." She wiggles her fingers before slapping them down at her sides. "I'll look it up tonight. I owe you."

"No, not at all." I shake my head. "Let me know if you have any questions after you do your research."

"I will," Moira says. "And you're obligated to come here Monday to answer them. What's your favorite soup, and I'll make it the soup of the day?"

"Tomato," I answer. I'm not turning down her offer if it tastes as good as it smells in here. The fresh bread and spices have me salivating, ready to head back to my hotel and rip open this bag.

Moira smiles in delight at my response. "Monday," she says.

I lean against the door and step out, and the entire way home I don't understand why I told her, "I'll see you then."

I meant the words, and I know I'll be back on Monday, even if I don't understand why I'm comforted by the knowledge I'll return.

CHAPTER 4

EMRY

I wake up in Sebastian's arms when the sun and moon both hang in the pink sky. Life would be perfect if his touch was the last contact I had for the rest of my life. My body relaxes when I remember it's the weekend, and I have two solid days where we can be alone in our house, no one reaching for me or touching me without my consent.

If only it were the last weekend of the month when the entire city shuts down. We sometimes even turn off our phones, only leaving the emergency line open, and spend the entire time together, talking and making love. Those weekends are perfection, but this morning is close enough.

The sunrise from our back patio beckons me to watch it, and I smile into Sebastian's chiseled chest, turning over the idea of waking him. Reaching up to graze a finger over his lips, he leans up and puckers, kissing the palm of my hand.

"Good, you're up," I say.

"It's early," he whispers, his voice cracking from the morning. "I thought I wore you out enough last night."

A blush forms on my cheeks, and I can't stop my wide smile. "You certainly did."

Exhaustion seeps into my bones, but when there's nothing to do but drink a cup of coffee and watch the colors change in the sky, I'm willing to get out of our comfortable bed. I'd grumble and roll around on a workday, but this day is mine to do with as I please. The silk robe wraps around my naked body as I stand, noticing I'm a little sore between my legs from last night.

"You go back to bed." I kiss his forehead, and he brings me to his lips, slipping his tongue inside and running rough fingers through my hair.

"I love you," he says. His words are a promise, never perfunctory. He means them each time they're said.

I place my hand on his chest and lift myself up, tracing a fingertip along his collarbone. "Love you, too."

Why would anyone fight this lifestyle if they knew how mornings like this felt? If Alison only took a moment to try, she would see this wasn't giving up the race. It's realizing the race is for fools.

My phone sits dead on the counter, left there from the night before when Sebastian yanked me up from the kitchen table and carried me to our bedroom. I grab it along with a cup of coffee and set it on the charging station by my favorite outdoor chair.

The crisp air cuts through my thin robe, but the briskness of the morning awakens my senses more than the caffeine. I curl into my seat, resting my head back on the cushion and stretch.

A few seconds later, my phone blinks with messages and alerts, most of them from Alison. I grumble but pick it up, always worried she's been abandoned at some half-rate reception she went to last minute.

Probably because that has happened.

More than once.

ALISON

Thought you might find this interesting.

There are three news articles about bonding research. As a geneticist, I let the science behind these studies intrigue me, but as a sensible human who can do the math, it doesn't change the facts. There are too few bondmates in the world to get proper data and fewer still that offer their genome to research.

The government keeps upping their payouts for cooperation, making bonded couples the wealthiest in the world. They give some blood and who knows what else, cash in, and scientists scratch their heads.

I shoot her back the article about a couple from last week, highlighting the section where they both were out of town and met at a breakfast spot by chance.

EMRY

Looks like finding their bond mate only cost them $15.29 instead of whatever those reception companies charge. Food for thought.

Damn the early hour. She needs to get the message.

I sip my coffee when my phone pings again a few minutes later.

ALISON

Check this out

Italian couple meets by random chance after decades of searching.

She's not getting the message. She thinks we're swapping love stories, but I can't help but click the link and keep reading.

Matera, Italy — July
Lydia Morton didn't expect to find her bondmate on a girls' getaway in Italy, and if she did, it certainly wasn't when she went to visit her extended family in the small town of Matera. With a population of less than one hundred thousand, she strode through the streets with distant cousins, oblivious to who was and wasn't making contact.

I call bullshit. Women who are searchers and for decades, make certain that every new person touches their skin. I shake my head and keep reading.

When Emiliano Ricci bumped shoulders with the teacher, the spark they felt was undeniable. "It felt like fireworks inside my body," Lydia tells The World Report. "There was this bright light, and I thought there was an attack on the city because I was blind. But I knew it was something wonderful, you know. How could an attack make my world spin upside down in the most amazing ways? I felt... him, and then I knew. After attending over a hundred receptions, I finally meet my soulmate on a side street in a place I booked a week before my trip."

"I felt pulled to her," Emiliano told us (translated). "My body had to hold her and keep her forever. We are two halves of a whole, and now we can live many years together. Many more than I thought possible."

The couple has agreed to give bi-annual labs to the country, but under Italian law, they will keep their test results proprietary. Still, the results of their bonding are apparent on their faces, and friends and family are shocked at the differences.
"It's sad to know I'll get older than my father," Emilio's son told us (translated). He's fifteen and co-parented with Luna Sartori. She was not available for comment. "But I'm happy for him. Who wouldn't want to live for hundreds of years?"

I look at the picture included in the article. The differences don't surprise me anymore, but the sadness when I look into the young boy's eyes sends an ache into my heart. Does he feel his father loves someone more than him now? Is he jealous? Is he sad?

I zoom in on Lydia's before and after. In a matter of days, the fine lines around her eyes disappeared, giving her fuller and brighter skin. Her cheekbones appear more prominent with the hollows filled in. Her hands hold the starkest difference, though.

Every dark spot and vein has vanished, and the loose skin is now tight and full. Bright clear nails tip her fingers, and I zoom over Emilio's, finding the same changes.

Reverse senescence is impossible, but I'm staring at it, and after a hundred years of this, we're no closer to knowing why.

Alison's text pops up on the screen.

ALISON

Maybe you have a point.

I start typing her back when another one shoots through.

ALISON

But I'm still going to the receptions until I can't anymore.

I groan and throw my phone back on the charger, frustrated when I realize I missed the entire sunrise.

"What happened?" Sebastian asks. I scoot over in the chair and he slides in, bringing me onto his lap and nuzzling my neck. "It's too early to be throwing phones."

"It's too early for you to be awake and cooking breakfast. I smell the bacon."

He trails his fingers down my arm and I sink into the touch, letting him calm me. "You love bacon. What's the problem?"

"I've been on edge lately," I admit. "I'll be glad when the end of the month comes and we have a few extra days off."

His finger tips my face up to his, and his full lips meet mine, making my nipples peak and sending a shiver to my core.

"We have two days," he whispers into my mouth. "Let's make the most of them."

The smoke alarm goes off inside the house and we both leap up, running inside.

"Fucking bacon," Sebastian says, half laughing.

"I like it crispy," I admit, waving the smoke out of my face.

After turning on every fan and opening all the windows, the alarm turns off, with our house still standing. We eat standing in the kitchen, Sebastian popping charred bits of bacon in my mouth and making me another cup of coffee.

Even the threat of fire doesn't interrupt the peace I feel with him.

He's my home.

The workweek comes with a vengeance full of commuters, unwanted touches, and thankfully, caffeine. We make it to Friday, ready for the long weekend. Alison and I check the drop list with steaming cups of coffee in our hands.

"Eight-hundred and sixty-three," she hums into her cup. "Who won the pool?"

"Mitchell, that weasel," I answer. "We shouldn't let staff from admissions join. They can sniff out the deserters, and now I'm out a hundred dollars."

Alison laughs and leads us across the lawn. "What time is dinner?"

"Why don't you just come over after your last class?" I ask, looping an arm into hers. This week, our friendship feels like it's held together by a thin string, ready to snap if either of us oversteps. I'm hoping our dinner doesn't cause a catastrophe, but it's bound to have a hiccup or two. "We can catch up—"

"On our reading," she interrupts.

This woman sent me over twelve articles about bonding this week, and I've only responded with witty banter, dripping with sarcasm. She's said without words that she expects Sebastian's brother to come over for company or to talk about co-parenting, and nothing else.

"Is there a point you're trying to make with the incessant research? All I can determine is that the whims of bonding have no reliable data. It's random, Alison."

"I find the research soothing," she says with a shrug. "And I get the sense it annoys you." A sly smile creeps up on her face, and I rip my arm from hers, giving her a smack.

"Good conversation starters for dinner," I offer.

Alison's eyebrows shoot up, and she stumbles where the

grass meets the cement. "You'd be okay talking about bonding at dinner? With you, Seb, and his brother?"

"Why not? It's the only thing anyone wants to talk about anyway, and we all have it in common."

"But we don't… have that in common. And plus, he wants a wife," Alison argues.

"We all deal with it every day, I mean. And maybe you don't know what you want until it's in front of your face."

She purses her lips together and waves goodbye at the fork in the sidewalk without rebuttal, but she's late for her class. I won't accept a win until she's laughing at my brother-in-law's jokes and falling for his charms. I've already sent him Alison's likes, dislikes, hobbies, and dinner conversation blunders that are bound to come up. There's nothing she can say or do that will put him off at this point.

I failed to mention she's vehemently against choosing a partner, but I was honest that she attends the receptions. He does, too, or did. I'm not sure where anyone stands day to day anymore.

My classroom looks sparse compared to the first day, and I'm pleased. Students struggle with my class scientifically and ethically, and there's no room for anyone who doesn't truly want to be here.

Everyone perks up when my heels click across the wood floors, and there's an extra crane in their necks when I remove my jacket, showing the tattoo scribbled across my wrist. That topic will get discussed another day when we all know each other better.

"Good morning," I call out.

There are several grumbled responses, more alert than I expect this early in the day.

"It's drop day in case you missed it," I say, turning my back to grab the remote for our lesson. "Before I dim the lights, does anyone need to visit administration? This is your last chance."

No one moves behind me, and I make the room dark and flip on the projection. This is the group, for better or for worse, and I laugh to myself at the joke I don't dare say out loud.

A holographic couple stands in the center of the room. My syllabus always starts here for those that stick around.

"I won't bother telling you who these people are, because if you don't know, you shouldn't be in the damn class to begin with."

A few chuckles echo throughout the room, and I sit on my desk, crossing my legs and clicking on the next image. The same couple beams to light over a dozen times, years underneath their shoes while they float a few feet in the air.

"Christa Sanders and Leo Thomason came to the Mayo Clinic for separate ailments over one-hundred years ago. Who can give me a synopsis of the medical file?" I ask.

Numbers light up on my remote, signaling students who have tapped their desk buttons to answer. Good. We'll start this year with some eager learners. I call out a number and a young man speaks up.

"They both had pancreatic cancer. After undergoing the pancreaticoduodenectomy surgery, they came to the hospital for experimental treatments."

He smiles and clasps his hands at his front, content to have started off strong.

"And what commonality do they both share which affected their genome?" I ask.

The young man clears his throat. "All biological parents of Christa and Leo were treated with Emily's Oncolytic prior to their conception."

I click the remote again, and the infographic lights up above Christa and Leo's many heads. "Emily's Oncolytic was created as a vaccine for over sixteen types of genetic cancers. Emily's parents, the infamous virologists, had no way of knowing the generational effects, and we still know little about the long-term impacts."

"It eradicated cancer," a student calls out.

"It did not and do not interrupt," I snap back. "This isn't a discussion. It's a lesson."

"S-sorry," the student responds.

"Now, if you want more about the vaccine, the virology class is in another building, but this is the most important and honestly the only piece of the bonding puzzle we have. Everyone who has the variant genome derived from parents who were given the drug." I click the remote again, and the number 13,345,994,672 appears. "That's how many vaccines we delivered in a ten-year span. It's a very wide net."

Jaws drop open, gaping at the number and the couples standing before them.

"Emily's Oncolytic is within all of us, rapidly changing our genome in ways we are still seeking to understand. Christa and Leo stepped into the hospital close to death, and described the bonding as we know it today as a feeling of joining between the two when they held hands in a chemotherapy unit."

I step through the images, standing next to their admission pictures at the hospital. "This was the day the Mayo Clinic admitted them."

Hollow eyes and sunken cheeks stare back at the students. Both bodies appear skeletal, as if they're waiting for death to take them both at any moment.

"This is three days after they met," I say, waving my hand over the next image where they're smiling, and sallow skin stretches across their faces. It's not a complete transformation, but anyone can see the changes. Bright eyes look out at the classroom, and the bones jutting out days before are less pronounced.

"This is two weeks," I say, stepping to the side. It's a different man and woman to anyone that didn't know better. The only evidence of who they were is the loss of hair that's already sprouting new growth at the roots. I would guess they could run a marathon or swim across an ocean with the energy beaming out into the room.

Separate images of the couple all look the same with different clothing and hairstyles, but, as the decades pass on the dates under their feet, their youthful faces only show the slightest of changes.

"Christa and Leo are one-hundred and forty-three and one-hundred and forty-seven years old today," I declare, setting down my remote and walking through the images.

The students gape at the faces that almost refuse to age and bodies that appear stronger with time.

"Here," I point to the final image, "you see, they both have some wrinkles returning. They've volunteered for studies to help determine the aging process after the bond. They'll live about five-hundred years by our estimation."

I give the students a minute to examine the room, their eyes scanning each couple, studying the last one with awe. I'll admit I've looked at their most recent portrait for hours, memorizing every age spot and wrinkle, mirroring it to mine. They're five times my age, but they look not a day over thirty.

"Your first assignment will be your initial assessment based on your acquired knowledge, answering only one question." Everyone straightens, ready to take notes on their devices.

I ask, "Is it evolution or the vaccine? And I do not want ten pages about how it's both. Environmental agents cause a variety of changes, but that's not the question. Is it evolution or a radical event that started this process?"

I clap my hands at my front and everyone's attention snaps back to me. "We need intelligent minds like yours in evolutionary biogenetics, not just so you can be like Christa and Leo. No matter how much money people pay to test and store their blood, we're no closer to unlocking the code that brings back cellular regeneration when a couple bonds. My challenge to you this year will be to think beyond the bond. What other repercussions are in store for our children? What if there's something more than the bond that we need to uncover for the generations that live and die as humans always have?"

A few people nod while others still gape at me, surprised by what they've seen. People know of the bond, but when you live in small towns, and never see the clear picture of it like I'm displaying, it feels like magic.

I step back to my desk and flip on the lights, sending away the holographs. "Our focus will not be finding the key to the bond. I have sent your syllabus over, and if it's a disappointment to you, today's still the drop date. Have a good afternoon."

CHAPTER 5

THEO

Working with Robin this week is a relief I can't describe, even if I have some concerns that she actually killed the old man.

"He's at his vacation home with his family," she tells me on Friday. I finally asked her his whereabouts, and she informs me his daughter is with him.

"Smart," I reply and she juts her chin at me.

"What do you mean by that?" she asks. She knows exactly what I mean, but she wants her ego stroked.

I lean back in my chair, crossing a leg over my knee and rock. "You set that up. His daughter's a searcher, and you arranged some sort of reunion under the guise of his renewed contracts with Adherence."

Robin bites the inside of her cheek and looks back at her screen. "I'm sure I don't know what you're talking about."

"I bet," I chuckle. I'll need to refer her to my consulting company. They could use someone that makes things happen, especially after I'm gone.

"I think we're about done here. Fifty buses all scheduled for the reception in a week will buy you another six months, but that's just scraping by," I warn her.

"It's your job to get it better than scraping by," Robin deadpans. Her words aren't accusatory or even cutting. Every syllable this woman utters is serious, and she's right.

"Initial taxes for vendors at bonding events are steep, but it will level out. Your city has the highest rate I've ever seen, but there's still lots of money to be made," I say, closing my laptop and getting up from the table. "You keep the old man vacationing while I fix the mess."

"Done," Robin says without looking up.

Thank fuck.

I head into my office, tossing my things on the desk, and open the closet to grab some clothes and change when there's a knock at my door. My shirt is unbuttoned, but I tell them to come in thinking it's Robin who barely looks up from her laptop.

"Theo?" a shy voice asks. A young woman from marketing steps through the entryway, and when I look over her shoulder, I see the line.

"Fuck, I promised. I'm sorry. I'll come out," I tell her. Her shoulders drop in relief. I don't let my annoyances cascade onto her. It's my fault I keep avoiding this necessary task clearly outlined in my contract. "Let me change, and I'll run through you all."

"We formed a line," she murmurs. "To make it easier."

I pull open my shirt, working the buttons on my sleeves and flashing her a forced smile. "I appreciate that..."

"Leena," she responds.

"Thanks, Leena. Two minutes."

She nods and shuts the door. Although I don't think the line of workers will come through with my pants down, I lock it behind her. My heart flutters in my chest and I rub my palm against it, pushing down on the muscle, focusing on my breath.

Going through a building and allowing everyone to touch me isn't new, and in most cases, it's something I get over with by day one. These employees didn't want to make a show of it in front of the old man, and I thought with all the people that brushed by me in the hallways, everyone already got their chance. I crack the blinds in my office window and see the line that stretches down the hallway and around the corner.

Guess they didn't.

My heart finds its rhythm before I step into the hall, but it beats harder than normal, sending a rush of blood to my ears and drowning out the chatter. They walk by me while I stand with my arms exposed, hands running over my skin while I stare at my shoes. Every time I look up, I see the never-ending sea of people, so I focus on the ground, forcing myself to count my breaths and wait until it's over.

"Theo," the shy voice says again.

"Are we done, Leena?" I ask, the bite in my tone concealed as best I can manage.

"Are you okay, um..." She trails off, unsure why I'm so uncomfortable.

This company may pride itself on being settlers, but in their hearts, they want the bond and think everyone else does as well. She doesn't understand my hesitance.

"Yes, we're done. Can I get you anything?"

"No. Have a great night."

I step back into the office and grab my bag when she speaks again. "Could I ask you a question?"

I don't smart back that she just did, but nod instead while she hovers in the doorway.

"Are you a... searcher, or..."

"Neither I suppose," I answer.

She tilts her head, squinting her eyes in confusion. I'm a paradox to myself and everyone else, unsure what I am or where I fit.

"What do you want... for your future, then? To co-parent, or..." Leena asks. Each word is softer than the last.

"I want a life," I answer. "Have a good weekend."

I find her mystical expression amusing, but I don't owe her explanations. I owe myself a homemade pizza that Moira promised, and that's all that I think about when I brush by Leena minutes later and head out the door.

"She's already accepted, and I'm excited but sad, you know," Moira tells me. I'm on my fourth slice of pizza that she drowned in basil and truffle oil. It's heaven on a plate, and I'll let her drone on about her daughter forever if she keeps feeding me like this.

"Actually, I don't, but your emotions make sense," I mumble through my chews.

"Such a pragmatic man," Moira chastises. "Well, she'll be doing her studies, staying in touch with me, and meeting thousands of new people. We all win. I can never repay you for this or thank you enough."

I get the impression she knows I pulled a few strings to get her daughter accepted, but I'll never admit that. In my experience, when people know you can give them something, they never stop taking.

"Keep cooking for me while I'm here. If you can't thank me enough," I say with a smile.

Moira laughs, and it fills the space with warmth. I'm not a fan of making friends in the towns I visit. Why bother when it's a temporary assignment and my next job will keep me too busy to stay in touch? Somehow Moira slipped in, and her kindness is something I'll keep with me no matter where I go.

There's a steady pump in my heart, soft and slow, and I'm grateful for the feeling of calmness. It's rare and short-lived when a dozen people enter the shop, spot the stranger stuffing his face with pizza, and proceed to poke and prod me until they satisfy their curiosity.

"You get so tense when that happens," Moira points out.

I wipe my face with my napkin and stretch back, running my hand across my full stomach. Staring at the pizza, I wonder if I can fit in one more slice. "Doesn't everyone?"

Her eyes become saucers. "No, Theo. Most people find it exciting. You never know when it could happen."

I decide to box up the rest, sighing at Moira's response. People flood the streets with their commute home, and I'd rather the crowd thin before I'm thrust into their clutches. "I don't. Find it exciting, that is."

Moira cashes out one man, and the group leaves. She moves her attention back to me. "Are you a settler?"

"This again," I groan.

"It's a fair question," she retorts.

"Give me that towel, and I'll wipe down the counter," I say.

"One you don't want to answer?" she lifts an eyebrow.

"It's fair. It's just the second time it's come up today. No one likes my answer."

Moira taps her nails on the counter and waits, unbothered by my warning.

"I don't have a preference, really," I continue. "I don't really think about finding someone. People don't believe me, but it's the truth, as odd as that sounds."

"So what do you think about?" She's puzzled beyond belief, her face open with genuine curiosity, but I don't sense judgment. Moira wants to pick me apart, but won't turn her nose up at my harsh edges.

"Money," I answer. "Lots of fucking money. Enough money to do whatever I want, go anywhere I want."

She freezes, nails mid tap, and then a laugh bubbles from her lips, small at first, and then she bursts into a cackle. "Really? Money?"

"I'm close, too," I tell her. "Two more years, and I can retire. Live out my days in paradise. Blow every fucking penny on exuberance by myself. I can't wait."

Moira's laughter doesn't stop, and I'm joining her, my cheeks hurting. "I love it. I love the idea of someone aspiring to something under their control. That's wonderful."

Her words fill me with satisfaction. She understands and doesn't chastise my choices. For everyone in this world, it feels like the options come down to two paths. You settle or you search, but why? Being alone is a choice. Not burdening others with my bullshit or breaking someone's heart when I die, which we all we do eventually, is a choice.

I shake my head. "I only have enough for one ticket, or I'd take you with me, Moira."

The words are true because she feels like someone I would enjoy spending more time with. She listens and doesn't burden me with what she thinks I should do or say. She's the first friend I've had in many years, and a born caretaker. Her daughter is lucky to have her. So many, myself included, didn't get a mother like her.

"But what about you?" I ask her. "What do you want?"

Moira sighs, her forehead wrinkling when she thinks of how to answer. "For the longest time, I wanted a child, but now..."

"Do you regret it?" The question rushes out before I can take it back. "I'm sorry. That's not—"

"Oh, no, it's fine," she says, tossing me a towel for the counter. "Lots of people want that check, but not the responsibility. I wanted both, if I'm honest."

"Right," I say, the laughter stopping. "She's leaving, but you'll always have her."

"Maybe I'll go back on the search. I don't think I can be like you, Theo. There's a part of me that wants someone to be with forever. Even if it's not the bond. I guess that makes me..."

"The dreaded settler," I answer.

"A minority in this town," she sighs.

"By far. I've done the research. But that's because the town is young. There were some big government grants to have children here. People tend to come around to the idea of settlement after the kids grow up."

"People my age," she corrects.

"You aren't much older than me, but if you want to put a number on it, yes," I admit. "The graph declines in searchers after the peak of thirty-nine. People..."

"Give up," she deadpans.

"I don't see it as giving up when you're going after what you want," I disagree. "Motivations change with age. That's normal."

The counter sparkles after a few more passes, and I hang the towel on the sink to dry.

"You're right," she agrees. "I don't see you as someone who gives up. You're different. You're driven."

She doesn't know how right she is about me. I'm more than driven. Some might call it obsessed. I'm playing with the cards life dealt me. That's not conceding to a life alone, but accepting the fact.

There's an erratic beat in my heart when I sit back down,

and I bring my hand to my chest and pat the spot, as if the drumbeat of my palm can soothe the rhythm.

Looking out the window, I see the sun dip, and fewer people fill the street. It's time to relax all weekend by myself, free of hands and disappointed faces. I stand up and give Moira a hug.

"Do you want me to get you tickets to the Adherence event?"

"Maybe," she shrugs.

"I'll hold a few just in case," I promise.

"Theo," she calls when I grab my pizza box to leave.

"I'm taking this," I wave it at her.

"Of course, but another question." Her voice turns serious and thin. "Maybe it's the fact that my daughters leaving I don't know, but... what about your parents? You said you want to be alone, but do you see them?"

"Mom's a searcher until the day she dies, and dad's, um, he's gone. I buried him last year."

"Oh, I'm sorry. That seems so young."

I fight the lump in my throat that threatens to give away my sadness when I speak.

"It was." I turn to the exit before we keep talking about my father, the man I miss more than anything.

The billboard outside blinks, reflecting its letters across the windows of the shop and beaming the words across my chest.

Fulfillment is companionship.

"Tomato soup on Monday again," she says when I open the door to leave.

"Th-anks." The word cracks, and I rush out into the street, ignoring the hands that graze across my skin. No one asks if I'm okay as I barrel down the road, jaw tight, fighting the memories. They only care about themselves and finding that spark.

I'm grateful for the loneliness of that. No one asks what's wrong, because for someone who's touched by every passerby, I'm invisible to them all.

CHAPTER 6

"I think dinner's going well," I tell Sebastian. We're in the kitchen, grabbing dessert.

Looking back at Lucas, Sebastian's brother, I notice the smile on his face while listening to Alison continue her mortifying story about me. She's talking with her hands and about to leap out of her chair, giggles rising from her throat in between sentences.

Sebastian thins his lips and looks down the hall, examining the table. "I disagree. It's a fine evening, but Alison is doing everything she can to argue with him. She's sabotaging any hopes you're carrying around in that beautiful head of yours."

"Fuck yes, she's trying," I tell Sebastian. "But he's still here and smiling at her. He'll wear her down."

"He's not a river," Sebastian scoffs. "This isn't a game."

"Oh, you fool, of course it is." I grab the dessert from the pantry and place it on a serving tray, elbowing Sebastian off me as he tries to take over. He concedes by rubbing his palm across my ass and nuzzling my neck.

"Well, how do we know who's winning?" he asks, finally getting me to move to the side so he can fix the cake. It's lopsided on the tray, and the chef of this kitchen won't settle for anything less than perfection.

"Last man standing at the end. It's like a cage fight, but in our dining room."

"This sounds bloody," he says, picking up the tray. "I like it."

I kiss him on the mouth with a smack, and he slaps my ass with his free hand, carrying the tray around like a maitre d'. I yelp and giggle, following him with another bottle of wine.

Alison's reached the peak of the story. "Oh, you're just in time, Em. So, Emry here has been at the university three weeks at this point. She's gained the nickname Escapee Emry, but she doesn't know this. There are a few folks in the historical department that call her Evader Emry, but it doesn't stick."

I pop the cork on the wine and roll my eyes. "Neither nickname stuck," I correct her.

"Oh, hun. They stuck," she smarts back. "Anyway. Escapee Emry is crossing the grass, making a figure eight to avoid anyone touching her. Mind you, it's the third week of classes, and everyone has made it their fucking mission to get their hands on her. Students are taking bets. There's a poll amongst the professors that haven't gotten to her yet. Plans were made to lock her in the bathroom."

"Which is kidnapping," I shout.

"Not according to the law professors," Alison retorts. "So, she's walking fast, and then jogging, and then running in this crazy back-and-forth motion, trying to avoid a few kids that want to touch her. And then a few kids become three dozen. And then someone sounds the alarm because they think there's been an attack or accident or something because a pack of students—"

"Wild animals," I interrupt. "They were wild fucking animals!"

"—are running, picking up every passerby as they go, chasing escapee Emry with university alarms blaring everywhere. By the time the Dean found out what was going on, the administration made her contract include how she would no longer exhibit distractive behavior unbecoming of a geneticist of her caliber. Direct quote."

"Fuck that guy," is all I say in response.

"And they made her stand in the theater while everyone touched her."

"It was very anti-climatic," I admit into my glass of wine.

"I'll agree with you there," Alison huffs.

"I'm so sorry, Emry," Lucas says. "That's awful."

His words make Alison scoff, but my wine glass twitches in my hand, a subtle tell that my indifference is all a front.

I don't find the story funny.

We joke about it, but I'll never forget how violated I felt standing in that theater. I worked so hard to teach at the university. It wasn't just the schooling, but the mental hurdles I had to go through to get my degrees. There were days I couldn't imagine getting out of bed, but I did it, and I kept going. All of that for the faculty to treat me like an insolent child.

Sebastian takes my glass and kisses my palm. The men sympathize with how awful that was for me, but so few people understand. The thrill of having that many new hands on you should feel electrifying, settled or not, but it didn't feel that way.

"We all do it on the first day of the year, thanks to Emry. It's easier if you ask me," Alison chirps.

"Do what?" Lucas asks.

"We greet the students as they arrive on day one, by the entrance arch," Alison explains. "All the professors pull up chairs and sit with a book or whatever to distract ourselves for eight hours and let the new students touch us."

Lucas's face contorts in rage. "You have to do that for your job?"

"Thanks to Emry," Alison answers.

"Cake!" I announce.

Alison may not sense Lucas's indignation, but I could reach out and touch his rage. It's decided then. Lucas sits firmly on the side of settling and finds Alison's story traumatic, not funny. My hopes of a sister-in-law are gone in the span of a dinner.

Alison doesn't understand, and it's not because she won't, it's because she can't. It's not in her to have empathy for those that want to settle or desire solitude. That's not who she is, and the flicker of hope I'd held all evening evaporates while I cut through the buttercream.

"Small piece," Alison says. "You know I have that reception next weekend."

"I know," I say, and plop the biggest piece of cake on her plate and scrape her off some extra icing.

Dishes from dinner stay in the sink while I crawl off to bed. They can stay there until Sunday night for all I care.

Relaxing with a man that knows my body better than I do, who brings me to climax more times than I can count, means the dishes can stay dirty until I'm forced to face reality.

Sebastian must read my mind, and he follows me into the

bedroom. The sound of his clothing softly hitting the floor is music to my ears.

"Not the evening you were hoping for?" he asks, stepping behind me. His warm hands slide around my waist and fingertips press into my skin. The wine from the night makes my head buzz just enough to make me sway in his arms.

"No, but I can admit it was the evening I was planning for. I should have known they weren't a match."

Sebastian's lips tickle my neck, creating a trail of goosebumps in their wake. I don't want to talk about Alison and receptions, or think about my failed attempt at a set-up. All I want is to pretend the work week is far away while we're in our home and secluded from the outside world.

That's why we bought this property. It gives the illusion of living on an island, surrounded by trees and silence, far away from reality.

Sebastian pulls my top over my head and unhooks the back of my bra. It falls to the floor and his hands reach up to cup and massage my breasts. His hot chest presses against my back, and I lean my head back on his shoulder, letting out a breath I may have been holding all night.

He's my safe place.

He's what makes these walls a home.

"Are you too tired?" he whispers. He knows I'm not but loves to hear me ask for him, beg for him if the mood strikes us.

I reach in between our bodies, feeling for his swollen cock through the fabric of his jeans. "You know I'm not."

He groans, hitching his hips forward into my touch.

I spin around, and our mouths meet, both of us removing what clothes we have left in a rush. Sebastian picks me up and lays me down on the unmade bed, his lips trailing down my exposed skin as I inch upward, urging him to come closer. He crawls over me, a mischievous smile on his face.

"What are you thinking about, Mr. Crowe?" I giggle. I'm cold without covers or Sebastian's touch, and I reach up to his neck, wanting to pull him into a kiss. He resists, that smile growing wider before he moves downward, tossing my legs over his shoulders and diving between my legs.

My back arches when his hot mouth meets my center, his tongue sliding over my opening, slow and controlled. It's a familiar sensation, but one that I'll never tire of.

"Oh, yes," I say, combing my fingers through his hair and pulling at the roots gently.

My husband's skills only improve over time, learning everything about my body, treating it like an instrument he loves to play. It doesn't take him long to slide a finger inside me and suck my clit with the perfect pressure until I'm whimpering, pressing on the back of his head without thinking.

He speeds up, licking and sucking while my thighs shake beside his ears, the climax barreling toward me. A hot tingling rises at my core, and I'm trembling while he doesn't relent.

"Don't stop," I rush out. He won't. I can tell he isn't in the mood to tease, and I'm so close, shaking so hard my muscles will be sore tomorrow.

Before I realize it, I'm screaming out his name, my body convulsing while he holds me in place. The wave of the orgasm sweeps over me, my nipples hardening to stiff points and the slickness growing between my legs. He laps up every bit of my release, moaning against my pussy before he lets me go, my body falling limp.

I'm flipped over to my belly, my arms and legs a tangle of limbs from exhaustion. He moves a pillow under my hips, and I have maybe a second to adjust myself before I feel his thick cock enter me from behind, his hands clasping on the sides of my hips as he thrusts.

I cry out, my voice muffled by the mattress. The feeling of him filling me completely, showing me with his body that I'm his and all that matters is us, makes me moan with pleasure.

My hands clutch at the sheets, balling up fistfuls of cotton as he speeds up. The motion of us fucking rocks the bed underneath us, a steady and rapid rapping on the wall. He's so deep that I lift to adjust my hips, and he pauses.

"Baby," he says breathlessly.

He tries to pull out, but I move with him, keeping us connected. I whimper at the feeling of this new position, how full I am of my husband.

"Too much? Are you..." He's out of breath and he rests a hand on my bare back, his thumb grazing over my scar. I don't flinch when he touches me there anymore. I trust him completely, and there isn't a part of my body that is off limits to him.

"Are you okay?"

"It was... a little too deep," I admit, and even though I can't see him, I know he's nodding. He wraps his arms around my chest and pulls me into his lap, his cock still sheathed completely. I tremble, touching my clit while I rock against him.

I'm wrapped in his hold while he lets me take control, sliding up and down on his thickness, feeling my next orgasm rise in my belly.

"That's good, baby," he whispers into my ear. "Fuck, you're so tight like this."

His voice strains from effort, and that only makes me clench onto his shaft and move faster. I want to feel him explode inside me and make him lose control.

I work myself while I fuck him, and his hot breath against

my neck grows uneven just before his growl escapes and hot cum floods my insides. My fingers press hard against my clit while I scream his name.

"Sebastian! You feel so good. I love it when you fill me up. Fuck, Sebastian." My body shakes from the climax, but he holds me tight against him, his fingertips digging into my skin while we peak together, my orgasm cresting while he pulses inside me.

Fuck, that was so good.

I want to say the words out loud and tell him how amazing he makes me feel, but I don't have the strength. I sigh, realizing it's hard to catch my breath wrapped in his tight hold, and I tap his forearm to remind him to let me go.

He loosens his grip and tells me he loves me before his cocks slides out and he lowers us both to the bed.

"I couldn't breathe for a second," I finally choke out, but I'm laughing when I say it.

"Who needs air?" he jokes. "Overrated. Only need sex."

We talk for a bit, mostly about all the plans we don't want to make for the weekend, and when Sebastian rolls over to grab a book, I get ready for bed, a smile never leaving my face.

I don't need Alison to fall for Lucas or the world to change.

Everything I need is already here.

We spend our mornings off in bed for as long as possible, not starting the day until we're hungry enough to leave the room.

My phone pings with another article from Alison. She's been sending them to me all morning, but I don't respond, deleting it without opening, and turning back to my book.

Seb's head turns at the sound, his arms crossed underneath his temple while he lies on his stomach. He looks at my phone, and his eyebrows stitch together. I shrug at him and turn a page in my book.

"Have you thought about my question from yesterday?" he asks.

"You mean your question from two years ago that you bring up every few months?" I lick my finger and turn back a page because the words I attempt to read don't register. It's a feeble attempt at distraction, and I feel the flush in my chest rise from the conversation that's about to take place.

Sebastian moves to his side, one hand reaching inside the book, closing it, and setting it down between us. "Yes. Have you thought any more about it?"

"I think about it all the time," I answer. It's honest, but not the yes or no he wants. Neither of those would be acceptable, either, because this is bigger than a simple yes or no. The answer brings on more questions, but my head spins, not knowing what to say.

"You are on your way to getting tenure at the university," he starts. "That was your last argument."

I swallow hard and shake my head. "I'm not arguing about it."

Am I?

I don't know what I'm doing anymore, and I'm out of excuses.

Sebastian sits up, the sheets sliding down his immaculate body, forcing my eyes to cast over every muscle and cut. He rubs his jaw and takes in a deep breath, expanding his chest and calming himself. "If you don't want to have children, I understand. All I need is you, but this limbo of maybe — it's purgatory, Em. It's difficult for me."

"Right," is all I can get out. My skin prickles with nerves, and I scoot down on the bed, bringing the sheets to my neck.

His large hand rests on my stomach, spreading his fingers and staring. I imagine he's thinking what I would look like pregnant, my belly swelling with his child.

"You're not your mother," he says. "And we aren't your parents. It won't be like that."

I nod, knowing he means well, but that's not what stops me. Children change things and not always for the better. I'm a selfish person, a needy, self-centered bitch, because I can't give him a reason other than it doesn't *feel* right. When the thought of being a mother surfaces, my stomach fills with dread, and the excuses I've given myself have run dry.

There was trauma when we first met that I had to work through. Years later, we started dating and decisions like this felt far away. Then, we were a new couple and should enjoy each other. After that, I wanted to save more money, and then work toward tenure.

I'm out of my well-crafted list of reasons. None of them were the whole truth, and all that time gave me no answers about why I feel this way.

"I don't know why I'm so hesitant about it. I understand we won't be like my parents. Your parents are wonderful and together, still in love. We could be like them."

"But?" Sebastian raises his eyebrows, waiting for my excuse this time.

I turn to face him, searching his eyes for the answer. Our child would be beautiful and loved. There's a picture in my mind of what he or she would be like with Sebastian's soulful heart and my wit.

"I wish I knew why it doesn't feel right," I admit. "I'm sorry."

His face falls for a moment, but he recovers, leaning forward to give me a kiss and stroking my hair. "Why don't we say no, then? If you change your mind, you bring it up. I won't ask you again."

"It's not that—"

He places a finger on my lips and shakes his head. "I won't ask again. Sometimes I think I know you better than you do yourself. I see you, the pain that you feel the last few times I've brought it up. We're happy... just you and I. That's enough."

He grabs my book with one hand, opens it to the bookmarked page, and hands it back to me. "Pancakes for breakfast?" he asks.

"Anything but bacon," I whisper.

CHAPTER 7

Alison appears outside my classroom just when I'm about to start my final lesson of the week. The room is buzzing with chatter now that everyone's settled into the routine of school, cliques of friends forming, grouped together in new formations.

Another week is almost over, and I've survived. Things settle more each day, but it doesn't fix my exhaustion. I thought I would feel calmer about the school year by now.

I stride over to her, curious about the interruption.

"Hey," I rush out. "Everything okay?"

"Can I borrow your green dress for this weekend?" she asks. "The one with all the straps."

"Are you fucking kidding me?" I snarl.

The room quiets, a few students hearing my words. They hush to listen in on what we're discussing, so I step through the door and close it behind me.

"You interrupted my class to talk again about another reception this weekend? I thought you were wearing the blue dress for the fifteen-minute ride before you got naked and ran through hordes of people."

She crosses her arms at her front and pops one hip. "I'm excited about it. I have a good feeling, so can I borrow the green dress?"

"Borrow whatever the fuck you like. Except for Seb. Thanks, bye," I huff.

I turn to leave, and she grabs my elbow. "I'm really sorry the thing with Lucas didn't work out."

That's not why I'm frustrated, but it's all she's able to surmise. Over the past few weeks, I've been on edge, frustrated at nothing and everything. I could speculate part of it is the mishap with Lucas or the overall problem that, as friends, we have two different fundamental beliefs about life. There's also Sebastian's push about having a baby, even though, true to his word, he hasn't brought it up again and I know he won't. My chest has a constant ache I can't place, and I don't want to take it out on Alison.

"It's not a big deal," I shrug. It's not, but something is and the tension in my gut rises, making it hard to catch a breath. My heart beats too fast for someone standing in a hallway having a conversation about a low-cut green dress.

I close my eyes, feeling the room spin a bit, and take in a few long deep breaths, rubbing the pain from my chest. When I open them again, Alison stands with a sorry expression, still convinced she's hurt me in some way by refusing my offer of sister-in-law on a plate.

"The thing with Lucas was a long shot, and that's not why I'm annoyed. You're obsessed with these events."

"Excited," she corrects. "I have a really—"

"Good feeling," I chime in. "Yes, I know. You've said it a million times. I don't want you to get heartbroken again."

"I'm interviewing potential co-parents. That's something that has nothing to do with the bond."

I sigh and smile, giving her a side hug. "That's right. You have a key. Go on over. I know you're done with classes, but I'm not, so I'm going back in there."

"Could we get a coffee after you're done? I just want to spend some time with you, and we won't see each other or talk all weekend."

That's guilt talking and I don't hide my eye roll. "It's fine, Alison. I'm fine. We're good. Please go get the dress."

She grabs my wrist, her eyes pleading. "Please, Em. Every time we're together lately, it's kind of tense. I-I don't want to go another weekend feeling like you're mad at me."

"I'm not," I tell her, but I can tell by the way her face deflates, my answer isn't enough. So I relent. "Coffee sounds good. You know I can't turn down caffeine. One more class."

She skips away, and I enter a dead silent classroom.

"I'm so glad I have everyone's full attention," I say, clasping my hands behind my back, sauntering to the middle of the room that likely heard part, if not all, of our conversation.

It's the third Friday of the school year, and that means it's a free-form teaching day. I dread it every semester, and even submitted a document to administration, citing the reasons we should abolish the practice. My efforts yielded no results, and calling in sick only pushes it back.

"We all know what today is," I grit out, attempting enthusiasm about the students choosing the lesson today.

They all shift in their seats, my desk lighting up with the votes for today's plan. Walking backward, I glance down at the nominations.

Bonding Genome Theory — 13%
Genetic alterations throughout history — 4%
Natural Selection Theory — 11%
Variant Genes — 8%
Sexual Selection — 14%
Constructive neutral evolution — 8%
Selected Bonding in society— 42%

Well, fuck.

"I see we have a resounding winner. Selected bonding in society, also known as settling. Also apparent is that it's the choice I made many years ago." I hold up my wrist, displaying my tattoo. Students scoot forward in their chairs, eyes piercing at the marking.

They always choose selected bonding in society, hoping they can get me to tell my story. Why would someone in my field settle? Inquiring minds want to know.

Taking my remote, I scan over my wrist, copying the image before I dim the lights so it displays in the center of the room. The word Crowe appears in bold script letters.

"My given name was Emry Crawford, and I married Sebastian Owens several years ago. We met when I was sixteen and he was nineteen when he was on a mission with a unit in NeXus."

A unified gasp echoes throughout the room. We all know about NeXus for the research and discovery of most everything published so far about the bond. NeXus is at the top of its field in this hemisphere, and there is a waiting list for years to even get a job interview.

There's a subdivision where Sebastian works, taking down rogue groups that attempt the bonding research themselves in nefarious ways. I let the class think what they want, their speculation growing by the second, knowing I'm married to someone I met while they were on a mission with NeXus.

"I lived in government housing for reasons I will not discuss in this classroom, and he checked on me every month for several years. We began a mutual relationship with the understanding of monogamy, and married a few years later."

The study of selected bonding in society isn't solely about me, but I see the way my students gawk at my tattoo every day. Their curiosity makes me uncomfortable, and it's the reason most of them chose this topic. I'll quell it and move on with their lessons and hopefully, be done with the invasion of my personal space and privacy.

"This city has less than ten percent of its inhabitants choosing this lifestyle, and even then, some of them still divorce after infidelity. It's by far the unpopular choice," I grimace.

That's an understatement. This city views me as a freak, an outcast. The average age in this city for settlers is sixty-seven, and Sebastian and I might be severely pulling down that average. Shaking off the annoyed feeling, I continue. "Centuries before, they observed marriage with what? Who can tell me the symbol?"

Lights beam on my remote, and I click on a number. "Rings on the left hand," a young girl answers.

"Yes. Rings have been around for thousands of years as a symbol of fidelity and marriage, going back to ancient Egyptians. So, what changed? Why are we now branded?"

My remote doesn't blink. Either no one wants to answer or they don't know. The study of selected bonding isn't big news when the world's focus is finding the true bond.

"Wow," I exclaim. "No one?"

A single number appears, and I click on the student. "The divorce rate?" he raises his voice in question.

"That was a catalyst," I respond. "Very good answer. When the bond occurred, and the early receptions began, called raves at the time, infidelity became rampant. Divorce rates went from twenty percent to over eighty percent in a five-year time, and eventually, the states became overrun with paperwork and civil disputes. Governments demanded extensive sessions before they would marry a couple when the dust settled."

I click through my remote a few times and bring up a few images. I point to a group of couples and say, "These here are the first to get the matrimony marks. They were part of the Chosen Church of the People, a religious organization that started after the bonding. Today it's the largest organized religion in the world, but mostly because the others have disintegrated since bonding. That story is in historical religion if you care to take that class."

Everyone looks over at the couples who display tattoos similar to mine. They stand dressed in white, a cultural normality that's still part of the marriage tradition, palms facing up toward the camera.

"This spark of an idea quickly grew across communities. The tattoos are a combination of your names that are permanently placed on a visible part of your body, symbolizing the decision you've made to settle with someone without the bond. It was another twenty years before the government made it a mandate for marriage."

I click again, and a government document appears. "So, why would anyone do this?"

My remote blinks and I choose a student. "Tax benefits," they answer.

"That's a consideration. Although divorce is so costly, you'd have to be sure. It's bankruptcy for almost everyone if you decide to separate. Fees for divorce are ten years' joint salary. That's inconceivable. Why else?"

Numbers flash once more, and I click without looking.

"You don't have to co-parent," another student answers. There's a pang in my chest and I rub it, feeling the ache from my earlier conversation with Sebastian. "Right. There can be complications with co-parenting. But remember the class you're in. What evolutionary aspects could affect this choice?"

More lights, fewer this time, but I click again.

"We find pairs across species other than humans. It could be embedded in our genome to find a partner."

I smile and nod. "Yes, that's correct. Remember, the basics of our genome have a predisposition toward survival. There are nuances, of course. And bonding is the ultimate survival which has caused this huge rift in our civilization. Every cell in your body fights to keep it alive, and the bond does just that."

I'm energized by the conversation, happy it's morphed into a discussion about science and not just my marriage.

"What contingent could override our genetic response?" I ask.

A number appears, the only one to answer, and it belongs to a student who's never spoken up in class. I hit it and motion for her to respond. The young girl clears her throat before speaking, leaning hesitantly toward her microphone. She's small in every way, looking almost too young to be here, and appears regretful of hitting her number to answer.

"Yes," I urge. "Please, what do you think would supersede the desire to seek out the bond?"

The room settles down, everyone waiting for what she has to say. A few heads turn in her direction.

"Love," she says, her voice barely above a whisper.

The room grows impossibly silent, and I nod. Even in the darkness, I know they're stunned by her answer and questioning if she's right, wondering if such a thing is real without the bond.

I want to give all the scientific reasons behind that word, explain to them what the brain does when it finds a partner, how our genome desires the half that makes us whole, but I'm suddenly at a loss for words.

"Yes," I choke out. My heart thuds with a heavy ache. "Very good. Love."

CHAPTER 8

EMRY

As promised, we are strutting down the too hot street with iced coffees, talking about everything but bonding. Alison can't take it anymore, and I feel the conversation coming when her shoulders rise to her ears.

"I can't stop thinking about the fizzer this weekend," she finally says. She takes a sip of her iced coffee, then chews on the straw, waiting for my opinion she knows will come even though she didn't ask. I don't know why she's baiting me after we just discussed how tense it's been between us. Maybe she thinks calling it a fizzer will make it all a joke.

I turn my head when I roll my eyes, a failed attempt to keep my thoughts at bay. I shouldn't judge, but I do. This city bleeds judgment all over us with every billboard and window sign.

Your life mate is waiting. Are you looking?

Fulfillment is companionship.

Give your children the edge and test.

What you crave is with the one of your choosing.

Vote Lockstone. I'll find the key to the bond.

The slogans shoot out at every street corner, condemning the decisions we make, forcing us to pick a side.

Alison is clearly wanting to talk about her hunt for a bonded partner, and I'm judging, inadvertently rolling my eyes at some old woman who glares at us from across the street.

I wave to her, hoping for forgiveness, and her eyes slit at the sight of my wrist tattoo. When she waves back, I see hers is bare. She's a searcher, too. She's judging more than just my eye roll.

"Isn't the name *fizzer* a self-fulfilling prophecy?" I bite my tongue before I continue and force a tight smile back at Alison. She won't look me in the eye when she sighs.

Those who hope for the best but expect the worst call the parties fizzers, and they couldn't be more right. People go to find their bonded, paying astronomical fees to attend, but it's always a disappointment.

"This company had fourteen matches in London this year, and we're lucky they're coming through our city," she says.

I guffaw at her statement, knowing I can prove her wrong in a few minutes. She knows it too, but believes the propaganda. She wants a bonded, not the truth.

Maybe the argument that's about to ensue is what our friendship needs. We have to get it out and move on. I stayed quiet during the awkward dinner with Lucas, and she's sent me about a hundred articles about bonding.

It's so hot outside, and the temperature tests my nerves. That and the fact that I'm failing to dodge every passerby from sliding a grimy hand across my bare skin. A woman can only take so much.

"Okay, so how much will this letdown set you back?" I snip.

There it is, my sharp tongue lashing out at my one and only friend. I don't want to be this way, but I'm on edge out in public. I wish I would have gone straight home after the coffee shop, avoided the crowds and their incessant hands darting out at us while we walk.

Alison sucks in her cheeks at the question I have no right to ask. It comes from a place of concern, as do so many wrong things I say to the people I care about.

Regret sours my stomach, and I open my mouth, attempting to correct my misstep when she stops me.

"Emry, please don't..." she cuts me off, chewing on her mangled straw. "I have enough. Enough money and enough of your... worrying all over me."

I exhale, grateful she used the word worry instead of judgment. It's no surprise she brought this up when we are about to separate at the end of the street. This creates a short tiff instead of a drawn out back and forth.

Alison lives with two other roommates in a two-bedroom apartment. She's given every spare cent to this pointless soulmate searching mission. At dinner last weekend, she mentioned adding another person to her room to save more money, and for what? Another promise no company from London can keep and no one in this world has a right to make.

I let out a puff of air and toss my coffee in a trash can, my insides churning from the shift in our conversation.

"I have to try," she whispers, and her eyes meet mine. The pity in them — it hits me like a brick, and I hold my breath for a moment too long. We both feel just as strongly that the other is making the wrong choice. It's only that I'm more vocal than she is, always ready for a fight.

"I asked Sebastian to courier over the green dress," I tell her.

"That's really nice. I could have come by to get it." Her eyes move down to the street and she frowns.

"I wanted you to have enough time to get ready since you waited for me to finish my last class."

My heartbeat thuds in my ears, and we stop at the end of the street, ready to split and head home. Her to a cramped apartment she's happy to keep so every penny can go to these damned parties, and me to a home with a husband of my choosing.

She's my best friend, and we agree on everything but this.

And *this* is all anyone talks about, or thinks about. She believes I made the wrong decision with Sebastian. I settled in every sense of the word because I made a choice to marry someone I loved.

I decided to let mortality take its normal course, a sign of insanity if you ask most of this city. She thinks I gave up or gave in, but she doesn't know how it feels to have someone love you because they chose you. If she did, everything would change.

"That's really nice of you. Especially because I know you don't agree with it all," she says.

"I don't. But that doesn't mean I don't support you and what you do with your life. As long as you aren't hurting anyone, well." I shrug my shoulders. "It's that I don't want you to get hurt, Alison. That's all this is."

Her lips shake a little when she smiles, and she pulls me into a hug. It's almost too hot to wrap my arms around her, but I do.

"We can't all find a Seb," she admits, and I sink into her a bit. Maybe it's not that she needs a bonded as much as someone she knows will love her no matter what. That is hard to find with or without the genetic response of a bond.

"You do what you think is best. Just be careful," I say into her hair before I pull away. "When is it exactly?"

"Tomorrow night," Alison lets out a sigh of relief, chucking her empty cup in the garbage. We're dropping the subject, letting our friendship survive for another day. I haven't said all I wanted, and neither has she, but this is good enough. "Will you come over and hang out while I get dressed?"

I roll my eyes at her face this time, and she chuckles. Everyone wears as little clothing as possible to these events, desperate to have every available inch of skin ready to be caressed by *the one.* Covering your skin means you risk not finding that person, and most people go naked. Alison has a time or two.

"I know I won't be wearing the dress for long." She giggles to herself. "But you know—"

"Oh, I know," I stop her. She thinks I've never been to a matching reception, but I spare her the details of my past. She's never known me without Sebastian, and I prefer it that way. My life started when I met him and every horrible moment before felt like a dream. No, a nightmare that I need to stay buried.

"I'll come over and bring some food," I say and turn to leave.

"Nothing that will make me bloat," Alison sing-songs across the street.

I rush in the opposite direction with a chuckle. Her looks mean nothing at the receptions and she knows it, but maybe she hopes to find someone of her choosing. Maybe she could be as happy as I am.

The crowds all move in the same direction, and I'm pushed

along, my body bouncing back and forth like a pinball in a sea of people. They sway in a rhythm, everyone heading home for the weekend.

I try to ignore the touches, fingertips that graze against my bare arms, searching for a chance at the spark. Clammy palms and fingernails glide across my skin with no apology or regret. The only remorse is the constant disappointment that the moment hasn't come for them, and I'm another woman who won't give them what they want — what Alison wants.

The sun beats down on us, burning my shoulders while we wait to cross another street. I would have worn sleeves if the temperature wasn't rising by the second, making beads of sweat pour down my back.

It wouldn't stop them from pushing against me, sliding sweaty hands down my body. They all look for a patch of skin to slip a finger across, no matter what I try to keep covered. The horde moves to a beat they all dance to, circling each other while we walk, touching and testing.

Most days, my patience stays strong. I have the ability to grumble through the complexities of this city and have empathy for the people that call it home, but my conversation with Alison eats at me. All the words unsaid between us make my skin bristle and my blood boil.

We come to a crosswalk, and the timer on the other side of the street ticks slower with every second as the crowd circles around me, rubbing against my arms, sending pinpricks of irritation into my veins.

I watch the countdown slow, and I think of the old woman from the street. Her bare arm waving and her eyes judging.

Who the fuck is she to look at me like that?

I wipe the sweat from my neck and catch someone's hand in the crook of my elbow. They ignore my grunt of agitation when I shake them off. They don't care because I don't matter to them once they've touched my skin and didn't get what they wanted.

Ten — Nine — Eight

Wasn't that timer just at five seconds?

A man runs a calloused hand across my shoulder, and I yank it away, scratching my skin that's already burned from the sun. I never wear such little clothing, and I'm charring my body with every second that passes.

I had planned on going straight home, but I didn't want to disappoint Alison when she asked me for coffee. Now, stuck in a crowd of searchers, I wish I had.

I pull the ponytail holder from my wrist and tie my hair up in a messy bun.

Five — Four — Three

Someone puts their hand into my armpit, and I growl. An actual rumble emerges from my chest which catches their attention, but they shoot me an indignant look and keep walking and touching as they go. I finish my hair and look back at the timer.

It's blinking. Stuck on three.

Fuck this. I'll go the long way home.

My pulse quickens as I try to push my way through the crowd, begging people to part as I edge my way out. They won't budge but insist on touching me instead, adding fuel to my frustration. It feels like this group has multiplied in the thirty seconds I stood waiting to cross the street.

I should have told Alison everything I thought and been done with it. Done with our friendship maybe, but I would be free of this gnawing in my gut from guilt. She's never going to find a bonded. These companies lie to steal your money, and she'll die alone, searching for something she'll never find. She's wasting her life on a one-in-a-million chance, living in a crowded apartment and throwing her money into the wind.

"Please let me pass," I beg. I whip my head around and the timer still blinks on three. No one seems to notice or care, and that's the true sign of who has a partner and who doesn't. People who are searchers take every opportunity to do just that, while the few of us who decide to settle down have places to go and loved ones to see.

"Please," I repeat, and pull at a man's shirt, using my shoulder to wedge myself through.

I break free of the group, and my feet take flight, running down the sidewalks, avoiding hands that reach out as I pass. Their actions are normal, expected even, but today it's too much. I'm suffocating from every embrace, no matter how innocent or small.

A man's outstretched hand juts out on my right, and I evade him, sending me face first into an open shop door. I ricochet back, my ass hitting the cement. When I reach up to touch my nose, warm blood runs down my palm, and my eyes well with tears.

Fuck, Emry. What are you doing?

It's my fault, running through the busy sidewalks fueled by some anxiety ridden panic attack. I curl my free hand against the pebbled street, my fingernails picking up bits of dirt while I chastise myself for losing control, letting the motivations of these people affect me like this. I'm still at the mercy of stray hands at every corner, and now I may have a broken nose to add to my annoyances.

A bundle of white fabric appears in my blurred vision, and I resist the urge to jolt back.

"I'm so sorry," a man says. The outline of someone steps closer and squats down, shielding me from a passerby who slides her hand down his arm but can't reach mine.

"Is there a hospital nearby?" he asks. "I'll take you. Shit. I'm just so sorry."

"I don't see why," I grumble. "I shouldn't have been running."

There's an awkward moment between us where nothing is said. He knows I'm right, but doesn't want to say it to the bleeding woman sitting on the sidewalk.

"Was someone... chasing you?" he jokes.

I blink a few times, and a square-jawed man in a suit comes into focus. He's got a boyish quality, bristling with the youth of someone who hasn't been through the trenches of searching or settling.

My lips lift in a smile, mirroring his by instinct, and the taste of salty tears I didn't realize were falling hit my mouth. I let my hand leave my nose and blood drips down my wrist, trailing across the symbols of my tattoo.

"I'll ruin it," I say, looking at his handkerchief. I've never seen a man carry one, let alone offer one.

He scoots forward, still smiling. People passing by us don't ask if I'm okay, but touch my shoulder and his cheek as they stroll along.

I realize he hasn't reached out to touch me. It's been over a minute and our skin hasn't met, which is a damn record in this city.

"You're not from here," I say.

Tilting his face down, he chuckles. "That might be obvious, but I, uh, manage to get down the street in one piece."

"Ha. Ha," I deadpan and he shoves the fabric closer to my face.

"You'll ruin your clothes," he says, waving it in my direction. "Please. Take it."

His eyes are kind, pleading with me to let him do something. It's unnecessary guilt, stemmed from opening the door at the exact moment a wild woman dove face-first into it, but I appreciate the gesture.

He glances at my wrist, and I look at his.

His is bare while mine is not.

"Do you want me to call your husband?" he asks. There's a downturn of his lips when he says it. I'm a disappointment again to another soul looking for his partner, but at least he's less obvious about it.

"No. No. I'll be fine. Let me just get up," I tell him. When I rise, the dribble of blood slides under my chin and I wipe it away, making a mess on the other side of my hand.

"Please, just take it," he pleads, and runs the fabric against my neck, stopping the trail of blood.

I grab at his bare wrist to push him away, our skin touching for only a second, and that's all the time it takes.

It hits us both, a bolt of lightning striking two strangers as our essence becomes one, souls mingling in a way I never could have imagined in my wildest dreams or worst nightmares.

CHAPTER 9

THEO

The event this weekend means my extra days off are up in smoke, and I'll be spending tomorrow night awake at all hours ensuring there aren't any surprises on the transportation side of things.

Because the company is moving individuals to and from the reception, I'll be getting to sleep when the sun rises, checking that no issues popped up with this first job. The company can't afford a mishap that would negatively impact future contracts and these events, although profitable, are a fucking record-keeping nightmare.

Everyone leaves from one place, and heads home to somewhere else, shifting the needs of transport around different parts of the city. To make matters worse, it's not clear until the end of the night who couples off with whom, sending our buses in all different directions. The last thing I need is some woman getting lost on the wrong side of town and reporting it as our error.

I called in some sleeping pills to pick up on my way to Moira's shop. I need to sleep as much as possible so I can stay alert for the all-nighter. The touches haven't stopped all week, even at the office, so I asked for a sedative too. Tomorrow I'll be another possibility for thousands of strangers, and I need extra help to remain calm while they grope me at every opportunity.

The pharmacist looks over my file for too long, and I know the concerns spinning around in her head. "Can I speak with you in the consulting room?" she asks.

As if I have a choice.

"Of course," I force a smile. She can't deny me the sedative, but she can give me her lecture so she'll sleep easy at night in case I misuse the medication and stop my heart.

She leads me into a side room, laptop open and in hand. "Mr. Lorwerth."

"Theo," I tell her. "Call me Theo."

She looks back at the screen of her computer. "You're on quite a few medications that could have adverse effects with this depressant. Are you aware there are risks of co-mingling the drugs?"

"I am," I admit. "I'm under no pretenses regarding my health, and I understand the potential complications."

"I have to advise you not to fill this prescription."

I take in a slow, deep breath, licking my lips and giving myself a moment before I speak. It's frustrating to go through this conversation where I must repeat myself, and I don't owe her any explanation. It's my body, but I don't want to appear disrespectful to someone that's doing their job. She's advised me not to fill the script, and I disagree. It's a simple business transaction.

"Respectfully, I won't be taking your advice," I answer, and step toward the door.

"Mr. Lorwerth. Theo," she pushes. "Your condition—"

"Is one that I understand. It killed my father, and I don't intend to make any mistakes or take risks. I'll need the sedative for my work this weekend. I won't abuse the drug. Please fill it. I'd like to get home and go to bed."

Her face flushes with indignation because she's not winning the debate, but she never stood a chance.

I'm not afraid of death. In fact, I accept the inevitability and understand I can't do anything to stop it. That's a rarity in a world of people searching for the fountain of youth. It's no wonder she never saw my rebuttal coming.

"I appreciate your concern. I promise I'll be responsible," I say, opening the door and stepping through.

Moira makes another delicious pizza, and I'm pleased with the Friday tradition. This time I eat the entire thing.

"Hungry?" she points out.

"Yes, but I'm hoping to fall into a carb coma. I'll be up all night tomorrow for the event. Speaking of." I set two tickets on the counter for her. One is for entrance and the other is for transportation. "If you decide to go."

She picks them up and gives them a once over before shoving them in her apron. "You'll be there?" she asks. "The whole time?"

"Yes, but mostly in the lots, handling the bussing. I'll still get assaulted my fair share." I chuckle while a pit forms in my stomach. I ignore it, stretching and standing. "I have to head out."

The streets still crowd with people, but I'm eager to get into bed. I'll have it worse this weekend, so I might as well ease myself into the chaos. "If you go tomorrow, try to have fun.

They can get a little wild, but you know how to handle yourself."

"Yes I do," she replies. "What if you... find a bondmate?"

I roll my eyes, adjusting my suit. "I'm more interested in finding a cash bonus, which only happens if this weekend goes off without a hitch. And what if you do, Moira? You'd outlive your daughter."

It's the wrong thing to say, and I know it the moment the words leave my lips. Her face falls in sadness, the thought sinking in and making her realize the ramifications of that possibility.

Moira packs up a few things in a box, absently working while she mulls this over. I want to apologize, but it might be better if I drop it altogether.

"I hope she finds someone, bondmate or not, but if I could pick between us who gets the bond, I'd want it to be her. Life's so short..." she trails off, lost in thought for a moment.

I button my jacket and nod. "You're a good person, Moira. There's not a lot of those out there."

"I'm a good mother," she counters. "Most of the time."

"There aren't a lot of those either."

We laugh at the joke that isn't the least bit funny, and I wave goodbye, swinging the door open, when I hear a solid thud and feel it vibrate in my hand.

I step to the side, and to my horror, I find a woman on the other side, flat on her ass and holding her face. Blood streams through the fingers of her hand pressed against her nose.

"I'm so sorry," I blurt out, crouching down in front of her. I didn't look, swinging the door open like an idiot on a busy street.

Her long hair falls forward into her bloody fingers, and I want to reach out and brush it behind her ears, but I stop. The last thing I want to do is act as if my focus is on finding a bond, so I resist touching her in any way.

Pulling out my father's handkerchief, I offer it to her, the blood already threatening to stain her cream blouse. It looks expensive or well-tailored at least.

"I don't see why," she gurgles through her hand. "I shouldn't have been running."

She's coming from work, and I've ruined her commute home with my carelessness. I wave the fabric in her face again, hoping she'll take it. My father had several of them, and even though I don't want to part with any, he would want me to be a gentleman.

"Was someone... chasing you?" I joke, trying to levitate the mood and offering a smile. She's on the concrete in pain, blood spurting from her face, and I can't tell if she's smiling back. The red liquid spreads down her arm, dripping onto her matrimony tattoo.

How rare.

"I'll ruin it," she says. People keep touching both of us, not stopping to ask if they can help or if she's okay. My frustration boils at them and at myself for causing her pain, and my chest pounds with my irregular heartbeat.

"You'll ruin your clothes." I'm adamant she takes the handkerchief, that I do something to help. Her eyes shoot to the fabric, and then my bare wrist.

"Do you want me to call your husband?" I ask.

She shakes her head, wincing with the movement. "No. No. I'll be fine. Let me just get up," she insists.

As she stands, the blood trails under her chin, dangerously close to her blouse. I reach forward to wipe it away.

"Please, just take it," I offer again and sweep the handkerchief over her neck.

She grabs at my wrist.

Time stops.

It's a blinding light, and I'm sure it's happened.

My heart has given out on me at some sidestreet before I had the chance to live the rest of my days as I wanted.

I'll die just as my father did.

A split second later, a warm feeling wraps around me, lifting me into the sky, spinning me in circles.

She's with me, her essence, her spirit. I can smell and taste her — feel every particle of her body mixing with mine. The pleasure courses through my veins, sending me into an odd climax, stronger than any orgasm I've ever experienced and different, too.

This isn't death.

Could it be?

My heart, my fucking feeble heart, pounds like a drum, stronger than I ever knew possible. I think it might fly out of my chest it beats with such purpose, and I'm not scared. For the first time in my whole fucking life, I trust it won't stop and I know the breath will continue to fill my lungs.

It's a relief I never knew was possible, and I know I'm crying without feeling the tears. I buried my father and kept them at bay, but this serene moment of ecstasy makes them pour out, and I can't stop. My sight returns, and I open my eyes to see her, the one I want to touch and hold. My body leans toward her without thinking, desperate to be closer even though she fills me completely.

A moan leaves my lips, and I grip her arms, pulling her closer to me.

To my horror, she twists her body and pulls herself from my grasp.

No!

My feet stumble underneath me, chasing her down a

crowded street as people stare, their faces contorted in a mix of understanding and confusion.

Her matrimonial tattoo...

I shouldn't chase her. I'm going to scare her, make her frightened of the one person she's supposed to trust for... for hundreds of years. This is no way to start, but my mind won't listen, moving my body on its own despite my reservations.

"Stop," I cry out. She gains distance between us, weaving in and out of alleys I'm unfamiliar with, and dodging me at every turn. She sprints up the side of a hill into a treeline, a park I've walked only once.

What are you doing, Theo? Stop chasing her.

I slow myself down, but I can't stop. My feet move on their own, forcing me to follow her, and what's worse is I think I feel her fear. There's a sensation of dread that washes over me, but it's outside my body somehow. A part of me, but at a distance.

It doesn't take her long to disappear from sight, and the moment it happens, I fall to the ground, clutching my chest.

The air leaves my lungs, and I claw at the dirt, gasping and choking on the breath that won't grant me relief. My mind shifts from her to my erratic heart, and I panic, which doesn't help as I'm frantically moving through my suit pockets, searching for the medication.

Footsteps hurry in my direction, the ground vibrating with people that find me. They all touch me first, but I'm too far gone to care, still searching for the needle. I pull it out, but my shaking fingers betray me, the world blinking between darkness and light.

I fall to the side and turn onto my back, ripping open my shirt.

"This," someone says, holding it in my blurry vision. I reach up, yank the cap off, and point to my chest. They hesitate, not sure of what I'm conveying, unable to help the barely conscious man near death on the dirt moments after he bonded.

The fucking irony.

This isn't my end. I won't die amongst strangers, not when I'm so close to a life I've fought for with every beat of this frail, pathetic heart.

My hand clasps around the person's wrist, and I plunge the needle down into my chest, piercing in between my ribs and stabbing the chambers of my unstable heart.

I hear them gasp, and someone yells, "Hit the plunger!" before the world fades away.

My head lolls to the side, and the last thing I see is the blinking billboard across the street. I can't make it out, but I know what it says.

Your life mate is waiting.

CHAPTER 10

EMRY

The world spins for us both, blinding our eyes with white light.

I know because everything he senses radiates between us. We're an echo chamber of each other's thoughts and feelings, reverberating with such a force, I can't breathe or think.

The air leaves my lungs, and the ringing in my ears is so loud I don't hear myself scream even though I'm sure I did. It's a mix of invigoration and fear, stirring my insides and clutching at my heart.

I'm trapped by the tornado of sensations while this stranger's hand grips mine. Our hearts sync to the same rapid beat, thrumming in unison. Blood rushes through our veins with a pulse that dances back and forth.

The ache in my heart that has plagued me these past few weeks lifts, and it's euphoric, pure joy and relief — relief I didn't know I needed so desperately. Waves of delight crash through us, and all I see and feel is him, an unnamed stranger.

Something beyond excitement fills us like I've never experienced and can't describe. It's as if we're free-falling from an airplane, jumping from a cliff into clear blue water, or walking through a cloud on top of a skyscraper.

Seconds, minutes, hours... I don't know how much time passes until I register his hands wrapping around my shoulders and the sound of his moan in my ear. The sound is orgasmic, full of pleasure and longing, and I hate myself for sharing the lust that fills my insides. His grip tightens, and he pulls me closer.

Every cell of my body wants to fall into his arms, wrap my body against his, and never let go.

Sebastian.

His face comes to my mind. Those dark eyes that were the first to truly see me and his perfect mouth telling me he loves me. The mouth I promised would be the last I ever kiss. He's mine, and I'm his, and there's nothing that will break that promise.

Not even this.

It takes every ounce of strength and then some, fighting my impulses and urges, ignoring the pain it causes me to even think about moving, but I force myself to slide free of his grip.

I twist my aching body and find my footing, tears and blood streaming down my face. My body and heart scream at me to turn around, but my mind runs toward Sebastian.

There's a cry from the stranger's lips and the sound of staggering feet behind me, but I ignore everything else. The sound of his footsteps and the gasps of people that pass us disappear in my wake. Some of them scream out in rage, while others clap and make sounds of delight.

They felt what I refuse to acknowledge, what I can't bring myself to admit. The shockwave of our bond will hit others for a hundred miles, and there's nothing I can do about that except keep my feet moving away from the onlookers.

Away from my bonded.

My pace quickens, running faster through the thinning crowd. The tether between us makes me run with the weight of the world on my back, but I keep going, keep forcing myself further.

I'm faster than most, and I know it, using my speed to fly around alleyways and up the hills of the park without slowing down. His voice calls out in the distance when I hit the treeline and cut through toward home, letting mud cover my shoes and spray on my clothes from each kick of my feet.

Just get home.

The sounds change to children playing on swings in a clearing and the chatter of mothers who watch. Necks crane at the sight of me covered in mud and blood sprinting through their play dates.

The further away I get, the stronger my resolve. Distance from him gives me renewed energy, as if the invisible rope between us frays with every step.

My home is twenty minutes walk away, but I'm throwing myself through the doorway in what feels like seconds later. I turn and slam the door behind me, locking it with too much force, as if that would stop this.

This bond is stronger than a deadbolt, and I rest my forehead on the wood, staring down at the handle. My chest heaves, sweat dripping between my breasts.

How could this happen?

What am I going to tell Sebastian?

"I made pasta," Sebastian calls out from the kitchen. His deep voice makes me whimper and I turn, resting my back against the wood.

My hands run down my shirt, smearing the drips of blood

and mixing it with the dirt. The pull to the stranger is weaker, but still there, beckoning me from the inside. It begs me to turn back and run toward him. I don't even know his name.

I won't go to him.

I've made my choice.

"Do you want me to open that bottle your mother brought over or are we saving that for this weekend? I never know if she wants us to enjoy it or if she's frustrated we didn't wait..." He drops the wine glass at the sight of me, the shards tumbling down the hallway. His jaw hangs slack as he steps over the pieces, rushing in my direction. "What happened?"

I clasp my hands into fists and force them at my sides, taking in a deep breath and stepping into Sebastian's sturdy arms.

"Emry, talk to me. What happened? Tell me right now!"

My body won't melt into his like it once did. Stiff muscles force themselves to relax in his hold, but once my arms wrap around his middle, I'm home again.

My Sebastian.

The man I love.

"Nothing," I lie. "Everything's fine."

I know I can't keep this a secret forever, but the idea of telling him what happened makes me want to vomit.

He steps back, tipping my chin up with his large hand. "Your face," he gasps. "It's covered in blood. That's not fine. Can you make it to the bathroom?"

"I-I just fell. I—" I stutter over the lies I'm about to spin. This mess is a ticking clock.

No.

A ticking bomb.

During most of our weekends, we take a break from the world, turning off phones and newscasts, but I'm fooling myself if I think this will stay buried long.

Sebastian will find out, and soon. Looking up at his dark eyes that cast over me with worry, my heart breaks in two. It's physically painful, aching in my chest in a way I've never felt before.

I've ruined everything.

This will destroy him.

Destroy us.

"I'll get cleaned up." My voice doesn't sound like my own. It's soft and defeated, brimming with panic. I brush past Sebastian, passing up the bathroom.

"I'll get the first aid kit," he calls behind me. "Where did you fall?"

I ignore him and step into the living room. Sebastian's phone sits on the side table with his laptop, and I toss it behind the couch. He won't look for it right away. Sebastian's never a man to have his phone in his hand at all times. Maybe we can just have tonight before I tell him.

One more night.

"What are you doing?" he says, stepping into the living room with the kit. He wraps an arm around my shoulders, holding me against him, my blood staining his crisp white shirt.

"The sauce is bubbling over," I say, pointing to the kitchen.

Sebastian releases me for a moment, turning off the stove before rushing back over. "I'm surprised you can smell it," he says as we step into the bathroom and I catch the first glimpse of my face.

I look horrid. Dirt-streaked tears run through the blood on my swollen cheeks. I catch myself on the edge of the sink, hunching over and studying myself.

"Oh, god. I'm so sorry," I say to my reflection.

"For a little mess. Don't be silly," Sebastian says, running a washcloth under the warm water. "I think this calls for opening that bottle tonight, but I'll have to find another wine glass."

I don't smile at the joke, staring at my reflection in horror. When he wipes the blood from my chin with soft small strokes, I can't look away from the elevens that sit between my eyebrows.

Or where they used to be.

I scrunch my face, trying to make the wrinkles appear.

Nothing.

I reach for the washcloth. "Let me see that."

Sebastian hands it over, and I bring it to my nose. Rubbing the dried blood away with harsh strokes, I break down into sobs.

"Easy, Em." Sebastian takes the cloth from my hands. "You're going to hurt yourself like that."

But it doesn't hurt.

My wound mended in the few minutes I spent with my bonded.

This is real, and I can't deny what is looking right back at me.

CHAPTER 11

EMRY

"Em, please talk to me. What happened to you?" Sebastian pulls back the washcloth and turns me to face him. He runs his hands over my body, searching for a wound and checking me over.

"I just n-need a shower," I insist. "I'm cold. People fall all the time."

"Did you fall into a truck?" Sebastian asks. He's attempting a joke, but his voice rises with panic. Dabbing the washcloth on my nose, I don't wince, and I wonder if he notices.

My chin shakes, and my lip quivers when I try to smile. "I just... freaked out with too many people touching me. You know how I am. Please, come into the shower with me."

He nods, unsure of what to do, except start the shower and collect a few towels.

"Emry, baby..." he trails off. He knows something isn't right, and I hate myself for this betrayal, for the bond, and then for not telling him.

I've never lied to him.

Steam fills the room moments later, and he helps me strip off my clothes, dropping them in a pile on the floor. They leave a trail of dirt on the tile, and I fight the urge to wash it away. I want everything about today to disappear and pretend it never happened.

Standing in front of my husband, naked, with dried blood on my face and tears in my eyes, I tell him a jumble of half-truths to ease his mind. I stutter over my words, swallowing hard as I try to ease his worry, if only for tonight.

"I had a panic attack at a crosswalk." *True.*

"There were so many people grabbing at me, and I ran off, hitting an open shop door at full force and falling." *True.*

"I was so freaked out I j-just k-kept running." *True.*

"That's all. I'm fine." *Lie.*

I lie for his sake and mine, because I'm selfish, because I can't imagine telling him the truth and crushing his perfect heart. He'll never look at me the same way, never love me with the ease of a man secure with his partner.

"I freaked out and ran the rest of the way home. My anxiety... it just took over, but I'm home, and I'm fine."

His eyes scan back and forth over my filthy face, doubting my words, but unable to dispute them. I bite my lip to stop talking and over explaining myself. He knows when people are lying, but he would never imagine I would be one of those people.

"Okay," he says. "We're going to the hospital before you try to go to work. Please."

"Sure," I respond, nodding my head and feeling fresh hot tears drip to down chin and fall on my breasts.

Sebastian reaches behind the neck of his shirt, pulling it up and taking it off. He loosens his buckle and slides his pants down, his briefs along with them, piling them up on top of my clothes. "Sit on the bench and I'll wash you," he offers.

The puffs of steam cloud the mirror and take the shiver from my bones until all that's left is the dull ache in my heart. Each beat sends a pinch of pain when the blood pushes to every limb, struggling to do something that once came so naturally. It's a rock under my ribs that doesn't beat properly, and I wonder what the bond has done. No one's denied the force of it before, and I wonder if I'll die, refusing the match my body so desperately wants.

Sebastian's arms cradle behind my knees and back, walking us into the streams of water and setting me down on the seat in the shower. He angles the spray away from my broken face, finding a washcloth and gently wiping away the grime.

The water runs clear before I reach out for him, wrapping a leg around his back and pulling him closer. I grip his length in my hand, forcing his body to stay close to mine.

"What are you doing?" He grips my shoulders and eases me back against the tile with a gentle push. "No, baby. You're hurt."

"I'm okay," I lie. I need to prove to myself he's mine and I'm his. Sebastian is my choice and one I make every day. There's no bond that can tear us apart, and I'm desperate to feel him inside me, making us one in a way that no stranger will ever get because Sebastian and I are forever.

I decide.

I want him.

I need him.

"You've had an... episode," he explains. "I can't. I want to, but it's not right. Let me take care of you."

A whimper leaves my lips, and I scratch my fingernails down his chest, feeling every slick muscle, and I push my palm against his heart. Its rhythm is even and strong while mine feels suddenly weak and out of control.

"Please," I beg. "I want you."

His hand reaches my face, rubbing a thumb across my mouth, pulling at my bottom lip.

"Emry," he pleads. "What happened?"

He knows I'm lying, but won't say it out loud. That or he senses something's changed within me, more than the pain in my chest that's become a vexing ache I want to ignore, preferably with the help of Sebastian's touch.

My fingertips trace along his jaw, running a thumb across his lips and sliding it gently into his mouth. I move my hand between my legs, teasing him, wanting him to concede. He releases my thumb and grabs my wrist, pulling it down to the bench.

"Emry," his voice comes out with a shake, imploring eyes that bore into mine. "Tell me what happened?"

I let my head fall back on the tile, breaking our gaze and allow myself to cry harder. It's an ugly sob that pours out from my gut, loud and echoing in the walls of the shower. Sebastian lifts me, sitting himself on the bench and bringing me into his lap.

I wrap my arms around his neck and mourn the life I had a few hours ago, but he doesn't know, and I can't bring myself to tell him. I pull at him with all the strength I have left, my hands slipping across his skin from the water and soap. He wraps his arms around me, tighter than ever, his muscles shaking against my body.

"I wish you would tell me," he begs into my ear. "I'm here for you. Always."

His words shatter me.

I've ruined everything.

The water runs cold before I think of releasing my grip, and when I look at his bloodshot eyes, the pain in my chest doubles.

I stare at my tattoo, visible beside his face, and think of our promise.

This vow I make to you of my own free will, to never separate or stray. Our bond of mind and spirit will forever unite us as one. I will honor our commitment for all the days to come, from this day forward, until death do us part.

The weekend I look forward to every Friday proves near unbearable with each passing hour, and my loving husband never leaves my side. Worry creases his forehead with subtle looks and touches that last a moment too long.

Cliches of broken hearts plague me. Food has no taste, I can't sleep, and the throbbing ache in my chest never ceases. I rub the spot so hard it bruises, and Sebastian runs a gentle hand over it while we sit in the shower Saturday morning.

"What's this?" he asks. "Is it from the door?"

"I don't know," I tell him. It's honest when I've lied more times in the past twelve hours than I can count.

"It hurts." I point to the spot. "Here. All the time."

"Since when?"

Opening my mouth to answer, I realize it's been weeks, starting before our first class at the university. I shut my jaw and shrug instead, afraid I'm making him worry too much when he's about to receive the terrible news that his wife has bonded with someone else.

I'll protect his heart as long as I can, doing whatever it takes. He's stronger than me, and we're unstoppable together. My body needs time to get over the shock is all.

"We'll ask the doctor," he assures me when I say nothing more. "I think we should go see Jack."

That's not a surprise. Jack has been seeing me on and off since I was sixteen. Sebastian doesn't know what exactly is wrong, he wants to start with my old therapist.

I nod and reach for him again, kissing his lips and wrapping my legs around his middle. I feel his erection press against me, but he resists, insistent that I see a doctor first.

"I'd never forgive myself if I hurt you."

"You won't," I promise.

"Here," he says, grazing a thumb across my temple.

He's not calling me crazy or unhinged, and he never would. Sebastian has seen me at my worst, when I was close to death and begging for it, hoping he would put me out of my misery when we met all those years ago.

I nod, understanding all he wants is to take care of his wife, but I need his touch, his claim of me, and this constant refusal hurts worse than the bruise that spreads between my breasts.

We avoid the topic of my panic attack, and I try not to bristle when he asks if I'm okay every fifteen minutes.

I'm not.

Sebastian calls Alison when we get out of the shower with our emergency line, telling her I'm sick and I can't come over before her event. He makes mention he doesn't know where his phone is, but he doesn't try to look for it, either. I lie again, saying I don't know where it is.

Lie.

Lie.

Lie.

I hate myself. I hate this.

Alison texts me a few times, asking how I'm feeling, but I can't bring myself to respond. Looking at my phone creates another wave of panic, worried when the news will break with my face on some headline. I stuff my phone in a corner under a pile of clothes and ignore the messages. The excuse of being sick should work for the weekend.

We make lunch and sit on the back patio to eat. I spend every second trying not to see the stranger's face, to think of him, to feel his presence inside me. Five minutes with that man, and his existence is entwined with mine. He's in my every thought, invading my mind and seeping into the deepest parts of my inner self. I swear I feel him in my bones, coursing through my veins, squatting inside my thoughts.

I don't know his name.

I don't want to know.

My muscles tense until my back pops from the strain, and Sebastian breaks me from my trance.

"Em," he calls out, shaking my arm, his face inches from mine. "I've been saying your name for a minute."

His eyes look down at the armrest, noticing the scratch marks I've made into the wood. "I'm fine," I say to the question he didn't ask yet.

He runs a hand down his face, shaking his head and sitting back.

"I can call NeXus," he offers. "Get the on-call doctor—"

"No," I snap. "I just need a little time."

To learn how to control these feelings and urges.

"I'm still calming down from yesterday," I continue. "I'll go to the hospital Monday and see about some sessions or even medicine. I promise. Why don't you... go for a run?"

"Absolutely not," he argues.

"Please," my voice cracks. "Just. I just need..."

"I'll work out in the house." He leans forward and squeezes my hand, and I soften with his touch. All I need is him. He's refusing me, and it's making me spiral, but if we can just be intimate, I'll be fine. "I'm not going too far. Not when you're like this."

I lean forward to kiss him, wrapping an arm around his neck and pulling myself into his lap. He's hard in an instant, and I know by the end of the weekend I'll wear him down. He'll understand we can get through this when I show him how much I still want him. Fuck the bond.

He begrudgingly pulls his mouth away, but his erection throbs against my leg. I graze my fingertips across his groin, and his breath hitches before he steps away, giving me some time to myself. Maybe he's torturing me, knowing I'm hiding something and holding himself back on purpose.

No, I decide. He's not one to do something like that, and the realization makes me feel worse. He would never take advantage of me, and that's why he keeps at a distance.

I feel the urge to call Alison and talk to my friend, but she wouldn't understand.

Would she?

Stepping into our bedroom, I dig the phone out of the pile of laundry and see a message from her.

ALISON

Can I bring your sick ass anything?

My finger hovers over her picture, toying with the idea of calling her, confessing the sin I never thought I'd commit. She's my best friend, my only friend these days, but she'll never forgive me for this.

ALISON

I won't mention the reception for a whole week if that makes you feel better.

She doesn't know about the bond yet. Maybe the news hasn't broken or they're trying to vet the story. No one's refused a bond, so it's not plausible outside of gossip articles yet. I tap the phone before I talk myself out of it, still not knowing what I'll say.

When she answers, she flips it to video and I'm watching her tie the laces of my green dress.

"What do you think?" she calls out to me, looking at herself in the mirror.

There's my answer. She doesn't know.

"Gorgeous, as always," I tell her, my breath hitching a little. She would have said something if a story was out about a bond this close to home, I'm sure, and I force myself to calm down.

"Thanks. You think— Oh, fuck, Em. You look like shit. What happened to you?"

I've showered and eaten some food. My hair hasn't been brushed and there isn't a smirk on my face as usual, but I didn't think it was a total disaster. I sniffle, and although my nose doesn't hurt, there's bruising and swelling, making me look like I lost a fight. I touch the tip, testing how sore it doesn't feel, still bitter when I think about why.

"What's going on? Seb was fuzzy on the details." She hops around, sliding her foot into one shoe.

"Why are you dressed? Isn't this a night event?" I ask.

"I'm deciding on an outfit, so I'm not late. So, what happened to your face?"

I go back outside and sink into my chair, watching Sebastian through the open curtains inside my house.

"I had a panic attack coming home from work and ran into a door. Then I..." I pause and look back at my phone, watching Alison turn to see herself in every angle of the mirror. She's not in a place to hear this, and it strikes me she'll be upset at what she considers good fortune. This is all she wants — the bond, and I've snatched away her dream life even though it's my nightmare.

"Then I panicked more and ran home, looking like a maniac. Seb's making me go to the hospital before classes. I might miss one, but I'll give admin an email."

She turns in the screen's direction, tilting her head. "This hasn't happened in a long time? I mean the panic attack."

I bite the inside of my cheek, spreading the taste of copper across my tongue, and nod. She waits a moment for me to continue.

"Well, we all remember my long-distance run through the quad," I joke.

She gives a pitiful smile, and I look over to the window, watching Sebastian lift a ridiculous amount of weight. His muscles shake, and a sheen of sweat reflects from the sun.

"I think maybe one of us should walk you to and from school until you get a handle on that," she offers. "I think that would make you feel better. Don't you?"

I nod without speaking, still watching the man I love. He's caring and sexy as fuck, and I resist the urge to rub my chest, the pain still burning and aching from the inside out.

"Have fun tonight, and be careful," I murmur. "You look beautiful."

"You sure you're alright?" Alison asks. "I can cancel and come over."

It's my last chance to talk to someone, but I don't take it, too afraid of losing everything in less than a day.

"No way. I won't ask how much you've paid for this thing, but it's too much to cancel for anything less than a funeral," I insist.

"Okay," she sighs. Her concern comes through the phone, and even though it's not the right time to tell her what happened yesterday, I think she might be there for me.

Maybe, when the time is right, she'll understand and surprise us both.

"Take some notes when you interview co-parents. I'll chart out the pros and cons for you," I say.

She claps a few times and nods, happily agreeing to the project. Her excitement is palpable, and I wish more than anything she finds what she's looking for.

I'm too exhausted to care or fight her when she mentions her upcoming ad for another roommate. My lack of attention concerns her so much that she asks to go with me to the hospital, insistent I'm damaged more than I realize.

I agree, but when she calls the next day, I don't answer.

I don't answer her thirty-seven calls or twelve text messages, and then I turn off my phone.

Sebastian and I go through the same pattern we've had for years, but there's a ticking clock that looms over us.

For him, it counts down to when I'll see a doctor and he can breathe a sigh of relief.

My countdown feels much different.

That stranger is out there somewhere, watching and waiting, and I'm no closer to confessing this to my husband.

Successfully freeing him of the outside world this weekend, I've only put off the inevitable.

I claw at my pillow lying in bed Sunday night, feeling Sebastian's arm wrap around my waist, his knees curling behind me while he holds me close. I've erased the stranger's face from my head when I close my eyes, and I concentrate on my nails pulling at the fabric, a slow and steady motion until I lull myself to a dreamless sleep.

Tomorrow will come, and I'll have to face it, and at some point, face my bond.

CHAPTER 12

THEO

I hear the beeping before I open my eyes, a shrill sound that pierces my eardrums, followed by the steady click of typing. Someone hacks away at a laptop at my side, matching the pounding in my head with every stroke of a key.

My bonded's face appears in my mind's eye, offering a moment of relief. My skin tingles with excitement at the mere thought of her—the woman I dream about that permeates my soul, but I don't know her name. She's a part of me, buzzing in my veins and clouding my thoughts the moment I'm awake.

The person typing is not my bonded, and I blink a few times before they come into focus.

"R-Robin," I croak, disappointment dripping from my lips, and the memory of my bondmate running from me surfaces, her feet flying and ripping out my heart with her every step.

Robin doesn't look up from her laptop, her fingers flying over the keyboard. "Almost done," she says without raising her head.

I try to sit up, but it feels like there are a thousand pounds on my chest cementing me in place. There's a sudden need to get out of this room, this hospital, I surmise, and find her. The memory of that beautiful face contorted in fear comes back, as does the cardiac event I had when I tried to catch her. The pain in my chest doesn't come close to the feeling of rejection, but is that even possible?

No one rejects the person they bond with.

"F-fuck," I cough, my throat dry.

The steady beep continues when Robin closes her laptop, a first since we've been working together.

My bondmate is the first thing that came to my mind, but my second priority comes into focus with this slap of reality.

"My contract states—"

"I reviewed it," Robin cuts me off. "In the event of a medical event, you're docked the wages you're unable to work, but we cannot remove you from the project unless you're incapacitated for over two weeks."

I look around the white hospital room, searching for a date or time, or maybe the woman. Every cell in my body thinks of her, wanting her, needing her.

"It's day three," Robin tells me. She circles the bed, hands clasped at her front. "I don't give compliments... ever."

Her comment is the funniest thing she's ever said, given Robin isn't comical.

Still, I huff a laugh that sends a jolt of anguish from my chest to the tip of every limb, my hand flying to the spot where the needle drove in days before. Wires that stretch out from machines and connect to my arms tighten while I rub the dull ache there.

"But," she continues. "I wouldn't let you go if you were out for a month. That is — unless we thought you'd die."

Well, that's good news.

"How kind," I get out.

I bring my arms to my sides and push down, trying to sit up. The action hurts beyond belief, but I move an inch, and Robin's arms hook underneath mine, helping me lift.

I groan through gritted teeth, and she sets a pillow behind my back. The thirty seconds of movement sent a trail of sweat dripping down my neck and chest, and I reach for the towel at my side, another bolt of pain coursing through my arm that I ignore.

"The event went well," I manage. "Is that what you're telling me?"

"Beyond expectations," she confirms. "We have solidified fourteen more deals while you were... incapacitated."

"Is that why I'm granted the pleasure of your company?" I force a smile. "Is this your way of saying thank you?"

"No," she deadpans. "Half the contracts want your name on the deal. Companies you've worked with before. Now that you're awake—"

"You mean alive," I interrupt her.

Her eyes narrow.

"Both," she admits. "I'm briefing you about said deals so you can sign."

I rest my head back on the pillow and exhale. Robin's direct nature, which I typically find endearing, isn't something I need at this moment. I'd trade a bucket of money for someone with a bedside manner.

I'd trade everything I have, everything I am, for my bonded to be here instead of Robin.

Fuck, I wish I knew her name.

"If you want a caretaker, that Moira woman visits every day. Should I add her to the payroll?"

The ache in my heart softens for a moment with thoughts of my friend, and I turn my head to Robin.

"Anyone…" I pause a moment, not wanting to give anything away. "Anyone else come to visit?"

Robin shakes her head. "No, but I'm not here every minute. I have work to do. More than normal while you're in this state."

I swallow hard and accept the rejection, knowing the woman can't refuse it forever. The bond is surprising, and she's…

Oh, fuck. She's married. Her tattoo.

"Theo," Robin jolts me from my thoughts.

"Yes," I say.

The idea of paying Moira to help me might be a good one. I don't think she would turn down the extra cash considering the cost of her daughter's studying abroad program.

"Pay Moira as a traveling nurse, with overtime," I say. "Get some of the stock boys to work for her. She has a shop in town to run, too."

Married.

The memory of her wrist hits me like a truck, and I close my eyes, focusing on the letters.

Craw? Clover? Cowen?

"Fine," Robin agrees. "And yes, I read that clause in your contract as well regarding medical expenses whilst on the job. Very clever to add that without disclosing your heart condition."

My eyes open and pierce into hers, and she's taken aback by the fierceness behind them. I'm overly kind to clients, but my patience wears thin when they try to blame me for their lack of follow-up.

"I would have revealed it had you properly reviewed the contract and asked," I say. "Perhaps this is a good lesson in your company's hubris, especially that of your fearless leader. How is his vacation, by the way?"

"Long," Robin answers, and I wonder again if he's buried somewhere.

I wouldn't put it past this woman, but I have bigger problems.

"I'll let the staff know you're awake. Your computer is here." She points to a side table covered in flowers. I assume Moira left them. "I need an estimated date of return to work when you talk to your doctor. I pinned all the contracts in your inbox, and I need them reviewed and signed today."

"Understood," I respond to her back as she starts for the door.

She pauses, resting a hand on the door handle. "There's something else in your contract," she adds. "Something we ensured the hospital adhered to once we knew."

"Knew what?" I ask.

Robin turns, crossing her arms at her front and narrowing her eyes.

"About your bond," she says.

It doesn't take long for me to realize what all has transpired in the last three days.

So, it's out then. Of course it is.

I tick through the hundred-page document in my mind, narrowing down the possibilities.

"My privacy clause," I sigh.

"They haven't identified you as the bonded," Robin says without me asking. "Pictures of you are blurry, and you're from out of town. The store owners won't release the camera footage until the government sends an order... which will make its way through red tape soon."

Moira won't release it. Thank fuck.

"And the woman?" I ask, every cell in my body alert.

"Not identified for certain with her face busted up, but a few people came forward naming her. And don't ask me because I don't remember or care to know. You still have a job to do, and after that, you can live off the government all you want. Contracts work both ways."

I fight back the laugh in the back of my throat. I can't believe the nerve of her, these words, and the bullshit position I've found myself in. What are the odds of finding a bonded at all, let alone one that rejects you? All the while, Robin only cares about ink on paper.

I admit to myself there's something satisfying about that. When there's a signed agreement, everything feels more stable.

Like a marriage.

"You're here under the company's name," Robin says. "You vouched for Moira stating she was a trusted friend when you wrote a letter of recommendation for her daughter to attend Matchmade, so I let her in. No one else. Not that anyone else has asked to see you, but they will come, Theo."

"That was..." I trail off. "The right decision. She won't..."

I don't know how to finish. I'm only beginning to grasp what this means.

"I recognized you in the photos and kept that information to myself," Robin adds.

We pause our conversation, staring at each other with that admission.

"I appreciate that," I tell her. "Really, I do."

Robin uncrosses her arms and adjusts her laptop bag on her shoulder. "I'm not a completely terrible person, Theodore."

There's the smallest curve on one side of her lips that one might guess is her version of a smile, but it's so faint and quick that I can't be certain.

"So, you didn't murder the old man?" I ask. "He's really on vacation?"

She turns on her heel and flings the door open. "Don't be

surprised if someone recognizes you once you're out of this room, Theo," she adds, slamming the door behind her.

That guy might really be dead.

I'm still staring at the shut door, lost in my thoughts and worries when a nurse barges in a few moments later.

They go over my list of medications, take every measurement from my oxygen to my piss, and inform me I'm free to leave tomorrow, but I'm walking this earth on borrowed time.

Not new news, but not something I don't want to be reminded of while I feel like shit.

It is, though, another assurance that they don't know I'm the bonded.

Crawford? No, it was shorter than that.

"There's also the matter of the roll call," the nurse says. "It's standard for treatment, and outlined in the facility's admission protocol."

"Roll call?" I bite out. Every hospital gives it a unique name, but I gather it's some touching party that I'm in no mood to take part in.

She casts her eyes over me, biting her bottom lip. "Before you leave, there will be a round of testing."

"Touching," I reply.

"Yes, well..." She clears her throat and takes a step back. I'm seething with what little strength I have, and she senses my disdain from across the room. "Shift change is in a few hours, so they'll take you to the hallway in a wheelchair. It will only take about fifteen minutes."

Not in a position to argue, I say nothing, but look over at the wheelchair in the corner. I consider getting myself into it and attempting a grand escape, but it's hard to take in a deep breath, so I'll suffer through their roll call if they insist.

I'm not ready to admit that no one can match with me because I've already bonded. That information feels oddly private, and something I'll keep to myself for as long as possible.

The nurse scurries out, and I let a frustrated growl leave my lips, my head falling back on the hard bed.

"Not happy to be here?" Moira's voice sing-songs. She must have snuck in after the nurse. "From what I hear, you should be happy to be alive, sir."

Crowe!

"Moira, I'm glad to see you," I blurt out.

She opens her mouth to speak, but I cut her off before she has the chance. My eyes are wild and my weak heart beats out of my chest.

"I need your help. I need to find someone."

CHAPTER 13

"Give me three guesses who, but I'll only need one," Moira says, shaking her head and smiling. "This is wonderful news, you know. This is... it's a miracle, Theo."

"So you did withhold the footage?" I ask to confirm my suspicions. "Of me in front of your shop."

She nods and steps closer. "It won't stay hidden for long, but it's your business. I know this might be confusing, given your life plan."

She looks to the machines at my side, charting every beat of my heart and breath in my lungs. Her vocation may be shop owner, but it wouldn't take a genius to know something's very wrong with me.

"They wouldn't tell me much," she admits. "About your condition. I know you passed out shortly after the... meet and greet."

I chuckle at her simple joke, grateful she isn't hounding me for details.

"There's not much to tell," I shrug, the ache lessoning after a few hits of my morphine pump. "Hypertrophic cardiomyopathy. It will kill me before long, but…"

I trail off, not saying what we both know. "It's a big word for a genetic heart disease that killed my father. Mine's severe, and I had maybe another ten years, no matter how well I take care of myself."

Moira looks over at me in shock. A young man, powerful in every sense if you spot me on the street, but underneath the curve of muscle on my chest lies a heart that doesn't work as it should.

I don't consider myself a vain person, but there's some conceit that comes with the way I look. It's a direct result of my disease. Maybe I indulge in Moira's pizza sometimes, but I'm regimented about food, exercise, and sleep. Every decision affects my health, and it shows in my body.

None of that matters, though.

With the length of our transplant lists and how soon my death could occur, I don't stand a chance. No one would know my health problems if I didn't have a heart attack in the middle of a busy city, and she's taking a moment to register the truth.

Without my bondmate, I'll die, and soon.

"I'm so sorry you lost your father so young, but now… with a bond."

"I planned on spending my last years in paradise before I stroke out and die on some beach surrounded by beautiful women and all the drugs I've never allowed myself to have," I joke.

Moira doesn't laugh. Her eyes well with tears, and she nods a few times, taking in the shock of everything and the disappointment that my bondmate isn't by my side, helping me heal.

"I need," I stop short, realizing I don't know Moira very

well, and I may be asking too much. "A woman, Robin, she'll be contacting you. The company I work for will pay you, temporarily of course, a lot of money to help me out while I'm here. They'll provide hands at the shop, too."

Her eyes squint, and she tilts her head. The machines next to me beep a few times with an unsteady pattern, and I hit the button to shut them up, knowing it's the typical rhythm of my foolish heart.

"It's a lot of money, Moira. Triple what typical nurses make, and I won't make you do any bedpans."

Her eyes widen, and she takes a few steps over toward me. "I know nothing about nursing. I'd kill you," she confesses.

"I could die any second with the best minds in the world at my side," I admit. "I trust you, and what I need help with isn't medical."

"Ah," she sighs. "You need that woman. You'll be better once we find her."

"I can feel her," I say. "She's anchored inside me somehow. She has to feel that, too. If we're close enough, I might actually live past my expiration date."

Moira slaps the side of my arm, then raises her hands to her hips, thinking over my offer. "I've never heard of someone less than thrilled about a bonding. And you're nice to look at. She mus—" She stops short, remembering something.

"Love her husband," I say the words that hang between us.

"There's been speculation about who she is," Moira says. "A few articles that no one puts much stock in, but still. She's a settler. Half of her tattoo is in a picture, but I can't make out her name. Maybe no one else could and that's why they didn't print it?"

I'm tearing a family apart. That's the only explanation for her refusal, and the pain in my chest feels different at the real-ization. I'm a problem solver by nature, fixing broken companies and making them succeed, giving people their lives back. This ruins the life she's built with someone.

Every morning, she wakes up next to a person she's chosen to love, a person she vowed to never leave. I know the outcome even though that vow has never been put to the test. It's easy to say forever when a future that's too good to imagine never comes to fruition. She can't ignore this pull to each other.

I hate myself a little for that. Would it have been better for me to die on the ground last week? What would that have done to her?

"It doesn't matter," I croak. "We've bonded."

"I don't think this has happened before," Moira admits. "And with fewer people settling each year, it may never again."

"I'm not a fan of being an example," I huff. "This stays between us."

"For now," Moira's eyebrows raise and she pulls out her phone. "They don't have any clear video, but there are some pictures. People don't know you around here, but they will soon. I'm surprised no one has recognized you yet."

"They don't expect a bonded to be in the hospital," I say. "Bonded get better — younger."

She nods and tilts her head in agreement, her fingers tapping and scrolling through her phone.

"Here's one article," Moira says, her eyes scanning the story. "They wrote that the woman ran away, and no one gave it much merit. Very few shares and only a few comments, but it's been up for an hour. Shit, this one doesn't have her name."

"It's good that the story isn't going far, but I need that name," I sigh.

These articles spread like wildfire, usually backed by reception companies. They feed the masses news stories about bonding so they churn out more ticket sales. I doubt a story of a woman bolting from her bondmate would generate much revenue, and I wonder if they're killing the gossip on arrival to create their own version.

"A few witnesses gave their name," Moira offers. "Am I a nurse or a detective?"

"Detective with triple a nurse's salary," I tell her. "A very lucrative triple salary."

A speaker comes on in my room with a scratchy voice. "Mr. Lorwerth, we're approaching shift change."

I wonder why they think I give a fuck, and then I remember.

"We'll send a nurse in to help you into your chair."

I reach for the speaker to talk into and Moira holds it out for me. "Now?" I bite out.

"Yes, sir. We'll be in shortly."

"Detective, Moira," I groan. "They're going to make me sit in the hall while the entire building accosts me."

"You could just... tell someone here you bonded," Moira says. "Why put yourself through that? If you tell them, people will find her quicker than I can."

I place my open palm on my chest, pressing my fingers into the skin. The typical strain of my heart and agony when it struggles to beat now fills with a sense of need. She's flowing through me, and my typical decisiveness clouds with the desire to please her.

It would be easy to call the press and announce I'm the bonded to track her down, but the world would watch, and it would hurt her. I'm about to rip apart the home she built for herself, and I need to dislodge her walls piece by piece, not bulldoze them to the ground.

"She wouldn't want that," I confess. "We need to take it slow."

"And if you have a heart attack and die while we pace our way through this?"

"Then her husband is one lucky man," I answer. "Don't let anyone know the story is true."

Moira nods as a few nurses walk in, grazing their hands over me before they bring the chair and get me set up. Moira leaves without another world, and I don't know what I hope for as I'm set out into the hallway.

The idea of living longer than I ever imagined doesn't feel as euphoric when the price is to devastate the first woman I've ever cared about.

How can the bond feel so right and wrong at the same time?

"It's genetics," I tell myself. None of it's real. Just a mix of DNA that went haywire a hundred years ago, forcing us to abandon our promises to ourselves.

Promises to others...

If I die in the hallway waiting for Moira to find something, all the better.

It wasn't supposed to be this way.

CHAPTER 14

The grip I have on Sebastian's arm makes my hands ache, but I refuse to let him go. I'm walking into a volcano that's ready to explode at any moment. The earth feels unsteady beneath my feet, and I'm unbearably hot, my skin scorching as we ascend the stairs to the sixth floor of the hospital.

He notices, walking down every hallway with me in between him and the wall, protecting me from stray hands reaching for my skin. I wish that was the problem. I'd give anything to go back to Friday on that crosswalk and pull myself together enough to wait, cross the street, and go on with my life.

I wrap my sweater around my chest and bury my face in the collar, dipping my head and watching my feet as we walk. My face is hidden from onlookers who might recognize me, but that doesn't change how I'll have to tell him after this. I feel foolish for not doing it before we left the house. Now I'm stuck.

Our next errand is getting him a new phone because he thinks he's lost his.

I'm so selfish, so stupid, but I can't make the words leave my mouth. I don't even know where to start or how to answer the questions that will follow.

We step into the office, and Sebastian sets me in a chair. A few patients get up, and my pulse skyrockets, wondering what they'll say. They graze the back of my hand and sit back down without a word. He grimaces while I let out a slow exhale, then turns to finish my intake forms.

"How are you feeling, on a scale of one, to I'm-going-to-burn-this-place-down?" he asks, sitting down next to me. The words help me smile despite my trepidation.

I feel like my life is a time bomb that will explode all over everyone and hurt the ones I love beyond repair.

"I'm fine," I lie. A young man calls my name, and Sebastian stands with me. "I think it's best—"

He finishes my sentence, "If you go by yourself. I know. I love you more than anything. I'll be right here." He wraps his arms around me as he whispers the words into my ear.

They send a knife into my heart, and I fight the tears that threaten to escape. When we separate, I force a shaking smile he knows is fake. His thumb runs along my bottom lip, and I pucker a kiss before I leave. Every moment with him feels like my last, and this agony in my chest has to be my heart breaking.

I'm still in chaos when I leave him. I don't have a plan or even a clue about what happens next. Thoughts spin while we walk down an endless hallway. I could tell the doctor I never want to leave the house again and get diagnosed as an agora-phobic. I'd lose my job, but Sebastian is worth it. Maybe I can confide in Dr. Wells, tell him the truth. He's always been a support to me, and someone I trust. There's patient confiden-tiality, right?

Before I get to a conclusion, I'm standing in his office, the door shutting behind me with a thud. The familiar space hasn't changed. Same grey carpet and furniture. That clock in the corner ticks too loud even after all these years, and he's made tea, as usual.

I hate tea.

"Professor Crowe." His voice is calming in a way that suits a psychologist. He ushers me over to a large chair and offers me some tea, which I accept in my haziness.

I clutch the cup of brown water to my chest and sink into the cushions, staring at him with wide eyes. We have a long history, and most of it I'd like to forget. Not because of anything he did, but because of why I had to seek his help.

Jack Wells brought me back to sanity after Sebastian found me, and I never made his job easy. Seeing his face, I'm forced to relive the memories of the woman I was and accept the terrible truth that another life-changing event brings me back to this place.

"I won't bother with the formalities of what brings you here today," he says, taking a sip from his own cup before picking up his tablet. I freeze, curious about how much he knows. Dr. Wells works around the clock, never stopping for the pleasantries of breaking news unless it suits his field of study. He never had many friends outside his profession, from what I could tell.

"Your husband filled me in, and he called me this morning, leaving a long message."

I know because I stood outside the door while he used my phone, paranoid he would see a news article with my face on it.

"I have your files from our last sessions several years ago, but this event sounds different with an intensity that scared him."

He pauses for me to respond, but I sit motionless, letting the hot cup burn the palms of my hands.

"I know it's not the best circumstances, but I'm glad to see you again," he says. "Do you need a moment, or may I ask you some questions about the event?"

"I'm fine," I lie again. The cup trembles in my hands. I'm holding it together by a thread in my therapist's office. How will I handle the real world where my bondmate is out searching for me?

"You're not," Dr. Wells corrects. "Fine, that is. You had an episode on the streets, ran into a shop door, and then ran home bloody and bruised. Sebastian says you've spent the entire weekend in a fog. Distant and jittery. Would you say that's accurate?"

"Yes."

He taps a few times on his tablet. "You haven't had a depressive episode or panic attack in three years by my records. Is that correct?"

"Yes." This will take all day with one-word answers, but my only plan is to live out the rest of my life in this office. Maybe I could move in here?

"What would you say your state of emotional feeling was leading up to the hit to your face?" he asks.

I twirl the cup, pleading with myself to be helpful. I trust Jack, and I know he'll keep what we talk about between us.

"Claustrophobic. Erratic probably," I rush out, "I was running away from the crowd. It was my fault I hit the door, not..."

I stop myself before saying more and gulp my tea. It tastes like shit.

"You've been teaching for years, but school started

recently. Did you notice these feelings building up, or did they come upon you at the start of the school year?"

"I've never enjoyed being touched everywhere I go," I admit. "A buildup, I guess. I was... disagreeing with a friend and I wasn't completely honest with her. It was really hot outside. Just a combination of annoyances."

He jots down some notes before continuing. "Did you feel annoyed or panicked as you ran?"

"Um," I huff. "Both I suppose."

"And after the hit to your face," he continues. "Did your emotional state change or increase?"

A jolt of agony hits my chest, and I bring my hand to the spot, almost spilling my tea. My breath leaves my body, and a few tears escape.

"Am I being too formal?" Dr. Wells asks. "I'm determining—"

"—my mental state before and after the hit to my head triggered my pain receptors. I'm aware of the trauma checklist. I've been through this."

I want to set my cup down and call him Jack, talk to him like we did before. If I bare my soul out in this room, beg him for his help, he would stop everything and be there for me. He's done that before.

"Yes. You certainly have. We've been through this together." He puts down his tablet, sits back, and looks me over, taking another sip from his cup. The clock in the corner ticks, sending my nerves on edge.

Tell him, Em.

"What really happened Friday?" he asks.

"I, um," I stutter. "When I..." Silence follows, my chin trembling.

Say the fucking words.

"Em," he sighs.

"Dr. Wells," I whimper.

He leans forward, his elbows on his knees, and he runs his hands through his hair. "Call me Jack, and let's put this formal shit to the side. I've treated you since you were sixteen, and you aren't any better at hiding your auto-response signals when you're keeping something from me. You've crossed and uncrossed your legs ten times. You're breathing fast, and you keep scratching the right side of your neck under your ear. What happened Friday?"

Fuck.

I spin the cup in my hand and watch the liquid spin, hoping the courage will come. "To be certain, you can't repeat anything we discuss?" I ask.

"Not unless I believe you are about to harm yourself or others," he affirms. "Do you promise to look out for swinging doors?"

I chuckle and look up at him. He waves his hand, urging me to continue. He wants to help. That's all he's ever wanted, and in the past, he succeeded.

"You worked for NeXus, with Seb in the field... when you found me."

"You know I did."

"Doing what?" I ask.

"You know I can't answer that, Em. And I don't know if going back to the past will help you work through the here and now."

I set the cup down, liquid splashing to the side and spilling onto the coffee table. "Two years ago, you came to the school and spoke to my class about hormonal changes in bondmates. I sent a request for a speaker on the topic, and they sent you."

"It was lovely seeing you that day," he responds.

"Did you see my name and pick up the job?" I ask. "Or did you work in that field of study and you were best qualified?"

He shakes his head. "You know I can't answer that."

I scoot forward in my chair, persistent and growing impatient with these games. My mind has switched to the science of my problem, and it helps steady me when I speak with him.

"Let's assume you did some work with how people's emotions and hormones change when they bond," I lead on, not making him answer the question directly, even though we both know that he did.

He's suspicious, squinting his eyes and leaning away from me. I can read body language too, and something has piqued his interest. He's fighting me, crossing his arms at his front, defiant to head down this path, but I'll take us there kicking and screaming if I must.

"In your professional opinion—"

"I can't answer any questions about my work at NeXus or hormone studies that may or may not have occurred," he interrupts.

"In your opinion—" I push.

"Em, I can't," he hisses.

"As a friend!" My words are a cracked scream, and he feels it, taking in a shuddered breath and uncrossing his arms. "As a friend who found a sixteen-year-old girl that had been studied and f-fucking t-tortured for years."

The words catch in my throat and his eyes meet mine, full of sadness for the girl I was all those years ago.

"I know the studies done on me went to NeXus," I hiss. "All that data didn't disappear, so if you could bend the rules this one time and give me a fucking answer to a proverbial question."

Red creeps up my chest and the ache is back, throbbing into my ribs and piercing my heart.

"What if someone denied the bond?" I find the courage to

ask. "What would happen neurologically... hormonally? Would there be adverse medical effects?"

"That's not something... I w-wouldn't know," he stutters.

"In your opinion, Jack. Fuck. In a fucking for instance, what do you think would happen?"

His eyes widen, and there's a spark of understanding. He almost stands, but relaxes, his eyes moving rapidly over my body. "Em, what happened Friday? Why are you asking me this?"

"Please answer my proverbial question," I beg. "What if someone didn't want to bond but did? What could be done to suppress or stop the... the..."

"I don't think that..." is all he says. "Oh, god, Em."

"I know what you're thinking," I snip.

"I'm..." he pauses, rubbing the side of his face, making his palm scratch across his stubble. "I'm thinking you've been through enough and you don't want—"

"The bond," I say.

He knows.

I see it in the way his face contorts, working through the emotions. He's excited at the prospect of another bond, but scared and sad for me, knowing this isn't what I want or need.

I don't care what he thinks if there's a chance he can help me. "Adverse effects," I continue. "There's a drive to be with a person. Do you think some hormone blockers might help suffocate that? Is there a way... to break it–to stop it?"

He picks up his tablet and moves his fingers over the screen. "I'm ordering a blood panel. Em, I don't know. I want to help you, so I'll take a look, see what I can find out."

"Thanks." I shudder in a breath, letting a small whimper escape.

"How's..." he trails off, realizing the question he wants to ask is wrong in some way.

"Seb?" I ask. "I haven't told him."

There's silence when he sets down the tablet, except for that ticking clock. I want to throw my teacup at the face of it and shut it up. Minutes pass without words, and I slurp what's left of my lukewarm tea when Jack clears his throat.

"You have to," he says.

"I know. I will," I gulp. "I can't believe I've evaded it this long with the news and everything."

"You're lucky," he says, eyebrows raising.

"Am I?" I bite back.

"I didn't mean," he sighs. "Seb's stronger than most, mentally. Tell him."

I nod, biting my bottom lip, hating how I've failed my husband in so many ways.

"You've always been so different, going against the current," Jack says.

"I'm defiant in my old age," I smirk. "And I love Seb."

Jack nods and stands. "I'll walk you to the clinic to do your blood draw. We'll get started now. I'll cancel everything else for the day – for the week, maybe."

I hook my arm into his. "I love Seb," I repeat.

Jack places a hand on top of mine and leads us to the door. "In my professional opinion," he sighs. "That won't be enough."

CHAPTER 15

THEO

Endless groups of people mill through the hall, talking amongst themselves. They don't greet me when their hands slide across my skin, lost in their own conversation. They wheeled me up to the sixth floor with a few others, and we're crowded together so the staff can test out the fresh meat without wasting too much time.

Some of these patients have no business outside of their room, still hooked up to machines and looking barely alive. One man remains asleep in his bed, unaware of what's occurring around him.

I scratch the back of my neck and roll my eyes once more, grateful I'm doing better than the others. Feeling returns to my weak muscles after days of not moving, and the discomfort in my chest subsides. I check my phone when another hand plops on top of my filthy hair, and I flinch from their touch.

Fuck, I need a shower.

Stepping into the bathroom felt like an insurmountable

task earlier today, but it's all I want at this moment. My renewed energy allows me to stretch out my limbs and test out my legs. I sit up in the wheelchair and bring myself to standing, my heart beating a steady rhythm as I rise. I expect a few stumbles, but I lift with ease, raising my hands above my head and feeling the bones pop.

The hospital gown leaves little to be desired and when there's a break in the crowd, I step over to a supply closet where a nurse is packing a cart.

"Hey, could I get some scrubs?" I ask, pointing to the stack in the corner. She grazes a hand over my shoulder before she nods and hands them over.

I change, pulling my pants up underneath my gown while more people pass me by and feel their way through us.

"Do you know when this ends?" I call out to the nurse.

"In about an hour," she says.

An hour?

I grumble at her response but should have known the fifteen-minute promise was just to get me out here.

"Can I get you anything else?" the nurse says.

It's only been ten minutes, so I grab a few blankets for the other patients and pass them out while we wait. If none of the staff will bother to make us more comfortable while we sit at auction, I might as well make myself at home.

Checking my phone, I see the pinned emails from Robin and respond. Keeping her off my ass gives me more time to track down the woman. Articles that I find are bare bones and without detail, and all of them are written today. Adherence or some other company is blocking the story until they can control the narrative and find a gain in it somewhere.

Moira hasn't had enough time to talk to anyone yet, and I'm crawling out of my skin, eager to leave.

My nurse passes by with her lunch in hand, and I lunge for

her. "Hey, I know you said I could leave tomorrow, but any chance we can change that to today? I'm feeling better. A lot better."

It's true. My energy rises by the second, and my heart beats in a steady rhythm.

"Sir?" her voice raises in confusion. "How are you out of your chair? You shouldn't be walking around."

"It's Theodore. Call me Theo, and I'm fine," I argue. "I feel better than before I had my..."

"Theodore, sit down," she insists.

"I feel great," I say to her blank face. "I feel amazing."

This is ridiculous. My company paid their bills, and it's only a matter of time before someone recognizes me. I could outrun anyone who tries to stop me with how great I feel.

"But you need—"

I'm sprinting down the hall before I let her finish, hearing her bellow my name in my wake. My heart beats like a stallion, strong and even, letting me run faster through the halls.

I search for the exit signs and follow them down hallways, every step faster than the last. My heart doesn't skip or fail me, and it's as strong as when...

Oh, fuck.

My feet skitter to a stop, thoughts racing through my mind. The feeling sits within me, the pull to her, and I turn away from the exit.

Opening doors and knocking on windows, I scour through the building, and no one seems to mind as long as they touch my arm when I pass by.

She's close. That's why I feel this way.

Her name is a mystery, so I can't call to her, but she's here somewhere. I feel it, and that pull grows stronger the further I go. It's inside my gut, sparking life into my body, energizing my every step.

"Have you seen a woman with, um, a broken nose, or a bruised face?" I ask a few men, stumbling into a break room.

"There's a lot of people here that fit that description, man," one of them says.

"Right, thanks. What is this floor, anyway? I was here for the uh, the testing."

"Administration, phlebotomy, and the lab," he says, focusing back on his sandwich.

That doesn't help me much, but I thank him anyway, stumbling back out into the hallway. I'm certain I've passed the administration offices, having gone through rows of cubicles with employees wearing suits instead of lab coats. Maybe she works here, but that doesn't seem right. She didn't have scrubs on the day we met, but she dressed professionally, and if she wasn't in those offices...

If she's a patient, she wouldn't be in the lab. The rush of adrenaline sends me into motion just as the overhead speakers blare my name.

"Theodore, you're needed back in the testing hall immediately."

That nurse snitched quickly.

I ignore the announcement, chuckling because they legally can't give out my full name, and I follow the signs to phlebotomy and venipuncture. Every second feels better and stronger than the last. She's back inside me again, closer than ever, her essence filling me with euphoria.

My lips draw up into a smile, and I'm laughing like a kid, skipping down the halls, darting in and out of rooms.

Something brought her to me, despite her husband. We're meant to be together forever, and I want nothing else.

"Theodore, please return to testing immediately."

"There's no point," I call out to the ceiling. A pair of nurses at the end of the hall twist their heads in my direction. "Sorry," I tell them, raising a hand.

"Can we help you?" one asks. "Theodore, I assume." She touches a radio on her wrist, and I back away, finding an escape through another door. They won't care once I've found her, and I *will* find her.

There are fleeting moments of sanity in my hunt, ones where I remember the tattoo on her wrist, and who I'm hurting. Those thoughts don't stand a chance with the urging inside me, begging me to find her, forcing me forward. It's not possible to stop or see reason. I have a one-track mind, focused solely on my bonded, the one meant on every level to be mine forever.

My feet squeak as I slide through corridors, rushing into rooms full of confused faces. "Crowe!" I yell out, remembering the name on her wrist. "Crowe!"

The overhead speaker blares again, but it's drowned out by my cries.

"Crowe! I know you're here somewhere. Where are you, please?"

Fuck, I sound crazed, but I can't stop myself.

I barrel through another doorway, my heart's steady *thump thump thump* beating stronger than I ever thought possible. I see the people getting blood drawn through the wide glass doors of the lab. This is the end of the road. If she's not in here, I have to find my way to another floor, but that can't be right.

The connection is stronger than on the street. I can taste her, smell her, feel her.

Is she fucking hiding?

I spin in circles at the end of a hallway, the feeling of rapture wrapping around me and excitement in my every breath. It's the peak of the mountain, just like when I touched her a few days ago. It's almost orgasmic, and I'm jumping out of my skin from the anticipation.

"Crowe. I know you're here somewhere. Where are you, please?"

"Yes?" a man's voice says.

I jerk around, almost tripping over my own feet.

A stranger stares at me, his face hardening as he steps closer. He's over six feet of brawn and muscle, and he eyes me with contempt. Cocking his head and closing his fists at his sides, he moves in my direction.

"Mind telling me why you're screaming my name?"

CHAPTER 16

EMRY

Sebastian heads with us to the blood draw and catches up with Jack, talking to him about mundane things to fill the silence. The weather's great and everyone's jobs are fine, along with family. Those are the lies they say to one another. If anyone told the truth, this would be a walk full of tears and heartbreak.

I concentrate on the posters that line the hallways, drowning out their words. A picture of a man and woman with no apparent tattoos stands on a beach in front of three children. They don't embrace each other, but the children hug.

Give your children the edge and test, reads along the bottom of the photograph.

I'm grateful for Jack's acting skills, but there's a stiffness to him where there wasn't before. He's harboring an immense secret with me, one he believes will crush his friend.

Sebastian and Jack have known each other for over a decade, and their closeness only makes matters worse. They can't disclose what they've accomplished together at NeXus, but they've worked in tandem since before I came into the picture. When Sebastian found me all those years ago, he insisted I have therapy with Jack, even though his focus had moved to research.

Jack took my case as a favor for a dear friend.

A friend he's lying to by omission.

I'm spreading misery everywhere I go, but instead of the sadness that's infiltrated my soul these past few days, I'm... content.

More than that, I realize as we turn down a hallway. I'm happy, holding back a smile from the flutter in my heart. It's nonsensical, but the feeling washes over me, blanketing me with joy.

It might be because I've shared my burden with someone else and no longer have to carry it alone. There's a chance that Jack or someone at NeXus can help me. What if I could convince someone I'm a valuable case study? If there's a way to block the hormones that create this response to a bonded mate, could that help researchers find what sparks the bond in the first place?

Typically, to defeat something, a virus, or genetic abnormality, you must understand its creation, but who's to say we couldn't make science work in the other direction this time?

Part of me can't believe I'm considering letting someone put me through more tests, but that's how desperate I am. I'll submit myself to their labs for Sebastian, and he would be there for me once he gets over the shock.

There's hope in my heart for the first time since I ran into that man. My... bondmate. The thought makes my heart beat faster, and I reach for the spot that I've rubbed sore the past few days. Replacing the incessant ache is something else, something euphoric. The sensation spreads from the ventricles of my heart into every vein, every limb, and makes my head swim. I never partook in recreational drugs, but I understand the appeal if this is how it feels.

A voice blares to life in the hallway, startling me and jolting me out of my haze.

"Theodore, you're needed back in the testing hall immediately."

The speaker turns off with a buzzing sound. I imagine an angry nurse dealing with an unruly patient and hanging up the phone.

"They're pretty serious about phlebotomy," Sebastian jokes, pointing to the sign up ahead.

Almost there.

"Oh, that's not what testing—"

"Theodore, please return to testing immediately." The speaker cuts off Jack's response, and I chuckle at the nuisance.

"You were saying," Sebastian smiles.

"Testing is um," Jack fiddles with the screen of his tablet. "They set the new patients out into the hallway for the staff to test."

Sebastian's face hardens. "They won't do that to Emry."

"No, no," Jack assures us. "It's only patients that stay overnight. A condition of care, but you may get touched with the blood draw."

"It's fine," I tell Sebastian, running my hand up his thick arm. "I'm okay."

I'm better than just fine. The elation in my body lifts my spirits and I'm smiling, bringing Sebastian's lips to mine and offering a soft kiss. The touch sends pinpricks of ecstasy from my mouth to my toes, setting my skin on fire in the best way.

Did Jack slip a drug into my tea?

Fuck, I don't care if he did because this feeling is one I

never thought I'd feel again. It's peace and elation in a fucking hospital hallway and I can't explain—

"Crowe!"

We all freeze at the sound of the name being shouted into the air, our steps halting suddenly in confusion.

"Did someone just say Crowe?" Sebastian asks.

I share Sebastian's surprise for only an instant as the worries race through my mind. The joy and elation that sparks inside my soul, and the sudden pull to run towards those words, has me coming to only one conclusion. My heart beats wildly in my chest, threatening to burst while I hold my breath, wondering if anyone notices my panic.

Jack turns his head. "Yes, I heard that." His eyes look like saucers when they meet mine, and then he casts them down to the tattoo on my wrist, the only thing my bondmate saw that could identify me, and suddenly I know.

I know he's here.

The crash hits me in the gut when I realize he's found me, and I'm pinned in this spot, my feet in quicksand. I'm sinking, unable to free myself from him on the very first day I've left the house.

This happiness that's twisted its way into my soul with every step isn't relief. It's not the chance to make things right or stop the train from barreling down on me.

It's him.

"Crowe! I know you're here somewhere." The voice screams, louder this time, and more frantic with every word.

The euphoria doesn't fade when I sense him closer, and I hate myself as I hold onto my husband, knowing I'm caught like some cheater or liar.

Am I?

I kept this from him trying to fix it myself, and what a pathetic job I've done with my first attempt.

He's here, and I curl my fingers into Sebastian's tensing muscles, my fingernails digging into the skin. My wrist turns and my tear-filled eyes look at the tattoo, unable to meet Sebastian's eyes.

Crowe.

Beautiful letters they tattooed on our wrists after the vows we took, and a sob escapes my lips. Jack's hands shake holding the tablet, but I don't look up. I don't want to see what's heading our way, but I can't run either.

"What is this?" Sebastian asks. "W-what?"

He can't make sense of the man yelling our name or our reaction, because who would imagine the truth? It's a million-to-one chance, and he won't understand.

"Crowe. Where are you, please?" the voice screams.

He's at the end of our hall, and Sebastian removes his arm from my grip, placing me back against the wall and ushering Jack to stand next to me.

I'm shaking. My entire body vibrates against the cold tile wall, and Jack takes my hand, squeezing it until my fingernails turn white.

"Yes?" Sebastian says to him. His feet are heavy in the silent hallway as he approaches the man. I can't stop him. I can barely move.

"Mind telling me why you're screaming my name?"

There's a pull in my stomach to run toward the stranger, but I fight it, slapping my free hand against the wall, tears streaming down my face.

Jack brings his lips to my ear. "You won't be able to resist him," he says. "Do you understand? Any closer, and it can't be stopped. I don't know how you escaped the first time."

"I love Seb," my voice shakes. "I choose Seb."

"It won't matter. The bond strengthens with every interaction. If you love Seb, run. Now."

My brain tells my feet to move, but I'm fearful they'll disobey and throw me into the arms of the young man in scrubs who's talking to my husband. I can't hear what they're saying, and I don't want to know.

"I c-can't," I stutter. "I can't move."

A few nurses come into the hallway, jogging toward Seb and the stranger.

Theodore.

The man on the speaker they're calling back to testing is him, Theodore. He ran after me, but I can't let him catch me. I can't do that to Sebastian.

I turn my body away and take one step, and then another. It physically hurts the further I go, my heart seizing and stopping my breath. I trip at the end of the hall, landing on my hands and knees, fighting to crawl until I make it to the elevator, banging on the keys and begging it to move faster.

"No!" I hear a voice yell. "You don't understand!"

It's Theodore, and it beckons me to go back. I whip around, our eyes meeting once more. Nurses hold him back while Sebastian's hands form fists at his sides, every vein in his arms protruding.

The familiar pain enters my heart and sends a cry from my lips. I clutch my chest in agony and wonder if this is my end. Every beat tightens the muscles in my body, turning me to stone, ripping the air from my lungs.

No one's ever refused the bond.

Theo tears away from a nurse, his hand clinging to the same spot on his heaving chest, pulling at the fabric of his shirt. His groan of agony vibrates something deep inside me, shaking my bones.

Sebastian turns and steps between us, staring at the crumpled mess of his wife on the floor in front of the elevator. His sorrowful eyes break the trance between me and Theo, but in a flash, they turn dark. The man I've only seen once before, the day he found me years ago, appears before me.

"Seb, she doesn't want this," Jack says. He walks toward the men, Theodore not far behind Sebastian, thrashing to escape five nurses who keep losing their grip. "Let her go so she can fight the bond until we figure this out."

Face contorted in confusion and heartbreak, Sebastian brings his hands to his hair, running his shaking fingers through it.

"No," he groans. "No. No. No."

"We're going to—" Jack starts, but he's interrupted by Seb's fist slamming into the wall, causing one nurse to jump. Sebastian cries out a scream of pure grief as the tile breaks under his fist. He pounds again and again, the agony strong enough to reach all of us, making the bodies in motion stop and watch.

It's what I need to see.

His heartache is enough to cut the tether tying me to Theodore, and I step into the elevator and let the doors close behind me.

CHAPTER 17

The doors to the elevator shut, and the buttons light up, counting down to my escape.

$$5 — 4 — 3 — 2 — 1$$

Each floor lessens the draw to Theodore, granting me brief moments of relief. My fingers tremble, searching for my phone, and it takes three tries before I can hold it still enough to call Alison. She may hate what's happened, despising me a little for it, but that doesn't take away the love between friends. She'll help me.

She picks up as the elevator doors open and I step out, sucking in a sharp breath that burns my lungs while my heart beats erratically against my ribs.

Patients, nurses, doctors, they all brush by me, touching my skin but ignoring the torture written all over my face.

"I need you to come get me. Now!" I cry. My voice shakes,

and I say it again so I know she hears and understands. "Come get me, Alison."

A blast of air cools my cheeks when I step outside and dart away from a man's outstretched hand. I hear her getting up, the books and clothes always stacked high on her bed knocking over.

"I'm coming." Her voice is groggy but worried. "Where?"

"The hospital. Get here now. Now, Alison."

"The… the hospital. Are you hurt? Oh, wait, that's right. Is it because…"

A group of people stare and question if they should come up to me, but I doubt they want to ask if I'm okay. They want to touch me, see if this manic woman bonds with them. I all but hiss at them.

"Now, Alison!" I scream. My voice is enough to scare them away.

"Okay, okay," she rushes out. There's the sound of her rustling around, breathing into the phone she usually props up with her shoulder. "I'm getting shoes on. Okay, shoes are on. Are you okay?"

"I don't know. No. Please just get here."

"I am. I am. Hang on." Her voice is an echo. She's set the phone down, scrambling around her room. "Top. No bra. Don't need a bra. Stay on the phone with me. Okay, clothes are on."

I'm on the other side of the parking lot, my hand clutched to my chest, my dried tears streak my swollen face. A man reaches out for me.

"Don't you fucking touch me!" I seethe at him. His eyes meet mine, and his face softens for a moment, but he still calls me a bitch.

"I'm getting into the car." A car door slams, and Alison's engine roars to life. "I'm driving the car. Estimated arrival in six minutes. I'm speeding. Going very fast."

She can't see me, but I'm nodding, spinning in place, looking for Theodore or Sebastian, scared of seeing either. Alison's never heard me this unhinged, even though I'm not the calmest person. Running figure eights across our campus isn't my worst outburst.

"I — I saw what happened," she admits. "I didn't tell anyone it was you. I swear."

Her admission almost sends me to my knees, and I remember the barrage of her missed calls I never answered. I don't deserve her allegiance, given the way I've chastised her lately, but I'm grateful.

"Thank... Thank you. I need you to promise me..." I find a bench and sit down, still frantically looking for those familiar faces. "Promise me you don't hate me. I need a friend. I really need a friend."

"I am your friend," Alison insists. "And I'm not going to do anything but be here for you. I won't push you." There's a moment of silence filled with all the things we don't say to each other. We both disapprove of each other's choices, and so many times our friendship has almost ended because we don't see the world through the same lens.

We won't agree on this issue, and I know that puts what's left of this friendship at risk, but she understands those differences are why I'm devastated and crying in a hospital parking lot right now.

She may be the only one who will love me no matter what happens. The look on Sebastian's face, his complete anguish... I can't get it out of my head.

"Two minutes," she says.

"I'm on the bench on the side of the parking lot, facing the entrance," I tell her.

Sebastian steps out of the front door, alone. He jogs through the lot, looking around for me. I curl into myself, wanting to go to him but afraid of getting closer to that building.

Jack's right about the feeling strengthening the more I see the bonded. Even from out here, I feel it surging within me, boiling under the surface. Theodore's hurting, and the sadness permeates my soul, too. A step closer to Sebastian is a step toward Theodore, and I can't take that risk.

There's a pull to Sebastian with my heart and mind, but I can't describe the draw to my bond. It's nonsensical, beyond my control.

"One minute," Alison says. "I'm pulling in the lot. Is that Sebastian?"

"Don't let him see you," I beg.

"Too late," she grumbles.

I watch her car slow toward the front of the lot, and I hear her say hello to Sebastian. She has the phone on, letting me in on their conversation. If I were a better person, I'd hang up, but I'm desperate to know what he'll say to her.

"She called you, didn't she? To get her." Sebastian's defeated voice is impossible to ignore, and Alison must know he's only recently found out. That's not a man who's had time with his feelings.

"Yes. I — I don't know what to say," she admits.

I watch him place his hands on the side of her car, his muscles tightening as he rocks back and forth. Alison must look in my direction because Sebastian's head turns, finding me. He takes a few steps toward me before he stops, his head hanging when he turns back to the car.

No.

Come over.

I want to yell the words, but my dry throat won't speak.

"Take her to our home. She'll be comfortable there," he

croaks. "I'll stay with my friend Jack tonight and come over in the morning."

"Okay," Alison's voice squeaks. She's confused, but I understand. He's giving us both the night to calm ourselves before we talk. Our entire future hangs in limbo, and he's still thinking about what's best for me.

"Jack's emailing the university to tell them she's sick," Sebastian says. "Will you tell her that?"

"She can..." Alison stops and I see her reach her arm out the window, phone in hand. He takes it, staring at the picture of me on her phone, a horrible image Alison refuses to change. I'm flipping Alison off with one hand, a glass of wine in the other. It's not what I want Sebastian to look at before he talks to me the first time after...

After our world shattered.

"Hello," his deep voice comes through the line.

"Seb, I," my voice cracks. "I'm sorry." There's a pause where all I hear is his breath.

"We'll talk tomorrow," he says. "I need a night to think."

"I love you, Seb," I whisper. "So much. More than anything. More than..." I stop before I say it, afraid it might upset him.

I hear him smack his lips, a habit of his when he's thinking things over. He turns in my direction, raising his wrist, displaying his tattoo. The sight breaks my heart into a thousand pieces.

I stand up and hold my wrist out with the phone shaking in my other hand.

"This vow I make to you of my own free will, to never separate or stray," he says.

I choke on the sob in the back of my throat and nod, unable to speak with the lump in my throat.

"I love you too," he assures me. "More than anything. Forever."

Alison stares at me so much on the drive home, I wonder why we haven't wrecked yet. I would be okay with that at this point. A nice coma would give everyone some time to make a plan because I'm not doing well at cleaning up this mess.

We're a few minutes away when she speaks for the first time. She grips the steering wheel until her knuckles turn white. The light changes, and she turns onto my street. "I'm not wearing a bra. I always wear a bra. Since I was ten."

"I appreciate you coming so quickly," I say. My hands rub down my pants and back up, a repetitive motion to calm myself.

It's not working.

"He didn't know yet, did he?" she asks. "Did you go to the hospital to tell him? Afraid he'd like... keel over or something?"

"I was there to see my therapist, Jack Wells," I answer her.

The car slows as she pulls down my winding driveway, sending us deeper into my property. I love our home, tucked deep into the trees, hidden from view. We built a life here where I have peace and privacy far from neighbors and noise.

"When you were sick this weekend, was it, um?" She struggles with how to ask if I went crazy, but I'm already there, spiraling into insanity.

The car comes to a stop, and I step out. "Let's talk inside."

Alison trails behind me while I step through my door and straight to the wine, popping open the bottle my mother sent and pouring it into two glasses. When I set them down at the table, Alison looks me over a few times before taking a sip. It's more of a gulp, and she sets the half-empty glass down at the table, licking the side of her lip.

"You don't look great. I know this might not be helpful

right now, but you're kind of my rock. You always have things together and…" She takes another sip of wine, close to emptying the glass. "And you look like shit."

"I should have told him before today," I whisper to myself, staring at the glass.

She doesn't nod or speak her thoughts, her eyes fixated on me and listening.

"I had a panic attack after we talked on Friday and ran off from a crowd of people. You know how I get sometimes," I say.

She shrugs her shoulders, twirling what's left of her wine in the glass. "I'm sorry, Em."

"Me too," I tell her. "I ran into him. Literally. I'm sure you saw a picture or something."

Alison swallows hard and sits down next to me. "You're not… recognizable. Unless someone knows you well."

"Okay," I say. "That's something."

"But going to the hospital," Alison sighs. "There's video everywhere, and it's owned by the government, and, I don't know. If you wanted to keep it a secret, why did you go there?"

"I know it can't stay a secret," I scoff. "I wanted one weekend with Seb. Just one last moment before it all went to shit. Then I would tell him, but I never did. I'm such a coward."

Alison pours more wine into both our glasses, shaking her head. "You're not. It's an impossible situation. Don't be so hard on yourself."

"Seb insisted I go see Jack about the panic attack," I explain. "And I agreed because I didn't have a choice."

I clutch my glass so hard, I'm afraid it might break. The urge to shatter it on the wall almost takes over, but that won't solve anything. Instead, I lower my head to the table, letting my wet cheek rest on the wood.

"How can you be my friend after this?" I ask her. "You should hate me."

Alison reaches her hand forward, gripping mine. "Never. I would do anything for you," she insists.

"You won't stop going to the receptions." I'm trying to add a smile to the situation, but it only sounds judgmental.

She snorts into her wineglass. "Got me there," she says.

"I'm bonded," I blurt out, saying the words we both know, but I've kept inside since it happened. "I bonded Friday night with a man whose name I learned today. He opened the door to a shop, and I ran face-first into it. He touched me, and it happened. I ran from him through the park, and when I got home, I told Sebastian about the panic attack, but not about the bond. The first person I've told is Dr. Wells, and he was trying to help me, but Theodore found me at the hospital."

Alison's fingernails dig into my hand, her eyes unblinking, boring into mine.

"And I don't want it," I break down. "I don't want a fucking bond. I don't want another thing in this world forcing me to do something against my will. My choice was Sebastian, my husband, and I want the life we have together."

"It's okay," Alison interrupts.

"It's not fucking okay because of me, and I hate myself for that. My entire essence is drawn to this fucking stranger, and I hate him for it, but I also... I also think I love him. And I wish I could undo it and go back. I wish it more than anything, and I'd do anything to fix this."

I'm bawling, tears dripping onto the table at every worry that pours from my soul.

"I have to fix this, Alison. I want Seb. I choose Seb."

Alison brings her glass to her lips, tears brimming around her eyes, and drinks until it's dry.

We sit at the table, listening to the wind and my quick breaths in uncomfortable silence. She never lessens her hold or looks away from me. I'm a freak to her. The woman who never wanted to bond, found by her match against her will, and the only person in history to reject another four hundred years of life.

"Say something," I beg.

She releases my hand, slamming back into her chair with a thud. She blinks once, twice, three times, and a few tears escape and stream down her cheeks. She takes a few attempts to say anything, her mouth opening and closing with no words escaping before she speaks.

"Open another bottle."

CHAPTER 18

I thought he'd be running, chasing after her when she crawled into that elevator, but he's almost hesitant when he hits the button and steps inside after her. All I see is his tattoo. With every step, the words etched onto her husband's skin sway forward and backward.

Crowe - Crowe - Crowe

They picked a name between them, placed it on their bodies forever, and carry it wherever they go. I've never had that kind of love. My devoted father wanted me, but that's a different sense of belonging, something out of obligation. I was a piece of him, his legacy, and I longed to make him proud. He died, saddened that I might share his fate, destined for a life shorter than most, hoping that there might be better options for my weak heart in the future.

His hope was always a bond, but my plan was to go out in

style. Spend every dollar on my last days knowing I may have had a short life, but it was mine.

He wouldn't be proud of this.

I'm tearing apart a family, ripping their heart out to fix mine. It's not right, but I can't stop.

Her husband's pain will be temporary, and there's always that chance that he could bond. It's a possibility.

No. That's just an excuse I'm giving myself to do what I want — to live — and I shake my head in shame and place my face in my hands.

The nurses gossip all around me about what they've seen, and I know she can't hide from me this time. There are witnesses everywhere.

What a show for the world to hear about in the next news story, one that won't go unnoticed. A bonded woman who married someone else first. People will chatter nonstop, but they'll all come to the same conclusion, no matter how much it hurts her or her husband.

No one refuses the bond.

"Her name is Emry," another man says to me. He's studious looking, especially compared to me. I haven't showered in a week, and I stand before him in mangled scrubs. "And you're Theodore." He holds out his hand for me to shake.

I take it, biting my cheeks and fighting the urge to sprint after Emry. Everything inside me pulls in her direction, but I have an ounce of my pride left, along with respect for her husband, who used his fist on the wall instead of my face. I can't say I would have had that much self-control, so I ignore the urges that beg me to find her. I'm growing weaker by the second, her distance draining the strength from my heart.

I meet his hand with a shake. "Theo. And you are?" Every word takes effort when my entire focus is on Emry.

"Jack Wells. I worked with Sebastian, Emry's husband."

A spike of anger stabs me in the stomach. It's unjustified, but the push and pull of emotions is beyond my control. I hate that Sebastian found her first.

Nurses leave us, looking back a few times before they disappear down a hallway. I suppose taking me back for the testing is no longer important, given the circumstances.

"Would you... like a ride?" Jack offers.

"Why?" It's the best one-word response I have in my confusion, but if he's Sebastian's friend, this man has no reason to take me anywhere but a ditch.

"You don't want to be here much longer," Jack says. He points to the line of cameras tucked into the ceiling. This isn't a privately owned business, and both our faces are clear as day in this brightened building. "Those nurses already called it in, and it won't take the news long to find you both."

"Fine. Take me to her." The elevator has closed, sending Sebastian down after her. "We can all... talk."

The words sound ludicrous and come from the part of me that needs to be near her. I head to the elevator when Jack's grip on my arm stops me in my tracks.

"Do you know why she was here?" he asks.

"That's a dumb fucking question," I seethe. I pull my arm back, but his grip is tight, and I am weakened without her next to me. "You know I don't. Why don't you tell me?"

"She asked for my help to break the bond," he carefully says the words.

My arm throbs from his grip, and I stare at him in disbelief. *That's not possible.*

"Then my bonded is a fool," I say and turn away from him.

He follows me as I stomp down the hallway. "Why were you here?"

"That's none of your fucking business," I answer, slamming an elevator button.

He looks me over while we stand in front of the elevator, noticing my unkempt appearance. I'm strong, keeping myself covered in lean muscle, but after only three days of being unconscious, I notice how thin I've gotten. Every second away from her makes my heart thud with an uncertain beat, and I sway, catching myself on the wall.

"You know, I could just pull your file. I'm a doctor here," he warns.

"I don't know you," I hiss.

"You don't know her."

I step into the elevator, turn, and pound my chest. "I feel her. That's enough."

"Is it?" he asks as the doors shut in front of his face.

He's right, but I won't give him the satisfaction.

How quickly I have gained enemies already. The husband's expected, but who would want to help a bonded separate their link? If you ask the right circles, it's murder.

I realize Jack's right again when the doors open on the lobby floor. There are two men in suits waiting for me, hospital name tags on their belts.

"Mr. Theodore Lorwerth?" one asks.

That didn't take long.

A clear scan of my face was all they needed, and I've been outed to the world.

"It's obvious you know who I am," I say. Stepping out, I slam into one of their shoulders, knocking him off balance. There's a fleeting moment of energy that rushes through my body. She's closer, and I break out into a jog, the two men trailing behind me.

"We just want to get a comment," one yells after me. "This is unprecedented news. We haven't had a match within five hundred miles."

Hands graze over my skin despite my appearance and

growls of protest. Running in circles, I find patients and nurses, almost getting hit by a car, but she's nowhere. I've lost the two men, but more will come. Everyone will want to invade our lives and considering the special circumstances, this news won't die down soon.

Sprinting through another row of cars, the exhaustion hits me, and I stumble, hitting one knee. Oxygen burns my lungs, and my heart which beat so perfectly, that had finally found its rhythm, falters. The strain of the muscle makes my eyes water, and I gasp, trying to catch enough air.

Someone touches my shoulder, and I smack their hand away.

"Stay still," his voice says. It's Jack with a needle in his hand, and I slide back, banging my head against the side of a parked car. "It will help."

I have no choice but to trust him, unable to stand on my own. The pinch of my skin turns to relief in moments, and I suck in a loud breath just as blackness starts at the corners of my eyes.

He sits down beside me, crosses his legs, and pulls out a stethoscope.

"I thought... thought you w-were." Every word is difficult, and I close my eyes to concentrate on slowing my heart that beats out of control.

"You thought I was what? Well, Mr. Theodore Lorwerth, I'm a man with a few doctorates and fewer friends. And after our chat, I pulled your record, which gave me reason to grab an emergency bag, and here we are. Don't talk."

The cold metal glides across my skin, and a few people stop to touch me.

"Don't swat them off, just breathe," Jack orders.

I keep still, simmering with rage at them, at this life and this place, at my weak heart that won't beat right without

Emry. "She was in the other lot. You turned the wrong way off the elevator."

I shoot him a gaze of indignation, but he only raises his eyebrows, listening to my shaking breaths and foolish heart.

He sits back, nodding. "You should go back to the hospital."

"I won't," I bite out.

"I know, and by the looks of the two trucks that pulled up, they're already searching for you." He plays with the rubber of the stethoscope and sighs. "Bonding is a big story."

I clench my jaw and turn to face him. "Want that ride, now?" Jack asks.

My heart rate calms, finding a tempo that won't kill me.

Won't kill me today, that is.

"What will it cost me?" I ask. Nothing is free in this world, and I stare at the news trucks that unpack their equipment, talking to the two men I saw from the elevator. "I bet our story will sell for a lot."

"So will my research," Jack deadpans. "And I'll need you together to complete the studies she wants."

"To break the bond," I add. It's an important piece he's leaving out, but I'm not a fool. We all want something here, and I want to be with Emry.

He swallows and nods. An honest answer gets him a chance, not that I have a lot of options.

It doesn't matter what his intentions are. If he's trying to break something we haven't begun to understand, let him try. Those efforts mean I get close to Emry.

I nod and lower my head, accepting Moira won't get here in time to save me from the swarm.

"Good," Jack agrees. "I'll get the car."

CHAPTER 19

Alison downs the bottle, but I can tell by her pacing and manic eyes, she's sober. It's adrenaline or anger that burns the alcohol up before it takes any effect. She's asked every possible question about the night I bonded. I've described the euphoria of the moment and the desperation to be next to him, how it strengthened the second time, and how my body no longer feels like my own.

She wants to ask the one thing I don't know how to answer, glancing at my wedding portrait and tattoo several times before I bring up the subject.

"If there's a chance they can break the bond, I've got to try," I whisper. "I don't think I can go on living with Seb hating me forever."

"That's not possible," Alison says, coming to my side and reaching for my hand. She runs a finger over my tattoo, smiling down at the word Crowe. "He's loved you forever. Since before you were legal."

I shove her shoulder with mine and nod. "It wasn't like that, you know."

She smiles and nods. "Lots of people are friends first. I get it."

I shake my head and bite the inside of my cheek, tasting the tang of blood that pools onto my skin. She knows we met when I was sixteen, but I've kept the details about that time private, burying it away and pretending it never happened.

Tears flood my eyes again with renewed guilt. "I chased him. He didn't want us to be together... like that. My second year of school, I got myself together. I mean..."

I struggle with how to explain that I went from a depressed mess who never washed her hair or got out of bed to someone at the top of her class without Alison asking why.

"We were friends for several years. He checked up on me, but always kept a safe distance. I noticed when he started to look at me as more than a friend and I chased him. I asked him out, more than once before he said yes. I did this to him." My lip trembles. "I think it was a pity date at first, but then..."

"Then he fell in love with you," Alison finishes my sentence. "And that's wonderful. He knew you for years first, and that's amazing. You all will figure this out."

"He would have been so much better off if he'd never met me," I say, and I believe every word at this moment. He spent years worrying about me and then I practically forced him to fall for me. He never wanted to take advantage, thinking I might have some savior complex, but I don't know how to explain that to Alison. I'll have to fess up. There's no other way.

"Em," Alison worries. "This has never happened before. You can make your own rules. Seb and you have been together for so long, and have loved each other for your entire adult life."

"I lied about how we met," I whisper.

"To me?" she asks.

"To everyone."

Her fingers interlace with mine, and she tilts her head. "Okay, I'll bite. How did you meet?"

The memories I keep hidden about that day, the anniversary Sebastian wants to celebrate, flood back in a rush of sorrow. I lost years of my life in that place, starving and sleeping for days, weeks, and months on end.

Sebastian's face when he opened that door is my one happy memory in all the years they kept me trapped there. It's the solitary moment of joy in a building built for torture. They tried to call it science, but I made my life about science. I dove into the true study of science to prove to myself and to them that their version was nothing more than desperate acts by pathetic people trying to live forever.

And what did it get them? No answers. No one knows any more about the bond. Maybe they can compare their notes in prison and see if they find any breakthroughs while they serve their life sentences.

"I did a short internship at NeXus, but he met me before that. He found me," I explain.

"Will I need more wine?" Alison lifts one side of her mouth in a smile and rubs my back. "You're shaking, Em. Take a breath and tell me about it. I'll open another bottle. What will it hurt at this point? Keep talking."

My shoulders relax a fraction, and I push my glass across the table, asking for another pour. "When the receptions started to get really big before they were organized... Remember when we were kids?"

Alison nods. "Oh, yes. Those big field parties before corporations took over. My dad still has a panoramic photo of one in his study."

I hiss in a breath. So many people loved that time before

there were ticket sales and planned parties. It was a chaotic mingling of every person who could make it there by plane, car, or foot.

And it was not a place for children.

"My mother took me a few times."

Alison spills the wine she's pouring, her eyes big as saucers. "Ick," she grimaces.

"More than a few times," I continue. "She really wanted to bond, and she would work non-stop for a few months and save every penny, and then spend the year traveling to the parties. She only got her government checks for me if she shared custody, so I tagged along a lot."

"A nomad," Alison says, pushing my glass back to my hands. I take a sip and nod. Nomads go from reception to reception, taking on odd jobs along the way. Most of those jobs involve sex, and my mother was never very original.

"It wasn't a great time for us, and got worse after my dad died," I admit. "They came out with the testing right about then. Remember?"

"Oh, yes," Alison says. "I remember peeing my pants from standing in line for so long to get tested. I'm still waiting for those results."

"It was just another way to get money," I shake my head. "They didn't know what they were testing for, but my mom thought she was being a good mother."

Alison squints and tilts her head. She's only met my mom a few times, but she knows what I tell her. The woman is selfish and thinks of nothing but the bond. Only a temporary moment of insanity would cause her to spend her time on anything other than that.

"While we were there, she got an offer from this place to do additional testing on girls right out of puberty. I had gotten my period right before and they paid her a lot of money. It was only supposed to be a temporary living situation, and I... I was tired of being dragged around. I wanted to do it, too."

Alison freezes, her body still except for her eyes that dart up and down my frame. I spin the glass at the table, gaining the composure to tell her the rest without upsetting her too much. She's expecting what I'll say, but that doesn't make it hurt any less. We all know what they did before NeXus found us. I've come to terms with it and won't give these memories one more tear, but for her, this is new.

"This was when testing your kids was the hip new thing and she only saw another chance to get me closer to the bond. I think she knew something was wrong with it, but she ignored her gut feeling. She kept getting video messages from me telling her how happy I was there and gave herself the out to travel to receptions without the burden of a kid." I laugh at the thought.

"You know," I smile. "I bet she'll be so fucking mad to hear that I've bonded. That's the only good thing about this mess."

Alison doesn't respond or move. She's waiting for the bomb I'm about to drop.

"It was the Genome Enquiry, as I'm sure you've guessed. They didn't release my name because I was a minor when NeXus came in and shut them down."

"How long?" Alison chokes out. "Did they keep you?"

"Over two years," I answer. That fact hits me again when I say the words out loud.

All my mother's excuses for why my stay kept getting extended fall apart with those words. I want to believe her, but in my heart, I don't. Sebastian told me about how many parents they fooled, but all that means is Genome Theory knew who to target. They found people who didn't want the burden of children, and she was all too ready to believe their lies and collect that check, forever searching for her bond.

"Two years of being poked and tested and tortured. Two years where they would inject me with a million things and then throw me in a pit with hundreds of other kids, hoping someone would bond."

Her eyebrows raise, and she opens her mouth but thinks better of it.

"No one ever did, Alison. No one bonded or found the reason we do. NeXus got all their research and you know what they found? Fucking nothing."

I gulp back the rest of my glass, letting the warmth run through my body. "Sebastian found me and he rescued me. I was no more than an animal at that point. He checked on me constantly, you know. He wrote emails and sent video calls. He never crossed the line. Not once. I was so fucking in love with him after like two weeks. He had a girlfriend for a year, and I used to throw darts at a picture of her face."

Alison's expression softens, and she leans back in her chair, taking in a shaking breath.

"I'm so sorry that happened to you."

A few tears fall down her cheeks, and she quickly wipes them away, a smile across her wet face.

She continues, "We always knew Sebastian was a saint, but damn. I get it now. I get why you married him. I'd rather live one lifetime with someone like that than have the chance at eternity with anyone else."

Those words choke me up because she understands, and I feel silly for not telling her before. There's a lot of shame in my past, most of those children taking their settlement and blowing it on drugs and other evils. So many took their own life not long after.

Sebastian set me up with a financial adviser and a therapist, Jack. He made sure I got grants from interning at NeXus and wouldn't touch a penny. This house is in my name, bought before we were married. He was sure I knew that he never wanted my money, just me. We were so careful with the start of our relationship. Look where that got us.

"What are you going to do?" Alison asks. "About that guy? Your bondmate?"

"Theodore?" I shrug. "I don't know. If I see him again, I don't think I can fight it. I know I love Seb, but the desire to be near him is impossible to fight. I'm in pain right now because of it."

Alison reaches forward, lowering the collar of my shirt. She purses her lips at the purple and green bruise on my chest.

"I know," I admit, running my fingertips over the edges of the bruise. "It hurts here since it happened."

"I noticed you rubbing it in the car. Could being apart hurt you? I've never heard of bondmates not, you know, bonded."

Another exhausted sigh from me is my only answer. Alison looks over my shoulder at my phone on the table. "It's lighting up," she says, pointing to it.

I jump from the chair, hoping it's Sebastian. I thought of calling him, but didn't know if he wanted to speak with me. There's no protocol for this, no way to know the right thing to do.

Jack's number lights up on the screen with a few messages.

JACK

> I'm taking Theo to a friend's house, a woman named Moira. Then I'm going back to get Seb. He's waiting in my office.

I squint at the message, not believing the words on the screen. Alison pops over my shoulder. "Can I read?"

"Yes," I tell her.

JACK

> Theo's agreed to researching a suppression of the bond, and I'll talk to Seb. You need to be on board.

I scroll further down.

JACK

> NeXus gave preliminary approval.

> I'll get blood in the morning while you're separate, but then you'll need to be brought together. The blood changes when you're together.

I feel faint, falling backward, and gripping onto the counter to keep my balance.

I type back once I gather my thoughts.

EMRY

> You said I won't be able to resist him if I see him again.

I wait for minutes, staring at the message I sent without a reply. When I set the phone down, a ping comes through.

JACK

> You won't until we break the bond, but I don't see another option. Talk with Seb.

CHAPTER 20

Moira has her daughter's bed set up for me when I arrive. It's full of everything I imagine a teenage girl would love. An entire counter covered in makeup, stuffed animals aged by the years and handling, and an entire wall decorated with pictures of her friends. Scattered through the smiling faces of school kids are articles about bonding, and I scan them, noticing how none of them hesitated for a second to love and cherish their bond.

I hate to impose, but Moira tells me she's gone to her dad's before she leaves for school, and they've said their goodbyes. She's still grateful I spared her from the receptions. Not that college kids are innocent, but there are far fewer orgies.

I'm too tired to think or speak, my heart barely keeping me alive under my strained chest. Without my bond, and the recent hospital stay, it's worse than ever.

"Do I have to worry about you dying in your sleep?" Moira cocks an eyebrow.

"I wouldn't rule it out," I admit.

Moira rolls her eyes and sets a glass of water by the bed. She holds up the medical bag Jack brought with him. "Am I supposed to know what to do with this?"

"He already loaded me up with painkillers and who knows what else," I tell her. "He'll be back tomorrow."

She lets out an exhale of relief. "Well, not that it matters now, but I talked with one person today who saw you and the girl."

"Emry," I mutter. My eyes grow heavier with every second that passes.

"She got a call from a news station while we were chatting. They wanted a statement from her."

I grunt, turning to my side and reaching for the water. Moira holds it to my lips and I drink.

"Don't die tonight," she repeats.

I shake my head and give her a wink. "The story will be everywhere tomorrow. Don't tell anyone I'm here. I'll get out of your way as soon as I can."

Moira smacks me on the arm. "I won't hear of that. If this place crowds with people looking for you, I'll make them buy something. Everybody wins."

The small laugh I let out sends a pain to my chest, and I palm the spot, annoyed with this incessant ache.

"Do you have anyone you'd like me to call?" A twinge of pity crosses her face. "A friend maybe. Co-worker."

I frown. "No. There's no one. I'll email work that I need to take a leave. I still have some time in my contract after I finish up a few things."

Moira sets the medical bag to the side, fiddling around the room, waiting for me to sleep. It won't take long, but my thoughts keep me awake. New ideas that I've never allowed before running into Emry.

"That's by design," I admit. "The fact that there's... no one.

No one to call."

Moira nods, folding a blanket in silence and allowing me to continue.

"When you think, I mean, when you know you're going to die, and I don't mean someday going to die. I mean—" I sit up on the bed, letting my head fall back against the wall. My words are a jumbled mess and I can tell she's waiting for me to work through my thoughts. "I never had a chance at a long life. Dead by forty if I'm lucky, and I've never been someone that believes in miracles."

Moira lets out a little laugh. "You seem pretty lucky from where I stand. Minus the running from the altar situation."

I grimace.

"Bad choice of words," Moira admits. "It's just an expression, because she's, well, running."

"Running to the altar," I sigh. "Back to it."

"I'm sorry," Moira says, and I know she truly means those words. She's right that my luck has turned. I've found my bond with Emry, but also a friend in Moira, and it's terrifying and wonderful all at once.

"I keep people away. Everywhere I go, in everything I do," I tell her. "I won't hurt anyone when I'm gone, not like my dad did."

She sits on the end of the bed with the folded blanket in her lap. "I'm sure his death was very hard."

"Not just for me. There were lines of people at the funeral. They did two services. Everyone was devastated and not just because he was young. He was really something. The kind of guy that would bring someone a meal every weekend just because he thought they'd like it. He would read at schools because there weren't a lot of volunteer dads, just moms."

A memory of my father flashes in my memory. He's smiling at me by a river bank, laughing about how few fish we catch.

Fuck, I miss him.

"I don't know. People walk around and touch each other and get nothing but disappointment, never looking at your face. Never noticing the person they're trying to connect with." I swallow hard, fighting back the lump in my throat when I think of my dad when people walked past him. "Everyone saw my dad. He wouldn't just let you brush by. He was a light. You couldn't look away."

"There are so many people that spend their life looking for the bond, that they never stay in one spot long," Moira admits. "When there's a pillar of the community like that, someone who connects with you even when you aren't a bondmate, they mean something to you."

"Like you?" I ask her. "Your customers all know you. They greet you by name and smile when they see you. You said you've lived here your whole life."

"Well, I guess," she says, crossing her legs and tilting her head in thought. "Yes, a lot of people will spiral into depression when I'm dead. Sucks for them."

We both sputter a laugh, and she stands, leaving the blanket on the edge of the bed. "You need sleep. I'll be here when Jack comes. We'll figure all this out."

"Thank you for everything, Moira."

She flicks off the light and stands in the doorway, tapping her nails against the wood. "You have it just like he did. I'm sure of it."

"Have what?" I yawn.

"The charisma. That spark. People are drawn to you, not just because you're new here. That's your dad, shining through."

Her words ease the pain in my chest, making me wonder what it would be like to plant roots for my life. A life more than a decade in the future — well past my due date. When I close my eyes and imagine how that might feel, all that comes to me is Emry. Her essence fills me as I drift off to sleep, and a part of me knows she feels it too.

J ack wakes me in what I think might be morning, but bright light beams through a side window like the noonday sun. He's talking with Moira, who stands in the doorway, rummaging through his medical bag.

"I feel like shit," I croak. Both of them look at me, worried expressions on their faces. "What now?"

"I'm here to draw blood, get some samples." He slides over, pulling my arm up on his knee and wrapping a rubber tie around my bicep. "Then I'll be taking you to NeXus and we'll continue studies."

I flinch when the needle hits my arm. "What about Emry? I'm not your lab rat without her."

"Emry is thinking things over," he admits. "But I think she'll come around. This is a lot for her."

I grit my teeth and watch the vials fill, one after another, until I'm sure he's done, but then he gets more. I'm not in great health, and he's drawing me dry.

"She doesn't have much of a choice," I murmur when he pops another vial into the needle.

Moira hears and crinkles her nose. "She does. You may not like it, but she is married, Theo."

"You don't understand," I explain. "I can feel her. We're connected in some way, and she won't be able to stay away from me for long, no matter what her husband says or does."

"Sebastian isn't the hesitation," Jack says, popping off the final vial and pulling out the needle. He's not gentle, and it burns, but he's a therapist, so he may not have drawn blood since medical school.

"I'm a decent guy," I smirk. "Not bad to look at and nice when I'm not crazed with an obsession over a stranger. What's she scared of?"

Jack puts the vials into a basket and drops them in a container. "Can you walk?"

"Can I or will I?" I mock. "Will Emry be there? What's the problem if it isn't her dearly devoted?"

Jack clasps his hands together and stares at the ceiling. "I'm aware that bondmates have a psychic link. It's said that there's the intuition of thoughts and feelings, but there are reports where they can unearth their innermost secrets without speaking a word."

"I make deals for a living, Jack," I inform him. "I'm not into riddles. We had a deal that if I'm close to Emry, you can play your research game. So what's your fucking point?"

"I don't feel guilty telling you this because you'll know it, eventually," he explains. "You won't be able to keep secrets from each other. Every thought and feeling will move between you."

Jack's eyes narrow, warning me he's telling me something I may not want to hear. The thought of something upsetting my bond sparks fire in my veins. Before the words are out, I know someone's hurt her, and I know I'll kill them without a single regret.

"Emry was a victim of the Genome Enquiry, and she's not excited about another situation where she goes through a battery of tests."

Moira brings her hand to her mouth and gasps. "Oh, that poor girl," she says.

Heat covers my skin, a rage boiling from my insides out, and I growl beneath my chest.

"What the fuck?" I say. Jack's hands touch my shoulders, holding me back down when I didn't notice I was standing. My fists clench and I remain sitting on the edge of the bed, ready to fight or kill. Sweat beads on my neck and chest, the fury growing by the second.

"You need to calm down before I continue," Jack orders. "Your reactions will intensify, but you can control them."

I take in a breath, counting the seconds as the air reaches my lungs.

"I trust Moira with this information because she could have sold your whereabouts to any news outlet and made a killing in cash," Jack continues turning to Moira. "I pulled up here today without one car in the lot."

"Oh, I would never," Moira says. "But that poor girl. Oh, what a life of heartache."

And I'm making it worse.

The Genome Enquiry tortured so many kids out of desperation to find the key to bonding. It was the worst scandal in the last fifty years and made all receptions require permits, security, manifests, and anything to ensure that never happened again. It's the reason only large corporations run them anymore, and partially why they are so expensive.

"She'll do this testing because she loves Sebastian," Jack admits. "I know how she thinks, and she feels like she owes him that. He found her, and he got her out. Made sure she didn't end up like a lot of those kids when they cashed out."

My head jerks up to him, and I blow out a harsh breath of air. Even though I hate the idea of my bond with anyone but me, I have respect for Sebastian, maybe even adoration. He helped her. If we weren't in this mess, I would like the guy. My dad would certainly like him.

Jack fixes a bandage on my arm, and when he's done, I bring my hands to my chest and close my eyes, thinking of her, seeing her face. I want to comfort her, knowing this must be so difficult. It's going to stir up all sorts of shit in her mind, and it probably won't even work.

She's with me, like I could reach out and touch her. She's a soft blanket that surrounds me, encasing me in her sweet scent and her warmth. The idea of having her next to me, skin-to-skin once more, is all I want. It's my only purpose every second I'm awake.

But when I think of her pain and what she must have gone through all those years ago, the agony makes me sink. I fall into a pit of sadness when I envision the picture in my mind of her face, younger but duller. All the life drained from her while she's caged away in the basement of some building makes me lose any will to live. Her suffering becomes mine. We are one in the misery, and in the memory.

"Are you feeling alright?" Jack asks. "Do you need a moment?"

He stands and turns to speak with Moira, but I grab at his wrist before he steps away. It's a stronger hold than I ought to have in my current state, and he takes notice, leaning down until we're face to face.

"I don't want to hurt her anymore," I vow. "I want you to promise me you'll do what she asks. You'll try to break the bond."

His hand moves to the top of mine, and he meets my eyes. I've made countless deals in my lifetimes, and I know when someone is lying or telling me what I want to hear.

He's honest when he tells me, "If there's a way to break the bond, we will."

CHAPTER 21

EMRY

This empty house twists my insides, and instead of sleeping, I pace the floors listening to Alison snore. She's had a few bottles of wine, so it was a toss up if she'd be throwing up or sleeping peacefully.

I'm grateful we have the latter... for now.

A week ago, everything was normal, boring some would say, but wonderful. Is this how a car accident feels? You're gliding along the road, singing to a song, or talking with a friend, and with no warning, it's carnage.

When the sun peaks through the sky, sending shadows over my living room, I give up on sleep. Coffee brews while I watch with bleary eyes, tapping my foot with the beat of the steady drip.

"The french press is better. Makes it stronger."

Sebastian's arms wrap around my middle from behind, pressing his chest to my back. I whimper, and my legs give out from underneath me, tears falling before I can say a word. He spins me to face him, and I move my lips to his. He's hesitant to kiss me, pulling back and placing his hands on my shoulders.

"Hold me," I beg him, and I claw into his chest, taking fistfuls of his shirt and forcing him to comfort me. I cry, "Why won't you kiss me?"

His eyes search mine, licking his lips with his tongue, and he takes another step back. "Does it feel... odd to you?" he asks. His question is earnest, spoken with soft words that want a true answer.

"Why would my husband holding me feel odd?" I close the space between us, placing my hands on the sides of his cheeks, and kiss him again. His hands clasp over my wrists, bringing them down and breaking the embrace.

"Why would you say that?" I ask. "I want you. I need you. Nothing will change that."

He rubs his forehead, creasing his brow, trying to create more distance between us. I go with him, not allowing him to take his warmth away.

My insides twist, and I worry I might get sick. Panic rises in my chest, and I'm overcome with the thought that he came here to leave me, to end us.

"I love you just as much as I did last week. That doesn't stop," I insist. My voice is shaking and pleading. It doesn't sound like me, but I don't know who I am anymore.

"I don't need you to love me anymore if you can't." He rehearsed those words and refuses to meet my eyes when he says them. It's something he's thought about all night, what he came here prepared to say.

No one married has bonded, and I don't know if love fades for your spouse when the bond grows stronger, but I have faith in myself and in us.

"I will not stop loving you, Sebastian." I take his wrist and place it next to mine, but he pulls it away before I can say another word.

"I don't want to do that." His voice lowers, barely a whisper. "I didn't come here for reassurances."

I turn back to the coffee and grab two cups, slamming them on the counter. "You snuck in here and held me. What is it you want to do, then?"

"I don't sneak into my own house," he grits out. "This is still our house."

The verge of an argument hangs in the air, threatening to pull us further apart, but I can't let that happen. I make his coffee the way I have for years, saying nothing, but nodding to myself.

"Let's sit down outside," I offer. "Watch the sunrise."

Sebastian doesn't respond. He opens the door for me to walk through, and throws away the empty bottles of wine before he follows me, a smirk on his face.

"I had help drinking that," I explain.

"I heard your help snoring from outside," he says. "But I'm glad you needed a drink as much as I did."

I hold my cup in both hands, curling my legs up in the large chair, and watch the colors change in the sky, sending beams of light through the leaves. This place still feels private and secure, far away from anyone else. It's always been enough to keep the world out of sight. I'm grateful for it today when people will look for me, wanting to be the first to break the story of the first married woman who bonded with someone else.

"I'm sorry I didn't tell you when it happened," I admit. "I didn't know how to react. I wanted one more weekend of just us and the idea of breaking your heart... I just couldn't do it. Every time I tried to say something, I just couldn't get the words out."

Sebastian takes a sip of his coffee. He doesn't look in my direction, but I can tell he hears me. I want to say more, explain myself, but I hold back and let him say his peace. This can't be me spilling my guilt all over him.

"I talked with Jack for most of the night," he says, looking into his cup. "Spent the rest of the time researching articles and asking him questions. I'm sure you know that no one else married has, um…"

"Yeah, I know," I admit. "But that doesn't mean—"

He holds his hand up, interrupting my stream of promises he doesn't believe I'll keep.

"Whatever happens, I don't want to be the last to know ever again," he says.

"I won't keep anything else from you," I promise. I reach for his hand, and he takes it, finally meeting my gaze. I see now his bloodshot eyes and swollen face, and I die a little inside. This is because I was too cowardly to tell him in the privacy of our home. His loving wife did this to him.

"I'm so sorry I didn't tell you here," I say. "I wanted more time before it all changed, and hours kept ticking by, and I… I—"

My words stop, and he squeezes my hand. "It must have been awful for you knowing you had to hurt someone you love," Sebastian sighs.

"It was," I croak. "Because I want you and I choose you. It's us forever."

Sebastian raises one eyebrow. "Even if you outlive me?"

My breath catches taking in that notion, one I'd not taken time to think about. If there's a future where Theodore and I were in enough proximity to extend our lives, I would outlive my husband. All I can do in response is nod my head.

"I haven't…" I struggle with what to say. "There's a lot I haven't thought about yet. I don't know anything about

Theodore." I struggle to say his name around my husband, fearful of what hurt that might cause, but we need to talk about things. No more pretending this isn't happening to us.

"I know a lot about that guy," Sebastian scoffs.

I tilt my head as he releases my hand, running his palm up my arm. I move closer to him, desperate for his touch.

"Theo," Sebastian says. "He goes by Theo. It's um, Theo Lorwerth. Quite a mouthful."

I freeze, ready to hear what Sebastian has learned. I'd be lying to myself if I said I wasn't interested in knowing.

"He's our age. Top representative at a consulting company on the east coast. He's brokered a dozen deals this year, all with large commissions. One of them was the project for college students to have safe receptions. Big news not too far back. He's light on any social media. No pictures of him at a reception unless it was for a client."

"You do know a lot," I admit.

Sebastian leans back and sets his cup to the side. "I'd like to say I broke into Jack's files, but I'm sure he left them where I could see them. He's not stupid."

"Neither are you," I add.

"Theo had a heart attack on Friday," Sebastian tells me.

I gasp, my steaming cup burning my palms, but I can't move to set it down. I'm unsure of how I feel about the news. The part of me bonded to Theo can't stand the thought of him suffering or hurting, and there's a gnawing in my stomach, sick over those words.

But there's another side of me, and one I hate to admit, that wonders how we would feel if he had died. Theo's existence complicates our life, turning everything upside down. I don't know him even though I feel him, so what would his death mean to me?

None of the bonded have died, yet.

"Seems he has something called Hypertrophic Cardiomy-opathy." Sebastian says the words slowly but perfectly. I imagine he's repeated them to himself many times, mulling over the diagnosis.

I touch my chest, the fresh bruise tender beneath my fingertips, feeling my heart rate pick up with news.

"He's got maybe another five to ten years," Sebastian says. "Probably less after the heart attack."

My stomach churns, and I worry I'll vomit all over Sebastian. More heavy tears threaten to escape and my skin burns with anger that my bonded might die. Sebastian's words confirm that my bonded leaving devastates me.

It defies all reason. I don't know this man, but the pull to him strengthens knowing that he needs me, needs our bond to get better. The cord that ties us pulls taut, yanking something deep within me, begging me to lift from the chair and run toward Theo. My breathing stops while I fight it, remaining still beside Sebastian.

It takes all my strength, and I let out a whimper from the effort.

"I've tinkered with the idea of us running off to the middle of nowhere. Find a cave in the middle of the woods and wait it out. Who needs running water?" Sebastian jokes.

I bite my lip and sink lower in my chair, letting my fore-head rest on the side of my coffee cup. A breeze rustles the surrounding leaves, sending a few sputtering up in circles.

A long breath leaves my lungs, and the cord to my bonded lessens a fraction, allowing me to focus on our conversation.

"I've killed people before," Sebastian utters.

"What?" I grit out. "For NeXus?"

"When we infiltrated the Genome Enquiry. It's classified information even from spouses," he says. "But no more secrets between us."

I don't know what to say, so I sit in silence, accepting that my husband had killed before. There's not a line Sebastian wouldn't cross to protect me.

"There were children," he croaks. "They were trying to get them out in this transport van, and they were all crying, screaming on the inside." His hand on my skin trembles a bit, and he wraps his fingers around my arm, urging me into his lap. I set down the coffee and ease my body onto his.

"I had a clear shot of the driver, and I took it. Then there was another guy in the passenger seat who didn't run from the van. Didn't know what he would do, you know. He could have taken a hostage," he explains.

I wrap my arms around Sebastian's neck, and in this moment, any thoughts of my bonded fade away. I cut the tether and focus on my husband, on the terrible things they forced him to do.

"I don't think what I did was wrong," he continues. "But I'm not a murderer. That's not who I am."

"Of course you're not," I tell him and cup his face, brushing my lips against his cheek. He laces his fingers behind my back, holding me against him. There's a steady shake of his chest, trembling with everything that's happened, and possibly other things he's left unsaid.

"I think you should go to NeXus with Jack and Theo." Sebastian swallows hard, turning his face so our lips brush against each other. "He'll die without you, and after seeing how weak you were this weekend, how different, I'm worried you might, too. I can't take another person's life, and I can't lose you."

Our lips crash together before a choked sob escapes my throat. Our mouths move in a familiar rhythm, but there's an undercurrent of longing and need. Lips press too hard, fingers scratch at the skin, and a moan escapes from both of us before he pulls away.

"I don't want any of this," I plead. "I want to go back."

Sebastian has never cried in all our years together, never let me see him lose control of his emotions. Today he's close, watering eyes boring into mine. I've known he loves me with every cell of his body, and he shows me in how he treats me every day. The big and small things that make up our life, let me know his love is there.

"I don't either, but this—" He pulls my wrist up, stacking it next to his. Our tattoos stare back at us, the promise I intend to keep. "—still stands if you want it. We'll do this together, but only as long as that's what you need."

"I can't do this without you," I rush out, pulling his hand to my chest, pressing the tattoo over my heart.

"It's us forever. Promise me," I beg.

"Then I'm going with you," Sebastian offers. "As long as that's what you want, we'll do this as husband and wife."

It doesn't go unnoticed that he doesn't promise me forever anymore, and I can't make him. That's too much too soon, but I'll keep saying it until he believes me. I'll make him see it's us until the end.

There's nothing more to say, so we sit together, watching leaves sprinkle on the ground. This is the last time we'll be in our home together for a long while, so we hold each other in silence, mourning the life we're leaving behind.

Alison woke up hungover and shocked to find Sebastian, and let me know my phone won't stop vibrating. It reminded me to give Sebastian his phone back, which he took with a heavy sigh, understanding the lengths I went to protecting my secret.

I don't answer Jack until mid-day when he's sent me over a dozen text messages.

JACK

> What did Seb say?

> We don't have a lot of time to decide. NeXus has agreed to house you and pay your wages.

> I'm with Theo.

> He doesn't have a lot of time if you aren't near.

The last message breaks my heart, not just for me, but for my husband, who's made Theo's life, and impending death, his burden. I suppose he may have a new lease on life after meeting me, and that's what Sebastian's thinking.

When Alison leaves, I tell her we're going to NeXus and I'll be away from work for however long this takes.

"All of you?" she worries. "That feels... explosive."

I don't disagree, but it's the best I can manage in this garbage fire. We hug and I thank her for not hating me. She laughs and reaches for her pounding head, promising she'll never drink wine again.

Well, at least not until another reception she has in a few weeks. She still has a key so she can raid my wardrobe at will, and with that, it's just me and Sebastian for a few hours.

I find him packing in our room, his expression focused and stoic on the task.

I send Jack a message that we're going, and put my phone down, ignoring the vibration of his response.

There's something I want before we leave, something Sebastian can't refuse me.

"Seb," I whisper, standing in the doorway of our bedroom.

"I started packing your essentials," he says with his back to me.

"Will you take the suitcase off the bed?"

"Sure," he agrees, lifting one and turning to set it on the bench in the room's corner. It almost slips from his hands when he notices I'm standing in nothing but my panties, and I'm lowering those to the floor.

He tosses the other suitcase to the side and takes two large strides toward me, yanking me against him. There's a moment of pause, where he hesitates, scanning my face for some sign. I don't know what more I can give him to make him keep going. I'm standing naked in our bedroom, asking him to clear the bed.

The hands on my back slide up between my shoulders, pressing me closer to him and his hardening erection, and I feel his breath on my lips.

"I need you," I demand. "Don't deny me this. Don't over-think us right now."

His lips touch mine, soft and gentle. I open my mouth to let his tongue slip inside, massaging mine when I'm lifted, and I wrap my legs around his middle.

It's effortless the way he carries me, setting me down on the bed. Looking up at my perfect husband, I let out a sigh of relief. His clothes come off with ease, and his eyes never leave mine.

My breaths quicken in anticipation. He owns me in the bedroom, and I love the control.

"Spread your legs," he orders, and I do, the excitement building. He reaches down to touch me, stroking himself with his other hand, and his eyes close when he feels how wet I am.

"Feel that," I say. "I need you."

He lowers his face between my legs, kissing the inside of my thighs, stroking my center with his thick fingers. I reach down and spear his hair with my fingers, pulling his mouth closer to where I need him.

Pushing one finger inside, he follows my lead, his tongue finding my clit and circling. The wet heat of his mouth and the pure desperation for him almost sends me over the edge, and I moan in pleasure, pushing myself against his face.

My nipples harden, and I rock against him, legs shaking as he sucks and licks. His muscular back flexes as he pleasures me, a growl vibrating against my most sensitive areas.

"Just like that." The pressure of his mouth increases, sending an ache to my core. I'm close, on the precipice of tipping over the edge and losing all control. "I don't want to come yet. Please, babe. Fuck!"

He lets up, but adds another finger, stroking me inside and making me writhe against the bed. Smoldering eyes look down at me while he brings his thumb to my clit, and I smile, eyes locked on the man I love, the man I want.

"You'll always be mine. This—" he looks down at my pussy, cupping his free hand over where his fingers are working me, "—is mine."

I nod, unable to speak. All that comes out are cracked moans of ecstasy. His hand reaches up and plucks at my hard nipple, pulling slightly and causing me to convulse. Both of his hands and all of his focus are on making me come.

So close.

"Do you want to come on my cock or my hand? Maybe my face?" he asks.

I whimper, wrapping my hand around his wrist that works my breast. "I just want you," I stammer. "Just you."

There's a flicker of sadness on his face, but it disappears in a flash. I can't focus on that when my body is about to explode from an orgasm.

"I'm not going anywhere," he promises. He slides his fingers out, and I whine at the loss of his touch. "I'm right here," he says, moving in between my legs and pulling my hips toward his waiting cock.

I reach out and wrap my hand around the base, squeezing the thick length up and down, letting a drop of pre-cum leak from the tip. He lets his head fall back and growls, running the pads of his fingers down my thighs, creating red marks on my skin.

"Put me inside you," he demands.

I don't hesitate, bringing him to my center and sliding the tip inside. I'm so wet and ready that he doesn't have to ease his thick cock past my opening. He thrusts forward, letting my soaked pussy take him, filling me inch by inch.

I gasp from the stretch, the completeness I feel when he's pushed inside to the hilt. My hands reach to his sides, feeling the corded muscle as he drives into me with relentless force. It's everything I need at this moment. Everything else falls away and the quiver of my orgasm grows with every push of his hips, slamming him inside me.

"Mine," he growls, lowering his heavy chest onto mine, his lips caressing my ear. "Mine," he repeats, thrusting harder, our bodies slapping together in rhythm.

"Yours," I cry out when I hit the peak. My legs tighten around his waist, and I moan for endless seconds, my body trembling in his arms, waves of pleasure taking over.

"Fuck!" he cries out, so loud that it reverberates between us. The swell of his cock is almost too much to take as I claw at his back until he's pulsing inside me, the evidence of his orgasm leaking out where our bodies meet.

The smell of him, woods and a hint of sweat surrounds me, and I exhale as his motions slow until he stops.

He hovers over me with his arms shaking by my sides, and kisses my neck, my chin, my chest, until he slips out and rolls to his side. Our slick bodies come together, holding each other in the bed. It's more than a climax we share during sex.

It's love.

I cling to that when Theo's face flashes in my mind the moment I close my eyes.

CHAPTER 22

THEO

"Are you comfortable?" Moira asks. She and Jack had to help me to his car, my body so weak with Emry's absence. The only relief is we're almost alone on the street. I hide myself in over-sized clothes Jack brought over and a ball cap, but no one gives me a second look.

"No," I admit. "Nothing you can do about it, though."

Jack comes around to the driver's side. He drives a car with the NeXus emblem, and I'm not surprised. They will fund our lives until this deal is over.

"We'll message you when we get there and try to arrange a visit," he calls out to her.

"You better," Moira orders, and I smile. "It will be okay," she tells me, but I think she's trying to convince herself. Part of me wonders why she cares, but she's so much like my father. There's goodness in her, and I'm glad we met.

"I'll see you soon," I promise and she steps back from the car, waving as we pull out into the street. It's dusk and Emry's on her way to NeXus with her husband. I push the jealousy down, reminding myself that we're going to break the bond, and I can only hope my time with her heals me enough to give me a few more years.

"Are you a searcher or settler?" I ask Jack.

"I don't know," he admits. "I've had a few kids. They're grown now, but that gives me a lot of fulfillment. My research does, too."

"I've seen how you look at Moira," I tell him.

"Oh, really?" Jack gives me a sideways glance. "In your condition?"

"I'm dying, not blind," I mock. "You like her."

He nods a few times to himself, weaving through the roads slowly, trying not to jostle me around too much. A billboard comes into view that stretches across every lane of the road, blinking its message to all the cars below.

Fulfillment is companionship.

I fight the urge to vomit.

"I like people that are genuine," Jack admits. "She seems to be."

"That bodes well for me."

"Why is that?" he asks.

"You have every right to hate me, but I don't think you do," I answer.

Jack nods. "The closer to death, the more honest people become, and you're knocking on the door of your last days. Honest people always have my respect. I don't mean to be rude. It's been researched."

"So you aren't going to drive me to a ditch somewhere and hide my body?" I joke.

"No," Jack answers. It's unnecessary for him to say it, but I won't deny I'm glad to hear the words.

"Even though you aren't plotting my demise, I'd like to see Moira while I'm there and have someone in my corner. You'll get her into NeXus now," I add. "Because you want to see her, too."

"Well, I won't turn her away," he admits with a grin. "We have a long drive. Care to give me a bit more intake before we get there?"

He's quick to change the subject, further cementing my belief that the way he looks at Moira isn't only in my mind.

"Not really," I mutter. "But I'd be fine with some tit for tat? That's how conversations work. You ask me a question and I ask you one."

"You are a deal maker," Jack comments. "Top performer at your company. Always bargaining with people."

I shrug as best I can through my pain, not surprised that a researcher found out as much as he could about his test subject.

"Okay, I'll bite," Jack agrees. "Why didn't you use your resources to find your bondmate?"

"Resources?" I ask.

"You're wealthy and have connections with reception companies. You have access to a thousand times as many people as the rest of us, and your life is on the line."

"Numbers don't add up," I explain. "I could touch millions of people in my lifetime, but all it would do is drain me dry and the odds of finding the bond were slim. Fuck, worse than slim. Not even a percentage point."

Jack seems to accept that answer, smacking his lips as we come to a stop. "So you considered it?"

"I looked into all of my end-of-life options. I'm under no pretenses that I'm on borrowed time."

"Not anymore," Jack comments.

"What did you do at NeXus?" I ask. He's pushing the questions, trying to lead me to talk more, and it's my turn. "Or what do you currently do? You must have a strong tie to get approval for this research in a matter of hours."

"No one leaves NeXus," Jack explains.

"Vague response," I snap back.

Jack gives a heavy sigh, changing lanes on the road with ease. I'm surprised to see him driving, given most cars don't require it, but it gives him something to focus on during this awkward ride.

"You're contracted for life. It keeps a paycheck coming and protects their confidential information. It's a symbiotic relationship," he explains.

"Like a parasite," I joke.

Jack holds back his smile, tapping his thumbs on the steering wheel. "I'm a researcher by heart, so it allows me access to their resources. Most of it I do as a hobby."

"So, you're a researcher for NeXus?" I reiterate my original question.

"Of sorts," Jack answers.

"Say someone came into your office that may be a benefit to NeXus's research. You may slip them a name from time to time," I surmise.

"Absolutely not," Jack affirms. "I wouldn't do something like that."

I raise my hands in apology as he picks up speed on the highway. Everything aches, but the stop-and-go motion of the city will cease on the open road.

"So this research on me and Emry, there's no big bonus for you at the end of it?"

"Don't think I can't count," Jack warns. "This is more than one question."

I don't answer, shifting in my seat to fight the pain that seeps into my bones.

Jack sighs after the silence stretches for too long. "We aren't all driven by money."

"We aren't all dead by forty, either," I argue, my words dripping with sarcastic frustration. "You still haven't answered the question, and my clock is ticking."

"Your question is broad." I grate my teeth at his response and he clears his throat. "May I answer what you meant to ask?"

"By all means. Psychoanalyze my turn." I knew better than to get in a small moving box with a therapist, but there's no escaping this nightmare now.

Jack frowns, easing into the fastest lane and switching on the auto drive. "Sebastian and I met at NeXus. We worked to find and extinguish the Genome Enquiry headquarters. I handled the psych team who helped the rescued children."

"And Sebastian?" I ask.

Jack takes in a deep breath, fixing his glasses that have slid down his nose. "He worked with the vanguard. Lots of muscle and heart. We lost old friends when we took down Genome but saved new ones. Saved Emry. He was barely an adult, and I was pushing thirty. Feels like a lifetime ago."

"Sounds like a decent guy," I bite out. "You both do."

"If circumstances were different..." Jack trails off, slapping his hands on his thighs. I know what he wants to say. I seem like a decent guy. We're all just good people stuck in a shitty situation.

The cars all move in sync over a hundred miles an hour, whipping by buildings and barreling us toward NeXus head-quarters. I can't feel Emry yet, and I wonder how close we need to be before I'll sense her.

"That's a lot of questions answered," Jack points out. "And if you want to know more, you need to ask Sebastian."

I roll my eyes at his suggestion. If I were Sebastian, I wouldn't be up for a heart to heart with my wife's bonded.

"Will you answer a few of mine?" he asks.

"Yes." I agree.

"Explain the bond in your own words, from the moment of conception."

"You make it sound like sex," I say.

"Isn't it, though?" he counters. "Sex is the joining of two organisms, in body, yes, but there are hormonal responses. Reactions inside oneself when the act occurs."

"Now you sound like a doctor," I joke.

He waits, cars flashing by us in the window, and I clear my throat. "It felt like that, I guess, like coming together." I bring my hand to my mouth, rubbing my jaw and close my eyes with the memory.

"I need a little more," Jack urges. "Physically, how did you feel?"

"Like I was free-falling, but I wasn't scared. I know that's not helpful."

"No," he corrects. "It is. In hypothesis, there's an adrenaline surge. No one has data from the point of contact. Every detail matters. What else?"

A wave of pleasure hits me, and I stifle a groan with my hand. "I could feel her in my body as if she stepped inside, filling me up. Her smell, her taste, unlike anything I've ever experienced. It was fucking amazing. Mind blowing."

"Did you orgasm?" Jack asks.

The words sound out of place, but they're not. It's the height of human pleasure, and the only way to describe something that feels as perfect as that moment did.

"It was better than that," I answer. "Meeting her tore us

into a million pieces and brought them back together. Every piece that fit felt better than any orgasm, any drug. I'm no saint, and that's a pleasure you can't buy."

"How interesting," Jack says, his forehead creasing in thought.

"The sensation of it was addicting. There's a connection when you have sex, but this was so much more," I add, struggling to find the words. "We never came apart. She's still swirling around inside me, filling me with a tingling."

There's a buildup of pressure in my groin, the blood rushing to my dick. I'm getting hard, and I adjust myself, trying to forget that moment and how Emry affects me. "Can we talk about something else?"

"Sure, we can get back to that," Jack obliges. "What about your heart? Describe the change as best you can."

"I've never had a great heart, so I can't say it felt normal," I shrug. "To me, I felt whole. Strong, I guess. It's never had that kind of power. I've always been a little out of breath."

I'm fully erect, and I lean forward, my hand running down my pant legs, trying to will it away.

What the fuck?

I shake my head, hoping I can push away the thoughts of Emry, and a wave of pleasure hits me, making me groan.

"Are you alright?" Jack asks.

"Vague question," I spit. The veins in my neck throb, and my erratic heart strums to life, beating faster, sending more blood to my throbbing cock. There's no hiding it, and it tents my pants. "Pull over."

"We're in the auto drive high-speed lane—"

"Pull over!" I cut him off.

Jack puts the command in the dashboard, signals, and maneuvers the car through the lanes, noticing how hard I am in his passenger seat.

"Is that from your memory?"

He's a doctor and as awkward as this should be, it's slightly less because he has a professional curiosity.

"I don't fucking know," I answer.

More pulses of ecstasy course through my veins, and I feel Emry when Jack gets off the open road, pulling off to the side in an empty parking lot. It's suddenly more than just her essence when we come to a stop.

I hear her.

Her moans penetrate my ears and send me over the edge. I open the car door, ready to exit.

"I'll get out," Jack says. "Stay there."

My only response is a growl that rumbles through me, and I grab my dick, unable to stop from rubbing one out in a parking lot where I'll probably get arrested.

That would make the news headlines go insane.

Jack shuts the door and strolls away, and I let out a cry of relief when my hand shoves down my pants and wraps around my throbbing cock, already leaking pre-cum. I've lost control with her voice in my head, moaning and begging.

"Just like that," she says. "I don't want to come yet. Please, babe. Fuck!"

My hand moves faster, the muscles in my arm clenching and burning as I run it up and down my dick. My other hand clenches around the seat of the car, making my arm shake. I smell her arousal, taste her mouth, her pussy, and it's intoxicating, sending me over the edge in a matter of minutes.

My heart strengthens its beating, even and forceful, pumping more blood to my groin. Her cracked moans of plea-sure continue, and I'm floating out of my body, the orgasm on the edge, ready to erupt.

"I just want you," she stammers. "Just you."

"Oh, fuck," I say to myself and when I think I've hit the

peak, a new sensation flows through me. One of completeness and fullness, making my balls draw up and I'm lifting my hips off the seat, pumping away, breathing hard and fast.

"Yours," she says and I sputter out onto my shirt, my chin. My hot cum pumps in succession with my thudding heart until the stream slows, and it slides down my hand, leaving me a mess in Jack's car.

"Fuuuuuuuck!" I yell out, slamming my fist into the roof.

It's one thing to go through this uncomfortable torture, but to be humiliated along the way is overkill.

Jack's standing on the edge of the parking lot, idly walking while he waits. He turns with my scream and I see him wave in my direction. The guy actually waves, and I close my eyes and grumble to myself.

"What the fuck was that?" I murmur, surveying the mess I've made in mortification. Something tells me Jack will find this newest development scientifically fascinating, and I hold on to the fact while I rip off my shirt and clean myself up.

CHAPTER 23

EMRY

The alerts began on my phone before I untangled myself from Sebastian. I had hoped I could live in bliss forever, ignorant of the outside world, but the device rattled on the wood. It's vibration a reminder that our secret isn't ours anymore, and I'll have to face the world. I grab the phone, my eyes adjusting to the light as the headlines scroll past.

Resist the Receptions — Bonding in the wild
Married or Mated? One woman's choice.
Left to Die — If Theodore Lorwerth's heart gives out, will there be manslaughter charges?

The last headline sends my pulse into overdrive, the fright creeping through my body like a snake. I open the article despite my better judgment and sprint into the bathroom.

"Em," Sebastian's groggy voice beckons me back to bed.

"Just a minute." I choke on my words and chastise myself for letting my emotions show. His feet are on the floor as soon as I close and lock the bathroom door.

My heart racing, I close the toilet lid and sit, reading while I hear his footsteps head in my direction.

Theodore Lorwerth reportedly matched with Emry Crawford, now known as Emry Crowe, Friday night in the shopping district.

The Oculus reported on the incident, but many news outlets disregarded the story. Why? Because Emry Crowe fled the scene after the bonding. New events have brought the story to light, validating The Oculus's breaking coverage.

Their match sent her into a sprint away from her bonded and into the arms of her husband, Sebastian Owens, now known as Sebastian Crowe.

If Sebastian Crowe sounds familiar, you're recalling the Genome Enquiry disaster some years ago. Sebastian, a member of NeXus, stormed the building's basement, taking on fire before the guilty attempted to flee to a second location with over three dozen children.

The Genome Enquiry killed four NeXus employees during the event, and the government awarded each member of the Vanguard medals of honor. Sebastian continues to work for NeXus.

He married Emry sometime later, and they decided on the name Crowe. It appears Emry Crowe, a University professor, didn't take those vows lightly, but what does that mean for her bonded?

No one has refused the bond, and although we understand the pairing of these lucky few extends life up to five hundred years, what happens if the bonded don't stay together? Will the separation have the opposite effect?

As a further complication, The Oculus reports that Theodore (Theo) Lorwerth suffers from a heart condition that will soon take his life. On the evening of the bond, he suffered a coronary event, causing him to be hospitalized for several days. It's not in doubt her rejection further exacerbated his poor health.

Some (this reporter) are questioning the legal implications in a world where bond mates have special rights, privileges, and laws, in exchange for their compliance with research. Local prosecutors for the city weigh in on the matter.

"There's the consideration that her absence would, in fact, take Mr. Theodore Lorwerth's life. The city is investigating the possibility of manslaughter if he passes because of her lack of cooperation." Mr. Lewis Stormbaugh, City Prosecutor.

The Oracle would love to hear your thoughts on the matter. Murder charge for marriage vows?

1,647 comments

"Em, are you okay?" Sebastian calls, banging on the door when I read the first one.

She's being so selfish. She's not just killing Theo, but other people who need more research subjects.

***I'll fuck Sebastian. Have you seen that guy? He'll be fine,
Emry. Throw him back.***

I think it's sweet. I want to find a settler like that.

I drop the phone, my hands shaking too much to keep my grip and rest my face in my hands. The doorknob shakes as Sebastian works the lock, and he swings the door open to find me crying on the toilet, naked.

Taking my robe from the hook and wrapping it around me, he crouches down and runs his fingers through my hair. He doesn't ask what's wrong, but picks up the phone, scanning the article himself.

"This," he says, waving the phone in my line of sight. "It's nothing to worry about. It's a headline, meant to draw attention. That guy is up for re-election and that paper is desperate."

"The prosecutor is quoted—"

"The prosecutor wants votes," he interrupts. "He's trying to get people to like him. And anyone fighting to find out more about the bond is the crowd's favorite."

I clutch the robe around me and lean my head on his chest.

"We're on our way to Theo. He won't die," Sebastian reassures me. The words are acid on his tongue, and he swallows them down with disgust.

"Why are you so damn understanding? Why don't you hate me? Or him?" I ask.

His head jerks back. "You didn't do this. This was done to you. Both of you."

He tucks my hair behind my ears and brings his lips to mine, his tongue exploring the inside of my mouth while his hand reaches behind my neck, keeping me locked to him.

When he releases me, I gasp for a breath of air, my lips tingling.

"I'll never hate you," he vows.

My fingertips trace his jaw, and I try to smile, but it doesn't come. My head pounds when I think about the day ahead, and my stomach churns from the stress. "Can you call Alison? Tell her I won't be looking at my phone for a few days, but she's free to come into the house."

"That's a good idea. Your mother... she's been calling my phone." He navigates through mine and frowns. "She's called you several times."

"I can't," my voice cracks. "She won't understand."

Sebastian nods. "Do you want me to call her back or leave it?"

What Sebastian isn't saying is that any contact with my mother will send her into overdrive, not calm down the situation. "I'm surprised she isn't knocking on our door already," I huff.

"She's nowhere close," Sebastian promises.

"How could you know that?"

"Reception... hundreds of miles away," he tells me. "It's a week-long event."

"And you helped fund it."

He sighs in a way that tells me he did. Most of the time I refuse to give her money, but in this case, I agree with him. She can't say no to a reception, and he's doing his part to help my anxiety by giving us distance.

"I'll suggest Alison stay here," Sebastian changes the subject. "More space than that cramped apartment." He stands, hooking his arms underneath my back and knees, lifting me from my seat.

"Um," I stop him. "I still need to pee."

"You're ruining my moment here," he grins.

I set my head down on his shoulder, and my smile finally comes. He kisses my forehead and squeezes me tight before setting me down.

"You might want to jump in the shower," he says. "We need to be heading out soon."

"Right," I agree, biting my lip, the smile quickly leaving with those words. I wait until the water is running before I let myself cry. Sebastian has enough to worry about today.

W e turn the windows of the car black to the outside world, but I see all the reporters at the end of our drive even if they can't make out anything more than my profile in the car. There's a flash of relief that we'll be safe inside NeXus's walls, unbothered by strangers. Everyone's constant obsession with the bond and now with me sours my stomach. I want nothing more than to be alone with Sebastian, and I sneer at them as we drive past.

The ride isn't long, and Sebastian makes this drive every day, weaving down roads with little thought, making small talk, and trying to lift our spirits. "We don't have to have your mother over for dinner anytime soon. I think this excuse is solid."

I haven't talked to her, but I will at some point, and her words will drip with guilt and jealousy. It's possible she thinks I care about her absence, as if going away for the week is a passive-aggressive stance about my bonding. In reality, I'm relieved. She would never feel empathy for my situation.

I sputter a laugh and notice my chest doesn't hurt. The bruise still shows on the curve of my top, a faded blue circle that peaks out from the fabric, but there's no ache.

Theo's close.

We pass a billboard entering the open road.

What you crave is with the one of your choosing.

Resting my head on the back of the seat, I stare at my husband. He's a threatening man to those that don't know him. Sharp jaw, and thick muscles on top of his huge frame, but underneath, he's the best of us. Betrayed by the universe and still joking about his mother-in-law. He's one of a kind.

We pass the building with the giant silver N on the side and goosebumps cover my arms. I flex my fists open and closed, and Sebastian notices, reaching over and holding my hand. He veers right, driving onto a road in a treeline no one would notice if they weren't looking. Slowing down on the down-sloping pavement, the world grows darker from the thick foliage.

"Where are we going?" I ask.

"Sorry, Em. I should have explained. We won't go to the main building." He pulls my trembling hand to his lips and kisses the back of my palm. "There's a facility for testing, underground. It's easier to secure that way."

"Right," I nod and darkness creeps onto the windows, sending a shiver down my spine. I tighten my grip on his hand and tell myself that I'm fine. We're going to break the bond.

But claustrophobia sneaks its way into my brain, speaking its terrible thoughts. Memories of my time at Genome Enquiry flood back full of white walls and small spaces. They always kept the doors locked, and I didn't see a window for years. This isn't the same, and I repeat that to myself, knowing I will calm down if I concentrate. I can do this for Sebastian, for us.

"Em," Sebastian whispers, slowing the car. "You're not okay."

He doesn't ask but notices how the panic that's always

squatting inside me creeps up and takes over. I'm breathing faster, my hand sweating against his while I shift from side to side in the seat.

"I'm fine," I lie. "Keep driving."

"I should have told you about this," Sebastian repeats. "I'm so sorry. We're turning around."

"No!" I bark, my fingernails clawing into the back of his hand. "Just let me focus."

He brings the car to a stop, pulling over to the side.

"You don't have to do this," he says.

Sweat beads on my forehead, and I press my back against the seat.

"Drive the car, Seb," I order.

"We can turn around and figure out another way."

I claw my hand down my pants and shake my head. "I'm doing this. We're doing this."

"Em—"

"No!" I scream at him. "It just took me by surprise. Drive the car, or I'm getting out and walking there myself."

"Okay," he whispers, kissing me on the cheek before he puts the car back in gear.

We creep forward to a gate secured with lights and cameras and a few men with weapons. Silver N's ornament their camouflaged uniforms, and they wear helmets that hide their face. They approach Sebastian, who knows one man for certain, greeting him with a familiar hello.

They circle our car, and one leans down next to my open window.

"May I have your name and identification?" he asks.

"I'm Emry Crowe, and we're here with Jack Wells," I say, handing over my information. The man hesitates a moment, and I imagine his jaw is slack behind the glass of his helmet. I bet news like ours travels fast.

He scans my ID and then my face, and I blink from the light, holding my hand up by instinct.

Someone scans Sebastian, the light of his device turning green. They say a few words, telling him us we're free to enter. They leave us, and a gate painted to conceal itself in the trees opens.

"Are you sure?" Sebastian asks before starting the car again.

"Drive through the gate, Seb," I say. My heart beats too fast, and beads of sweat form on my brow, but I force a smile and flick my hand forward, telling him to go. He grunts, creeping along at a snail's pace, looking at me every other second.

We pass through the gate, and my pulse soars into over-drive. I let go of his hand and clutch the seat, hoping he doesn't notice my shallow breaths and eyes on the brink of tears.

I don't think I'm strong enough for this, but I have to try until I break.

"Everything's okay. We'll figure this out. Together." I hear a voice that isn't Sebastian in my ears, and I sit forward and look around. We're the only car on the road, driving further down into the earth.

Turning to Sebastian, I ask the question I know the answer to, but I need to be sure. "Did you just say something?"

"No," he answers. "Are you okay?"

No.

"Yes, I'm fine," I lie. "Feeling better now that we're inside."

"You sound better," he sighs. "Calmer. A few minutes until we reach the valet and they'll shuttle us to the building."

I stare straight ahead, my heart rate slowing as I catch my breath. A wave of calmness hits me, starting in my mind and cascading down my limbs and out through my fingertips. I audibly exhale, my eyes fluttering closed. The claustrophobia dissipates, a forgotten memory of a young girl from long ago.

"There you go," the voice says. It's not my own, and although I'm grateful, it scares me.

"Theo. Is that you?"

Air fills my lungs, the long steady inhale continuing to calm me, sedating my busy mind.

"Yes," the voice speaks back. *"I'm here."*

CHAPTER 24

THEO

We arrived unceremoniously considering the media shitshow above our heads. Me without a shirt, and Jack talking to people in rapid succession, none of them being asked to get me some clothes or questioning why I'm only wearing pants. When I bring this up to him, he does his best to hold back a laugh, fails, and tells me a full closet is waiting in my room.

Employees emptied Jack's car the second we pulled up to the doors, no doubt checking our bags for recording devices or other items they deemed contraband. My things were gone before I could get fresh clothes.

I scowl, walking with him down a white hallway in an underground NeXus facility, clutching my semen-soaked shirt in my hand. Every few moments, my phone buzzes with a notification that my name is in a news article.

This experiment is off to a great start.

NeXus oozes money from its touchscreen windows to the gold embossed N's on the thick lab coats worn by everyone but us. Even Jack gets handed a lab coat while I stand and wait for him to talk to another NeXus friend... shirtless.

I'm not tired as we walk through an endless stream of hallways, and that tells me my proximity to Emry is closing in. She's getting nearer by the second, the ache in my chest easing, so I'm able to breathe in the recycled air deep within my lungs. The physical relief I get from her is almost worth all the emotional pain.

Almost.

Jack ushers me into a room that I'll need a map to find my way back to and steps inside after me. "I'll show you around after you get dressed."

"And showered," I add.

"Probably best." He bites his lip to keep from smiling. He held it together most of the way here before he burst into laughter at my embarrassment from the parking lot incident. I made him vow to let the subject die, not wanting to talk about it, and he begrudgingly agreed.

Sure, it will get noted in some file kept by all the curious minds in this place, and some lab coat will get a chuckle at my expense. But the least the man can do is drop it for today.

I like Jack, and we might stay friends for however long I have left to live. Friend or not, once I'm over it, he'll taunt me about this every chance he gets. I would if I were him.

"Bathroom's right here, full of products, towels. If there's anything you need, you send a message to the administration. You have my contact information, too." He steps over to a desk and hands me a tablet. "It's ready for you to program until you get your laptop back. Well, if they give it back. That might take a while. And this closet and dresser have your size clothing. Mostly scrubs and sweats. Nothing fancy, but it's cleaner than..." He clears his throat, doing his best to honor his promise.

"My cum soaked clothes?" I quip, holding up my shirt.

Jack takes in a big breath, holds it, and nods. "That chute right over there sends it to laundry," he says, letting his breath out with no laughter; a miracle at this point.

"Maybe this should go to the garbage," I offer, holding up my shirt. "I would feel terrible for the person forced to launder this."

"They've seen worse," Jack admits.

I toss the shirt inside the chute and circle the room. It's a stark difference to the building design. Soft lighting sends a glow across the floor, and the furnishings look like a luxury hotel, not a lab. There's a king-size bed with a lounge chair at the end, a bookcase filled with novels, and from what I saw of the bathroom, that's huge as well.

"This place is nice," I sigh. "Better than any damn hotel I've stayed in."

"You might be here a while," Jack tells me. "You should be comfortable."

I notice a tablet on the desk and presume it's for me. "I'll need to work from here. Can that tablet connect to my email?"

"Yes, but NeXus will offer you a spot on the payroll," Jack warns. "Be prepared for that."

"That's smart," I say. "Keeps their investments tied to them. Not sure what I could do for them, though."

"Oh, they'll find something," he muses.

Jack shoves his hands in his pockets and strolls around the room, taking it in himself. "The best and brightest are here. They'll help with what we've asked. The contract will be clear, but everything is about seeking the key to the bond with NeXus. That's the company's purpose."

Jack's full of advice today, and his lips turn in a frown at his last words. He's not required to caution me, and NeXus wouldn't like it, but Jack's not exactly a company man if he was honest in the car earlier.

"There's no money in breaking bonds. Who would want that?" I joke, clucking my tongue and offering a smile. "Ridiculous."

I sit on the bed and fall back, letting my body slap against the plush upholstery. "Why are you here, Jack?"

"Research is my passion—"

"Fuck, not here at NeXus. Here with me. Are you keeping your enemies closer?" My words aren't serious, not completely, but I'm the outsider in this situation. A stranger crashing in on his friends' lives, and especially Sebastian's. He sounds like a decent guy, and Jack speaks highly of him.

I stare at the ceiling, wondering how many miles down we are, tucked inside the earth. Buried secrets may not stay buried in a place like this, not if they find something someday, and NeXus has the means to succeed.

"You aren't an enemy, Theo." His voice is soft but firm. "You're no one's enemy."

I'm a good judge of people, and I think Jack's doing this for his friends, and partly, a large part, because he's a scientist. One that I surmise struggles with seeing his subjects as numbers on a page.

Yes, we'll be friends, I decide.

I rest my hand on my chest and realize what was left of the ache disappeared in the past few minutes. The steady throb of discomfort and struggle my heart suffers with every beat is gone, replaced with an even symphony of rhythm.

She's close.

"When do I see her?" I ask.

"We'll do a variety of tests without her. More blood — physical exertion, that sort of thing," he explains. "It won't be comfortable. If you can sense her when you can't get to her, it might even be painful."

His words don't frighten me. Despite my decision to help her break the bond, I'm too excited about seeing Emry to worry about pain. I've lived my entire life less than comfortable, pushing through the days with a heart struggling to beat.

"I'll remember that when they offer me a salary," I joke.

"There'll be several doctors," Jack tells me. "I have patients to attend to, but I'll be here every day. If it gets to be too much, just let me know."

"When are you going to have time to find your bondmate, Jack?" I ask. "Fourteen-hour days working doesn't leave much time."

"Maybe Moira can come have dinner a few nights," he offers. "I'm more keen on company than on an eternal treasure hunt."

"You're in the minority. Some would say an endangered species," I reason.

Jack shrugs, not responding, unmoved by my observation.

"What if we're not supposed to know?" I question.

Jack rests a hand on the footboard of the bed, one of his rings clicking on the wood. "I don't catch your meaning."

"Maybe people shouldn't understand the bond. Maybe it's beyond us. Humans use power for destruction, and time... time is power."

Jack makes a fist and hits the footboard twice, letting out a sigh. "You could be right. But that doesn't have a happy ending for you or billions of people."

"My ending won't be happy," I whisper, mostly to myself.

Jack tilts his head but doesn't acknowledge my words or argue them. He knows I'm right. Considering both outcomes, I lose either way.

"I'll be back in thirty minutes. Shower works like they all

do," Jack says. The door clicks softly when he leaves, and I lay for another moment, feeling the steady beat of my heart, enjoying the respite for however long it's mine.

My eyes close, and I concentrate on this day, this minute, this second. I can't control anything going forward. My body won't be mine when she's around. I'll do the best I can, trying to make my father proud and help a woman who's been through hell and back, only to have her world turn upside down because of me.

The strength of my heart when she's closer is a drug I happily take, even if it's short-lived, but there's another feeling that creeps inside.

Fear.

Not mine.

Hers.

It wraps around my throat, tightening its noose. The room feels too small, sinking in on itself, trapping me inside. I open my eyes, and it's the same large space with an oversized bed and ornate furniture.

I sit up, running a shaking hand through my hair, but the feeling remains. It's quiet in this space, even with a busy hallway just outside the door. I'm not one to get nervous in new environments, or worry about things out of my control, but I can't shake this sensation.

Getting up and heading to the shower, her voice comes through, clear in my head and impossible to deny.

"I don't think I'm strong enough for this, but I have to try until I break."

I'm not startled to hear her voice. I'm desperate for it. Every word that murmurs through my thoughts sends a quiver of pleasure through me, even though they're not words I want to hear. She's scared and worried, but her worries are mine, bonded together as one. I want to quell them, make them stop. I need to.

"Everything's okay. We'll figure this out. Together." I say the words out loud by myself in this room, but I know she'll hear them. There's an invisible wave that crashes back and forth between us, and when I send my words to her, I feel the relief flood right back. The dread that wrapped around my spirit softens, drifting until it falls away.

"*Theo. Is that you?*" she says to me.

I reach out, as if I could touch her. What would that be like? The moment we bonded, our skin meeting for the first time, the world exploded beneath my feet.

A part of me is curious if I'm losing my mind, creating her with me when she's done nothing but deny the bond. I shake off the worry, knowing we're speaking to one another, connected by the mysterious magic of the bond.

"*Yes,*" I tell her. "*I'm here.*"

CHAPTER 25

"We aren't staying together?" My panicked voice rises with each word.

Despite everything that happened last week, I'm not growing any more used to surprises that separate me from my husband. This room is gorgeous and huge, with a giant bed at its center, but I'm told I'll be staying here by myself.

A NeXus employee waits outside, rightfully terrified of me after the outburst I had about the news. Sebastian pulled me into my room with his apologies, and I kicked and screamed, grabbing his suitcase and throwing it inside before the door slammed shut.

I know part of this is acting out because I'm underground in another testing facility. It doesn't stop my actions, which feel more and more out of control.

Sebastian sets my things down at the end of the bed. "I'm across the hall," he offers, his lips drawing into a tight line.

He's displeased about this, too, but hides his distaste from me. "I'll be with you every night. All you have to do is ask."

"Why would I have to ask for my husband to sleep with me?" I bark.

Sebastian's calm, unpacking my items and kissing my forehead when he answers. "All patients have their own rooms. It's part of the protocol. I'll stay here tonight if that's what you want."

I shove him away with trembling hands, angered at how unaffected he is that we're being separated minutes after entering the facility.

All my sadness bubbles up into an anger that boils inside my stomach. This place and my situation — fuck all my unfortunate situations — create a ball of rage that has no way to escape.

"You'll stay here every night," I demand. "You're my fucking husband, and I have some say in my life. Not much I know, but don't make me beg anymore than I have been so you'll stay by my side."

He stills for a moment, a few of my clothes clutched in his hand. "You'll never have to beg," he bites out, moving to the side and placing the clothes in a drawer. He takes a few steps toward me, resting his large palms on my shoulders and sighing. "We don't know how you'll react to... exposure every day. You might need this room for yourself. I'd rather we take the doctor's advice and be separate in the beginning, just until things are more in control."

My thoughts spin with his words, and I pull away, looking him over in shock. "Do you think I'd want Theo in here or that I'd... bring him back to my room because of the bond?"

I don't bring up that Theo's voice calmed me before we entered NeXus, or that I hear him at all. That won't change anything and it certainly won't help my argument, but he's in my head, invading my thoughts without my permission. I focus, sealing off my mind, imagining a cage around it in case he's listening now.

Guilt fills my stomach at the realization that I'm breaking my promise to Sebastian so soon, keeping things from him when we said we wouldn't.

I'll tell him after this fight.

Sebastian doesn't speak right away, his face telling me he's holding back something that might enrage me, worsening this moment. That's not his way, and I'm not fighting fairly, baiting him with my harsh words. Even still, we need to have these difficult discussions, and I can't do them without being heated.

His hands form into fists at his sides, and his jaw tightens. "I want you to be comfortable enough to..."

"To cheat!" I scream.

His Adam's apple bobs up and down with a few hard swallows, and he straightens, turning his back to me. "There's not a definition for what this is, or what could happen," he offers. The empty suitcase thuds on the floor, and he glides it into a closet.

"The definition is very clear," I argue.

"Not for this." He closes the closet door a bit too hard, making the frame shake. Sebastian never loses control, careful with every word and action, but our situation pushes his limits.

"You're being ridiculous. You will sleep in this bed—"

"Enough!" he yells.

My words catch in my throat, and I feel the tears well in my eyes.

"Enough, Emry," he sighs, picking up his suitcase and stepping toward the door.

"You c-can't just leave," I whisper.

"I'm putting my things away, and then I'm coming back for

your consultation. I'll stay here tonight like I promised. And every night, but I'll wait for you to ask. I will not move in here."

"Why are you being like this?" I ask.

He hesitates to leave, rubbing his forehead and avoiding my gaze. "I'm being practical. No one has ever refused the bond, and I know why we're here. I want what you want, and I'm hoping with everything in me these scientists can do it, but there are no guarantees. And while we wait in this purgatory, you'll want him. You might even need him, Emry."

He reaches for the door, and I slap his hand away, or I try to. I'm no match for the wall of muscle clenched on the handle. "That's not true!" I yell at him.

"You can't promise that." His words shake, the handle creaking from his pull on the doorknob.

His chin juts forward, blank eyes staring at the closed door. I grab his face and turn him to look at me. I need those dark eyes finding mine, and then he'll know that everything will be alright. We'll break the bond and be together just as we vowed.

"I love you so much," I choke out. "If I have to ask you every night to stay here, I will."

His face softens the slightest bit, and he leans down to kiss me. Our lips meet, soft and tender, reminding me of home — of him.

"No one would consider it cheating," he whispers into my mouth. "Not even me."

He yanks open the door and rushes through it, the air leaving my lungs in a gasp.

The door shuts again, Sebastian on the other side, leaving me alone in this space. There's an emptiness in the vast room full of furnishings and niceties.

I'm alone.

The only bonded person in the world, lonely less than a week after finding their bonded. The irony makes me laugh to myself, and it echoes in the room, bouncing off the walls and taunting me.

I do my best to block off the part of my mind that knows it can reach Theo, shutting him out. I'm not sure how, or if, it's working, but I tell myself I have to try. When faced with the possibility that wanting someone isn't a choice, I need these walls if I can build them.

There is biology that can't be ignored, and I know Sebastian came to terms with that sooner than I could, even though it meant he left before finishing our conversation.

I'm not sure how much more there was to say, anyway.

He'll come back.

He'll stay tonight.

I circle the room, noticing how familiar everything feels. The desk looks the same as ours back home, and there are paintings on the wall from one of my favorite artists. Stepping into the bathroom, I find my preferred brand of... everything. It's my face wash and deodorant, even the dry brush I like to use on my skin at night. I hold it in my hand, running my thumb across the bristles. There's a person who spent an entire day doing nothing but setting this room up, searching my shopping history, and creating a replica of my home.

The seriousness of my situation settles in, festering inside me, and I toss the brush to the side. It crashes into the tub, sending a loud clang throughout the bathroom.

There's nothing of Sebastian's on this countertop.

From the moment I touched Theo, nature has pulled him away from me and now I'm heaving with sobs because there's one toothbrush and not two, and he knows why. He accepts why, but I can't.

This place can't keep us apart. My body might fail me, sending me to Theo every chance it gets, but my mind knows the truth. No one will love me as much as Sebastian or have that kind of devotion by choice. He's not going anywhere, and I won't let him slip away.

"So, you're settling in?" Alison asks. I have a line in the room, and I know Alison's number by heart. I'm still avoiding my phone and the articles about what a freak I am, how I should be tried for murder, and all the women that will line up to fuck my husband.

Alison was the first person I wanted to call. Jack would be second, but I'm bitter towards him, knowing he's filled Sebastian in on the protocol of our living situation and my oncoming lack of control without consulting me. It may be his job, but this is my life.

Even if Jack's actions come from a good place, those decisions are tearing my husband and me apart, and we don't need any help in that department.

Alison and I talk about the room and my small tiff with Sebastian, and everything mundane that one would expect. There's a chance they record our calls, a large chance, but I don't care. I'll play their game but have no intention of veiling my conversations. They can have all of me if there's a chance they'll break this bond.

"Ask me what you want to ask," I tell Alison after she goes through every outfit choice for her next reception. There's a tray of snacks someone dropped off a few minutes after I peeled myself off the bathroom floor, and I'm mindlessly chewing on a variety of cheeses. Maybe if I'm physically repulsive to Theo, the bond will wane?

"Can you feel him there?" she asks.

"I can hear him," I admit. "His voice."

I stare at the door, wondering when Sebastian will knock.

My consultation is this afternoon at an ambiguous time. They left a message saying to go before dinner when we feel comfortable. This place isn't comfortable, and neither am I.

"What does he say?" she whispers into the phone. If anyone's listening, a whisper won't help, but her tone conveys how I feel.

Secretive.

Dishonest.

Unfaithful.

"He says he's with me. That everything will be okay and we'll figure this out together," I admit.

His voice swirls in my mind, and I hate how it pools in my gut with a need for him.

Alison breathes into the phone, her thoughts almost ticking through the line, a pendulum of *what if* questions swinging between us both.

There's no point in saying them out loud. I don't have the answers.

"Sebastian is handling this well," she admits. "But..."

"But what?" I ask, popping another cube of cheese into my mouth. It's spicy, and my eyes water, burning more than usual after all the tears I've cried today.

"He's probably tearing apart his room, destroying everything in sight," she says.

"I wish he was with me," I sigh. "He said it slipped his mind with everything going on, but he should have told me about the separate rooms."

"You should have told him you bonded," she says. "I — I didn't mean. Fuck, I'm sorry."

"It's okay," I tell her. Our normal back-and-forth banter hits harder with my current situation. We mock each other regularly, but there's nothing funny about my predicament, and her words slip out without thinking.

"I didn't tell him I heard Theo," I admit. "I will, though. I told him no more secrets."

"Just be careful," Alison says.

I scoff. "With the fact that my bonded is a few steps away. Roger that."

"With the truth," Alison says. She's no longer whispering, enunciating the words a bit too loud. "Don't hurt him unless you need to. And listen, from what you've said, he knows that there could be... missteps along the way. If he doesn't ask you something, don't offer it up on a silver platter."

"That's not what we agreed—"

"Don't," Alison argues. "Why break his heart with a sledgehammer when a knife is enough?"

CHAPTER 26

"Dr. Wells," I say when we reach Jack in the hall on the way to meet our team of doctors.

"How formal of you, Emry," he greets me. His polite smile lets me know he's not picking up on my frustrations.

"It's Professor Crowe or Mrs. Crowe," I say with an air of annoyance, but my resolve doesn't last, and I smile back at the bastard. I want to blame him for Sebastian and my separate rooms, but it's not his fault. Jack helped me in the past, and he will in my present.

And I direly need his help because as we make our way further down this hallway, the pull to Theo strengthens, and my need for my bond does as well.

"Who will be there today?" I rush out.

Another scientist steps out in front of us. She doesn't seem chatty, her face buried in a machine she's holding that grows brighter as we continue walking.

Jack places a comforting hand on my shoulder. "Just NeXus employees," he answers.

"The emissions are growing, Dr. Wells," the woman calls behind her. I hate how she hasn't introduced herself or bothered to look in our direction. I'm not a number on a spreadsheet. I'm a person. This is our lives.

"Emry, are you feeling the pull of your bonded?" she asks.

I hook my arm tighter around Sebastian's, staying close to him while we walk. I clear my throat that's suddenly become too dry to answer her question. She stops and turns, her eyes casting over us, and then she narrows her gaze toward Jack.

"Emry, please understand," Jack starts.

"It's obvious she feels the bond," Sebastian says. "Look at her. Look at the piece of fancy metal you're holding. It's lit up like a fireworks show."

The woman cocks an eyebrow as if to say without words, "I told you the husband was a bad idea," and then turns back around, pocketing the device and straightening her shoulders before she marches forward.

She isn't afraid to show she's agitated by the situation.

Aren't we all?

"They'll speak to you alone," Jack warns me.

Sebastian already broke that news as soon as he came back into my room. I greeted him by throwing my legs around his waist and spreading kisses across his cheeks and neck, all while he tried to keep me up to speed on everything he knew. True to his word, he wouldn't hold back any surprises from me if he could help it.

True to mine, I wouldn't cause him undue harm, so I keep the insatiable draw to Theo quiet. The line between blatant lies and lies by omission is hair-thin, and I'm walking it with clumsy feet, vowing not to crush my husband if possible.

"I'll just be outside," Sebastian says. "But they'll start

testing tomorrow, and I'll be at work. I think it might be... better that way because—"

I nod in agreement. We can't make it down the hall without him interrupting the scientist, and the entire day with me and Theo, whatever they have planned, would be torture for everyone.

"But you'll come to my room after." I cut him off. He's made up his mind, and if I must, I'll make sure he gets an invitation ten times a day to stay in his wife's bed.

"We'll talk tomorrow, and if that's what you want..." He trails off, careful not to start an argument again.

"It's what I want," I tell him, and we keep walking forward down this endless hallway.

"Here we are," the woman says a few turns later, opening the door to a large room that's half conference room, half lab. A dozen scientists stop their conversations and turn in our direction. The room smells like bleach and coffee, and I hold back the urge to gag.

I walk through the threshold, realizing I'm still gripping onto Sebastian's arm while he plants his feet on the other side of the door.

He pries me loose. "I'll be right out here," he promises.

I release him, our eyes not breaking until the door closes between us.

"Emry," Jack says. "I'd like to introduce you to the group of scientists that volunteered for the research study."

I wrap my arms around my middle and turn, flashing a smile in their direction that falters at the edges no matter how much I try. These people are my only chance, and if I'm nice and they like me, maybe they'll work harder to break this bond.

Jack begins from left to right, spouting off names too fast to memorize. A small woman with a dark bob and a Russian accent points to her nametag when she introduces herself, and I exhale. That's the only way I'll be able to remember them all, and she must have read the panic on my face. I mouth thank you as the man next to her goes into an excited speech.

"We're thrilled to take part in this case study." He talks faster than most, using his hands to exaggerate his words. "We never get this much data at the moment of inception."

"What inception do they have planned?" I mouth to Jack.

"We will get to all of that later," Jack interrupts the man named Bob, resting a hand on his shoulder, almost holding him back. "Today we go over the initial plan and have introductions. More blood draws. All simple things."

"The separation factor as well will show hundreds, no, thousands, of hormone imbalances and shifts in the spectrum," Bob continues, ignoring Jack. "Exciting nuances we've never—"

"Spectrum?" I say out loud, and the scientists share some awkward looks.

"Oh, oh, yes," Bob nods. "A spectrum is an emission of energy, typically linear—"

"I know what a spectrum is. I'm a professor of evolutionary biogenetics," I say. "Our fields may not align, but science is science, and I don't need you to speak to me as if I won't understand."

I adjust my stance, running my sweaty palms down the front of my shirt as I take in a slow breath. He's excited, and that's a good thing. There's no reason to feel offended. Especially when I should have asked a full question about their spectrum theory.

"I'm sorry. What I mean to ask is that, in all my study there has been no mention of a bonding spectrum, so I need you to clarify." Once the intellectual side of me takes over, the anxiety over my bond and being trapped in an underground box, yet again, disappears. If only I could get a lab coat and join in the fun, my stress would lessen.

Bob looks at Jack, who gives him a nod to go ahead.

"Many hypothesize that the bond creates a spectrum that may even create its own dimension for the bonded. Through it, anything is possible. Not only talking to each other telepathically, which we've proven, but sharing emotions. It could affect others on a cellular level if exposed to the spectrum."

He coughs, his eyes darting around the room before continuing. "And if we harness that energy, we could replicate it. Potentially, the created dimension could send out a rift from the bonded—"

"All in theory," Jack cuts him off, glaring at him. His eyes tell Bob that's enough, and the man steps back with a tight-lipped smile. My lesson may be over for the day, but I'll bring this up to Jack later.

"Emry, we are planning out the agenda one week at a time," Jack explains. "As you can imagine, we've never had a case study like this before. Most bonded are inseparable, and getting them into the government offices takes months, sometimes years."

I internally grumble at his reminder that I'm breaking every rule with my bond, but nod politely instead.

"Theo is being kept in this facility, but as far from this room as possible," Jack says.

My eyes grow wide. I feel the pull to him, weaker than the street or the hospital, but it's still ever-present, torturing me and twisting my insides.

Jack gives me a knowing look, understanding my shock.

"Vera here is going to ask you a series of questions regarding your feelings with this amount of distance and complete your general intake." Jack ushers the woman with the dark bob forward.

She taps on her nametag again, and I smile.

"Theo is going through the same round of testing," Jack continues to explain.

"This way," she says, her arm extended toward a windowless room against the wall. Bob lets out a deflated huff, stomping his feet as a toddler might. The rest of the scientists scatter back to their tables and monitors, and I notice how many have the name Crawford on their screens.

It should say Crowe.

The door clicks softly behind her, leaving Jack and everyone else outside.

"Is he not coming?" I ask Vera.

"No, my questions will be personal in nature," she explains. "NeXus finds it best to match you with a woman in this case."

"Explains why Bob is pouting," I joke.

Her shoulders shake in silent laughter. "Oh, you have no idea. Please take a seat. I'm sorry this will mean more blood."

"I would expect it weekly at least, daily at most?" I guess.

She snaps a small purple glove on her hand and tilts her head. "Something like that."

I grimace and place my arm on the table, elbow side down.

"Vera Alekseeva ID number 233583623," she speaks into the room.

"Welcome Vera," a smooth voice greets her.

The room lights dim with the background noise of running water and the woods. It's meant to relax me, but the voice is eerily similar to one I heard many years ago. A computer that read out sequences and test results while I lay on a slab in front of Genome Enquiry masochists.

I shove the worries down, squeezing my hand into a fist, and Vera takes a seat.

"Good. This will find the vein and take your blood." She sets a blood port on the inside of my arm, and it suctions to the skin and grows warm. A soft spray of numbing medicine wets the area, and I don't feel the prick when my blood flows through the tubing on top.

"Let's get started," Vera says, her voice an octave too high. I realize she's speaking to the computer, alerting it to start.

"Emry Crowe," the voice says. Vera pulls down a keyboard from the wall and slides it to her waist, ready to take notes on the screen that flashes to life. "If at any time you wish to cease the inquiry, please say so, and we will stop."

The blood stops pulling from my arm, and I clear my throat and look at the port, wanting it removed from my skin.

"It's going to run your vitals throughout the process, okay?" Vera explains, and I sigh, understanding it's not going anywhere until we are through.

"Question one of eighty-seven," the voice says.

Eighty-seven questions.

Vera must notice the shift in my mood, and she reaches over and taps me on the leg. "It won't be that bad," she promises.

"When was the last time you had intercourse?"

I glare at her, and she bites her bottom lip, avoiding my eyes.

"Last night," I announce.

"Question one-A of eighty-seven," the voice says.

Oh, hell, I'm never leaving.

The questions don't stop, sometimes going to the letter E if I answered in a manner that spurred necessary follow-up inquiries. By the time we get to number six, I'm resting my head on the table with my eyes closed.

I'm exhausted, and as long as they get their answers, I don't think they care.

I think I might drift to sleep when the computer says, "Question eighty-seven."

Finally.

"If bond weakening or separation proves impossible with Theodore Lorwerth, would you choose to cease the bond with Sebastian Owens on a molecular level?"

My head shoots up from the table. "No!" I scream at the device.

Vera's eyes, which hadn't drifted from her screen in hours, brighten with my statement and flash to mine before looking back away.

"Question eighty-seven A. Would you choose hormone therapy to resist the noradrenaline, dopamine, and phenylethylamine reaction to Sebastian Owens in order to ease a transition gradually?"

"No!" I repeat. "That's the same thing. Aren't you supposed to be a genius with this artificial intelligence?"

The computer ignores my complaint. "Question eighty-seven B. Would you comply with a course of action where Sebastian Owens ceases his love with you or engages in hormone therapy to subdue his chemical reaction to yourself, Emry Crawford, in order to ease his transition?"

I'm about to scream at the voice again, my mouth opening, but I clamp it shut, my teeth clicking in place. Vera's fingers hover over the keyboard, her eyebrows raised, waiting for my answer.

What if Sebastian was to fall *out* of love with me? The same force that draws me to Theo, begging me to connect with him, to love him, could be used in the opposite fashion.

Would that be unkind? He could stop loving me and let me go. It might kill me, but the idea that Sebastian could find happiness because of his indifference toward me is something to think about.

Is that even possible?

Is breaking the bond possible?

"Could you repeat the Question?" I ask. "Maybe ask it in a different way?"

"Question eighty-seven B continued. Would you, Emry Crawford, agree to hormone therapy for Sebastian Owens? In such therapy, receptors that replicate feelings of love in the subject, Sebastian Owens, would be dismantled. In theory, Sebastian Owens undergoing this treatment would cease to have romantic attachments toward Emry Crawford."

If we can't break the bond with Theo, would I set Sebastian free?

"I-I don't know," I answer, my voice a hushed whisper.

"Answer accepted," the voice says. "Questionnaire complete."

CHAPTER 27

"How did it go?" Sebastian asks.

He's tired from the day, collapsing on the bed with a thud and pulling his shirt off from behind his neck. I wonder what work put him through, but it doesn't matter. I'm the reason for his turmoil, even if he'll never admit the fact.

The realization of what I'm doing here, what we both are doing here, weighs on him, leaving my husband dreary-eyed, rubbing his temples with exhaustion.

Before all of this, Sebastian would usually arrive home before me. I would find him washed up and cooking dinner by the time I strode through our door. He's spoiled me for years, and this is how I repay him.

"It was just a lot of questions," I answer. "Eighty-seven, which turned into three hundred."

He chuckles to himself and moves his hand to rub the back of his neck. I join him on the bed and place my hands on the corded muscles of his shoulders, rubbing the ache.

"How was your day?" I ask.

"Let's not do this," he sighs. "The pleasantries. Let's be honest — like we said."

His words sting, but I appreciate them, knowing he's right. I rub harder into his muscles, finding a knot and pushing my thumb into the nodule. He sucks in air between his shut teeth before he continues.

"They sent me to the furthest district they could," he says. "Suddenly I'm urgently needed an hour away, and that's one way."

"That's ridiculous. Let's talk to Jack," I offer.

"No point," Sebastian shakes his head. "NeXus isn't wrong. Keeping me at a distance might be best, at least in the beginning. But it's a horrible commute. I'm exhausted."

I say nothing in response, but I flatten my hands on his back and let them glide down his skin. Leaning forward, I wrap my arms around his waist, and then do the same with my legs, holding him from behind as the big spoon.

"I don't know everything I answered today," I admit. "I zoned out for a while, and they kept the blood port on me. Felt like I was talking to one of those old-school truth teller machines. You know what I'm talking about?"

"A polygraph?" he asks.

"Yeah! Just like that." I laugh at the thought, as if this would be an instance where I would lie to NeXus. I need their help.

Sebastian scratches at his stubble, and I rest my cheek against his back. The warm skin expands with his breath, rocking me backward and forward. "They may have something like that, Em. They have everything at their disposal."

"So it's bad I lied about everything," I joke.

"Nah," he laughs. "Keep them on their toes."

I hold him tighter against me, and the words are there, but I can't bring myself to say them.

What if you didn't have to love me anymore?

The question bubbles beneath the surface as the endless seconds tick by, Sebastian rubbing my arms while I hold him. I take in a deep breath, daring to find the courage, and open my mouth to speak.

"Let's shower," he suggests.

My jaw shuts, and I nod, burying my face in his back.

I can't do it.

We make our way into the shower, and I tell myself I'll find the words once inside.

They never come.

The bathroom remains silent except for the running water. Sebastian washes me, lathering up a washcloth multiple times, rubbing this place off of my skin, rubbing away the day I spent talking about my bond with another man.

He goes to lie down while I comb through my wet hair, staring at myself in the mirror, mulling over that last question that could offer him freedom.

If he knew about a medical treatment to stop loving me, he wouldn't take it. It could be because he loves me, but it's more than that. These tattoos are more than just a word in ink to him — to both of us. I consider the possibility of him not knowing. NeXus would want his consent, but what if...

No, they wouldn't do that.

I couldn't do that.

It's too soon to talk to him about this. I'm not waving the white flag before the battle starts, and Alison was right when she said honesty for the sake of it may only hurt him.

When I step back to the bed, he's asleep on top of the blankets, one hand over his stomach. I crawl into bed next to him and rest my ear on his heart, listening to the steady beat.

It makes me think of Theo, and I wonder if his heart beats stronger now that I'm around.

T heo
My eyes open and my arms jerk up. I'm half-asleep, running my hands down my torso, feeling her warmth on my chest where my heart beats.

"Emry," I croak, reaching over to turn on the lamp.

Light blares into the room, my eyes taking a moment to adjust. There's no one but me in here, but I continue running my hand along my skin and throughout the bed, looking for her. The spot on the left side of my chest is warmer, and it tingles.

I look over at the clock and find it's only nine at night, and I'm asleep in my bed, still wearing scrub pants.

Get it together, Theo.

I must be imagining her, wanting her so badly I'm still dreaming when I wake up. Covering my face with my hands, I groan out loud before I slap them back down on the bed, swinging my legs over the side and getting up.

The day never ended with their incessant questions and devices. It's just the beginning, and I need to prepare mentally for what's ahead. Falling asleep the second I get home isn't a good start, and despite how energetic I feel with Emry in close proximity, today drained me from the inside out.

I need to check some work emails to keep Robin at bay, have a good shower to scrub this place off of me, and then find a drink.

My hands hit the sink, and I flick the water on full blast, refusing to see how awful I look in the mirror.

"Theo," a voice calls from the bedroom, and I jump.

"What the fuck?" I yell out. "Jack?"

"Yes, I'm sorry to barge in, but I knocked—"

"Come in, man," I cut him off, turn off the water, and wander back into the bedroom. "Oh, you're a lifesaver."

Jack is holding a bottle of scotch, and although I would rarely partake in drinking before since I was always on the brink of death, I'm ready to down the bottle tonight.

He opens a few cabinets before he finds some glassware and pours us both a double shot.

"Joining in?" I ask, reaching for the glass.

"I occasionally have a drink on special occasions," he says.

I raise my eyebrows and down the alcohol, slamming it on the counter and gesturing for another.

"And when I'm about to deliver difficult news," Jack continues, pouring me another double. "This, unfortunately, is the latter."

"Give it to me," I sigh. "The drink and the news."

Jack takes a seat at the desk chair, and I relax on the edge of the bed, leaning forward and holding the drink between my knees, wanting to down this one too even though I know I shouldn't.

"Did I fail my three-hundred-question quiz?" I joke. "I promise tomorrow I won't answer any questions with *how the fuck should I know.* That was my go-to response when, well, I didn't know."

"No, no," Jack shakes his head and takes a sip. He turns the glass in his hands a few times before he continues. "I saw the plans for this week. Tomorrow is easy, testing your reach of communication, talking to each other telepathically, things like that."

"Child's play," I say with a smile. "Just your run of the mill psychic ability."

Jack doesn't laugh at the joke, continuing to stare at his

glass of scotch. He's bracing himself to tell me something especially terrible. "The next day, you will undergo a small procedure. That is, if you agree to it. I didn't know about it until this afternoon, and I have to admit, I agree with the team that it would give us substantial data."

I sip on the scotch and sit up, cracking my back and smirking.

Jack sips and then takes the cue to keep talking.

"It's a device that is commonly used to send data on irregular heartbeats, open ventricles, and, if needed, restart the heart. It can inject medicine and even send video. You've never had it before because, well..."

"Because it doesn't exist," I say, deadpan. "You want to put a medicinal robot defibrillator... inside me?"

Jack takes another large swallow of scotch. "It's cutting edge, not exactly cleared through all the channels yet. We won't use it to restart your heart. That won't be necessary with Emry."

A rush of excitement courses through my veins. "So, she'll be with me?" I ask.

"Well, that's the thing," Jack sighs. He twirls the glass of scotch and crosses his ankle over his knee. "She wouldn't be there for the surgery. The idea with you two is getting this initial data, so after it's inserted, we'll shorten your distance from each other, see how your heart reacts."

"So, if I start dying, you rush her to my rescue?" I ask. It's partially a joke, but I see on Jack's face that it's more serious than I thought. They're testing the reach of our bond, and how she'll feel with my chest cracked open.

I down the rest of the scotch. "That seems a bit extreme." I smack my lips from the burn and get up.

"It does," Jack admits. "And we'd need you to sign some forms to continue."

I narrow my eyes. Those forms will state if I die from this experimental procedure, it's not NeXus's fault.

"That it? Anything else, doc, while I'm full of scotch?" I huff.

"I know it's a lot, but I'll be there every step of the way," he calls after me as I stride into the bathroom. "If it looks like anything is going south, I'll stop the procedure."

I flick the shower on and look at myself in the mirror, holding my hand over my heart.

I feel her here.

Today felt like torture and not because it moved at a glacial pace with a list of questions that never stopped. It's because knowing my bond is close, but not being able to see her, to touch her, destroys me.

Our bodies and souls long to be together.

Instead, I'm stuck in a tiny room talking to a computer about how many times I masturbate in a day. It's insane.

"How close will she get?" I yell over the water.

In the mirror, I see Jack pour himself a little more, and he shrugs. "I don't know that part yet. I imagine they'll start with her as far away as possible until they can read that data, then draw her nearer at intervals."

The thought of her by my side makes my skin flush, the pink rising in my cheeks when the image of her face flashes in my mind. My senses, dulled from exhaustion moments ago, wake up, alert at the thought of my bond.

"I'll do it," I agree.

Jack's back straightens at once, the drink he's holding sloshing over the side. I make eye contact with him in the mirror's reflection.

"Just don't make me wait too long for her," I tell him. "I know I agreed to break the bond, but until we do, I need Emry. I need my bonded."

CHAPTER 28

"Today's exams will be simple," Jack promises. He's giddy like a child at the idea of starting. This doesn't align with my memories of the man, although during most of those, I was in a deep hole of depression. Back then, he was pensive and careful with his words, showing no emotion and almost mimicking mine.

I don't miss that time, but I miss the simplicity of our relationship before. He's still my doctor, but everything's muddled, and I'm watching him pace from the excitement. It scares me a little, the idea that I'm his patient in a facility, and I'm forced to remind myself this isn't the Genome Theory and I've volunteered to be here.

"Simple for you or me?" I ask.

"For both," Jack assures me. "You're a professor of evolutionary biogenetics. This will be a piece of cake."

"I'm strapped to a table, Jack," I sneer. "This is far from cake."

"We can get you some cake," he offers.

"You scientists are so literal," I sigh. "What's the plan for today?"

"It's simple."

"You said that," I remind Jack. The helmet they've placed on my head weighs me down, making it impossible to sit up. It makes my scalp itch, and I'm eager to have it off, imagining all the wavelengths that are zipping through my skull.

"We know through your intake that you and Theo have mastered some telepathic speech," Jack explains. "We'd like to test those boundaries. Simple."

I struggle to turn my head with the bulky contraption, but I give Jack my best side eye before I remind myself they are helping, and this is the only way to break the bond.

Vera steps inside, tablet in hand, and draws Jack's attention to the screen.

"Okay, wonderful, we're ready to begin," he says, pulling a rolling chair over to my bedside.

"Are you comfortable with me administering the test and Vera sitting in?" he asks.

I chuckle to myself. "Yes, and the dozen other scientists watching on the other side of the two-way mirror is okay too, Jack." I wave to the people I know look onward. I imagine them all smiling and waving back, but they're likely confused and thinking I'm brain damaged. First, this woman refuses her bond, and now she's waving at a wall.

"Wonderful, let's begin," Jack says. He loosens the strap around my waist that he explains is there for safety purposes only. "Does that make you feel more comfortable?"

"No, but let's get going anyway," I admit.

I see Jack frown from the corner of my vision, and I reach out and pat his hand. "Just being honest because this helmet is horrible, but I'm not going to panic. I know this is different,

Jack. I know you've volunteered to administer this test because it's more comforting for me. I appreciate that. Let's do this."

His smile returns while Vera doesn't change her expression once. She's pensive, squinting her eyes at her tablet, carefully typing away.

"Questions will come from the computer just like yesterday," Vera explains. "We'll be reviewing data, but we may pause and interrupt with our own questions as needed."

Yippee.

I try to nod, but the helmet doesn't allow it, so I offer a thumbs up instead.

"Initiating Day two sequence," she says.

"System processing patients Emry Crawford and Theodore Lorwerth." A smooth robotic voice carries through the room. "Communications review is online."

"Before we begin, keep in mind Theodore Lorwerth should be the recipient of all your communications," the voice explains. "Envision him sitting in front of you, listening to you talk during a conversation."

"That's not how it works," I say. "It's not like that."

Vera taps on her tablet. "Can you describe it to us? We can alter the computer's programming."

"I don't really know what it's like," I answer. "I'm new at this, but I kind of... open a door for him. Inside somewhere."

"Okay, that's good," Jack says. "Whatever you need to do so that Theo is getting the message. The purpose of today is to measure the brain waves between you two. The spectrum, if that's what it is. Can we definitively measure the telepathy? Will these wavelengths then increase in strength over time?"

"Okay, I understand," I say. "The door is, um, open."

Vera taps on her tablet once more and the computer speaks again. "Test one of seventy-five."

I hold back the grumble and make a mental note to tell Jack a countdown is not helpful when they are this long.

"Think of an edible orange sitting on a white table," the computer says. "The scent. The color. The taste. It may help if you close your eyes."

They're already closed, and I imagine the orange sitting on my kitchen table. I'm standing in front of it, looking at the waxy peel and its lopsided shape.

"Do you have a visualization of the orange, Emry?"

"Yes. I see it." There's a pause, and I hear the subtle touches from Jack and Vera on their tablets. They're administering this same test to Theo, waiting for his responses in tandem with mine.

"Without communicating your actions, envision what you will do with this orange and, if possible, make it something unique. A human expectation is to peel or smell the orange."

Picky robot.

"Alert us when the visualization is complete," the computer instructs.

"Okay," I murmur and imagine myself picking it up in my hand. I look out the window of my kitchen, staring at the trees in the distance. Tossing the orange in the air a few times, I contemplate if I can juggle with one piece of fruit. Instead, I rear back and throw the orange through the windowpane, seeing the shattered glass pour over my counter in my imagination.

"I'm done," I say. Even though I didn't break the window, letting out a sliver of aggression gives me some relief.

A few seconds pass before Jack clears his throat to speak. "Please describe your vision."

I do it in great detail, keeping my eyes closed, and seeing it all on replay in my mind.

"Configuring results," the computer says.

"Very good," Jack whispers. "That's very close to what Theo saw."

Vera gives him a subtle hush before the voice comes to life again. "Test two. Inverse reaction, beginning with Theodore Lorwerth. Close your eyes and focus on the other test subject."

I do as I'm told, but they're only shut for a second when I feel him, the reach of Theo creeping inside. His touch thrums through me, and I feel the beat of his heart that isn't as steady as mine. It's better, but every once in a while there's a softer thud or one that's out of rhythm. It hurts me, making the ache in my chest return.

"Why do they tell us how many questions and tests there are? Just say, You'll be here all day."

I chuckle at his thought that I share.

"Emry?" Jack questions.

"He's here, or I can hear him," I tell Jack.

Theo thinks of a watermelon, but instead of picking it up or slicing it, he stands on it, balancing on top with one foot, daring it to explode from underneath him. I see what he does as if it's through his eyes. It's not like watching a show because I'm there. I'm him.

"Are you wearing loafers?" I ask.

A smile creeps up on my lips, and I feel Theo doing the same.

"I'm always working, or I was always working. It's what came to mind."

I describe the imagery to Jack and Vera, and the computer lets me know we're going to test three.

"This is moving along nicely," Jack says.

"Can you see anything? Anything that will help break the bond?" I ask.

"These are preliminary tests, Emry. We'll need to fully evaluate results," Vera explains. "It will take weeks and months before we can determine any new findings."

"You're doing great," Jack says.

He's pacifying me, and she's being a scientist. I can't decide which I prefer.

He continues. "We want to push the limits on this next test. We know bonded can speak to each other, share feelings and pictures already. Let's try a unified approach. You'll both be sharing an imagined thought."

"*Are you hearing this?*" Theo asks.

Theo's getting the same speech somewhere in this building, or he hears Jack.

"*They want us to create a dream together,*" I answer him.

It's the best way I can describe this before the computer speaks again. "Imagine yourself standing in an empty field. You're in front of a mirror. On the other side of the mirror is Theodore Lorwerth."

"*This would be a lot faster if she would just say Theo.*"

Theo chuckles at my thought and tells me he agrees.

"Now, create a space together. Take your time and let us know when you're complete."

"*How will we know when we're done?*"

Theo's already standing before me on the other side of a standing mirror. I see him asking the question, his lips moving when he says this, or maybe thinks this. It's an odd sensation, and I'm disorientated, but who wouldn't be when you're in someone else's mind?

Or is he in my mind?

"I don't know?" he says. "Po-tay-toe, Po-tah-toe."

"Right. The door is open. You can hear me," I say.

"That's a good way to put it," he admits. "An open door. I like that."

I smile and put my hands on my hips. "It's nice to see you again."

"Is it?" he asks.

"I don't know," I answer honestly. He's here, but he's not. We haven't laid eyes on each other since that fiasco at the hospital, and this experience is not in person, but it's eerily close.

"I'm glad to be here with you," Theo says. "You know, I missed you. I don't want that to sound odd. I know you're married. I just—"

"I know what you mean," I say. "Listen, Theo." I'm not standing next to him, but it's hard to breathe, and I wonder how I look to those watching me stretched out on a table. My face must be flushed and I'm breathing rapidly. "I really appreciate you doing this. Seb and I, we want you to get better. That's a goal while we're here. I want you to know that."

"Thank you," Theo says.

His breathing hitches, and his eyes cast over my body. Before he can say more, I change the subject.

"I'm not sure how to know when we're finished, but we might as well start," I say, shrugging and watching as his face falls. He's dressed in his work suit, a bit of watermelon on his nice shoes. I'm in the plain scrubs they provide at NeXus, and I pull at the fabric, bored with my choice.

"That's pretty," he says, noticing the yellow dress I picture myself wearing. It's something Alison has borrowed a time or two, but I've felt hesitant to wear it. When I sit down, it rides up in the back, but in a dream, I'm able to fix that.

The edges of the mirror between us fade away, and we're standing in a field, just the two of us.

"This feels private," Theo says.

"But it's not," I correct him. "Remember the helmet and all the wires?"

"Remember, we have to tell them what we're thinking about," he corrects me. "They can't see inside our heads."

The side of my mouth lifts in a smile. "Right. So, they want us to create together. Where would you like to go?" I ask him.

He shrugs, stepping closer. His suit fades to jeans and a white T-shirt, his feet bare on the green grass.

"Better," I tell him, and he nods in agreement.

"I've never been anywhere for long. Nowhere I care to go back to," Theo admits. "Why don't you take the lead? Where would you go right now if you could go anywhere in the world?"

A wall forms at my left side, bricks stacking together in sequence, growing taller by the second. We step back, our jaws hanging slack at the sight. A part of me knows I'm creating this, but it's magical, clearer than any dream I've experienced before.

Outdoor furniture spins in front of us, settling into place, and an overhead awning stretches out over the chairs. The slats of wood create breaks in the sunlight overhead. Grapevines wrap around each slice of lumber, the plump berries ripening and pouring down, casting more shade on the patio.

"Your home," Theo says.

"How did you know?" I ask him.

He touches his chest, patting it a few times. "I feel it somehow."

A window opens in the center of the brick wall, and there's a flash of someone on the other side. We step out of the grass onto the patio, an out-of-place oasis in the middle of nothingness, and I reach up, plucking a grape from the vine.

The person walks by again, holding a skillet in his hand.

"I didn't think of Sebastian," I say. I made a point not to

think of him, afraid of how I would feel with my husband watching me and my bonded alone together.

"I did," Theo admits.

I choke back the lump in my throat. "What's he cooking?" I ask.

"That I don't know," Theo says. "What would he cook for you while you sit out here?"

I take a seat in one of the chairs, noticing the sun rising on what would be the east side of my house. Rays stretch across my legs, sending long shadows west.

"Bacon," I say. "He always makes that in the morning. Why would you think of him?"

"He's a part of your home. He's a part of—" Theo waves his hand between us both. "—this. Of us."

Theo takes a seat, running his hand down his thighs until he rests his elbows on his knees.

"I love him very much. More than anything," I confess.

"I know," Theo agrees. "That's why he's here. He's not going anywhere."

I cross my legs underneath me and sink into the familiar feeling of the chair, closing my eyes and wishing I was home. When I open them, hundreds of trees appear before us, stretching out as far as we can see.

"Did you do that, or did I?" I ask.

"I'm not sure," Theo says. "What else should we make? Wine from these grapes."

"I've never done that," I admit. "Never tried, anyway. We could just... talk."

"Okay," Theo agrees. "I think that would be good. It's easier this way, you know."

"Right. The pull isn't like when we're really standing near each other because we're not really here. We don't have to worry about..."

Theo smiles, cocking his head toward me. "You cheating on your husband."

I nod, a heavy feeling settling into my chest. "I won't do that."

"I won't let you do that," Theo says.

I'm torturing him, too, and I hate that. I don't dislike Theo, with or without the bond. Something inside me senses that he's a good person. There's a piece of me that simply knows he's smart and funny, honest and kind, and a catch for anyone available.

It's unfortunate he's bonded to the wrong woman. Alison would have been the perfect match, but the world is unfair, and he's trapped here because of me.

"How long do you want to try?" I ask him. "To break the bond. How long can you put up with this?"

He clasps his hands together and leans back, giving my question some thought. Vera said they would need to review data for months to get anything useful, and although that's not a surprise to me, Theo doesn't work in science. He doesn't know how long these things take.

"It could be years," I admit. "Before they can do anything. If they can do anything."

Theo sucks in a long breath of air, scratching the stubble on his chin and nodding.

"I'm in it as long as you are, Emry," he says. "But if we can't take it here anymore, just talk to me before you do anything drastic."

"What do you mean?" I ask.

Our eyes meet, and that longing that I thought was absent because we're not really sitting together comes back. I fight the urge to get closer to him and let him hold me. I feel the same need in him, spiraling through me, wanting to be closer to his bond.

"We'll make this work," Theo says. He breaks his gaze and looks back at the vision of Sebastian working over the stove, a cup of steaming coffee in one hand. Two cups of coffee appear at the table beside us, the smell of hazelnut cream filling my nostrils.

"The three of us," he muses. "We'll make it work together."

CHAPTER 29

Another day in paradise at NeXus. My eyes are bloodshot from lack of sleep, and I can't stop yawning as Jack and I walk the halls this morning. All last night, the words I spoke to Emry circled over and over again in my mind.

The three of us can make it work together.

Why did I say that?

It's all I can think about until I'm walked into a room full of surgical equipment and a dozen doctors.

Fuck, the surgery. There's no point in backing out now.

It's when they strap my wrists to the table, telling me I'll only get localized anesthesia during the procedure, that I realize my mistake. The more I think about it, this endeavor with NeXus, trusting Jack, and promising to break the bond are all mistakes, and I'm on a roll with them.

Consistency is the key to success, or death, in my case.

I'm too exhausted to care, staring at the ceiling while doctors talk about my vitals and medicines as if I'm not here.

I think about yesterday, hoping it isn't my last with Emry. We talked inside our created dream for so long that we had to have lunch and dinner in the testing facility. She went on about her work as a professor, and how she helps our youth see past the bond into something more.

"It's evolution, but science-triggered," she went on. "We've only reached the infancy of what humans are capable of, or what we will become."

My work sounded trite compared to her passion. Only focused on money to reach my end, a nonstop party before I found death. I wished I'd done more with my time and my life. She assured me my reasoning wasn't selfish or ridiculous, and who knows what someone might do if they knew when their time on earth would be over. We all walk around pretending we'll live forever, and those who think they'll find a bond believe this.

Mostly, we talked about her life with Sebastian because that's the happiest part of her journey so far. I expected it to fill me with jealousy, but my joy expanded, happy she found someone who loves her so much and treats her so well. If there was an ounce of resentment, it was because I never experienced someone who cared for me that much.

My father was close, but that love was different, and he's gone. All I have are the memories of how he made me feel.

I wanted to talk about Sebastian more, how he saved her, their early relationship together, and how they spent their days. She was happy to tell me, maybe a little confused by it, but happy. When it was time to leave, I believed what I had said to her.

Somehow, we would figure this out together.

All three of us.

It doesn't change how foolish I was to say it. She must think I'm insane or desperate.

Maybe I am.

I try to fidget at the table, wishing they knocked me out, but these straps don't give as they pinch at my skin. My day job doesn't touch the medicine or science fields, so the reasons they give me why I have to have my eyes open and remain conscious during this nightmare might as well have been in another language. What makes sense is they are not cracking open my chest and sawing straight to my heart. That much I understand after Jack explains it in four different ways. It's a tiny straw that's doing all the work, sliding past my ribs and placing the device on my heart.

I shiver at the thought, beads of sweat collecting at my temple. Earlier today, waves of anger, fear, and sadness bombarded me, and I couldn't make sense of why. When I reached out to Emry, I felt blocked, like the door between us was shut.

Lying here now, I'm full of nerves, and there's nothing left for any other emotion. I push it away, forcing myself to focus on the next step that will bring her to me.

Jack gives me multiple opportunities to back out, so many I'm wondering if he's telling me in not-so-subtle terms not to do this. I don't pick up the hint because all I can think about is Emry. This brings us together, and my broken and bonded brain can't focus on anything else.

"I want you to understand the risks, is all," he insists. "They haven't done this procedure on someone with your condition, only healthy volunteers so far."

"Where's Emry?" I ask in response, my one-track mind leading the charge.

A nurse straps down my right ankle with too much force and answers. "She's with Vera on the west side of the building."

I want to tell this nurse that's so fond of bondage that I

don't know who the fuck Vera is and her location means nothing to me, but I bite my tongue. Jack pats me on the arm, and I shoot him a glare. He's decked out in head-to-toe in medical garb with a thick mask across his face.

"We're in the east sector," he mumbles through the fabric. "They'll need to activate the device and check on the data transmission before she's brought closer."

"Heart rate spiking," Nurse Bondage announces, pointing to a monitor.

"That's expected when anyone mentions his bond," Jack explains. "Nothing to be concerned about."

I can't feel my torso. Whatever they gave me to numb the area works, and I'm grateful. A large sheet comes down from the ceiling and folds along my neck. It's tucked underneath my shoulders, blocking my view from my chin down. If my heart rate didn't reach new heights before, it sure is now.

"Hey, Jack," I rush out. "Could we revisit the going to sleep discussion?"

"You'll be fine," he says.

"You just listed about a hundred ways to die, and I can't see my body or what you're doing to it," I argue.

He steps to the other side of the curtain. "You want to remove the curtain and see what they're doing?"

I think for a moment and decide I don't.

"No," I answer.

"Do you want me to describe it?" he asks.

"Also, no, Jack," I groan. "Hey, how close are you and Sebastian? This isn't a grand plot to torture me to death for bonding with his wife, is it?"

The bondage nurse standing by my head chuckles.

"I'm serious," I say to her, and her eyes grow wide.

"I'm in the business of science, not theatrics, Theo," Jack assures me. "I'm going to give you a countdown of time. I think that will help you know where they are without the unnecessary gory details. Remember, I'm here for your support. You can talk to me the whole time. My purpose today is to help you through this."

I let out a harsh breath of air I didn't know I was holding. "G-good — good idea. Thanks for, um, being here."

He nods, and I assume he's smiling behind the mask. I'm reassured this isn't all a revenge plot, but no one can be certain. "They estimate eighteen minutes from start to finish, and everything is done with a scope. You won't hear any noise. No bones cracking or saws for Sebastian's revenge."

I laugh at his joke and calm down enough to feel my shoulders lower from my ears. That's all I feel, and just then Jack announces, "Seventeen minutes."

They've started?

After that, I can only pick out the few familiar words they use during this procedure. The rest is medical garbage, so I tune it out and only listen to Jack. His countdown brings me closer to Emry.

Sixteen minutes.

Fifteen minutes.

Fourteen minutes.

"How are you doing, Theo?" Jack asks, his head moving around the curtain. He places a hand on my shoulder, but it only tingles.

"How about you focus on what they're doing to my heart?" I suggest. "Keep them on task."

"Dr. Lewis is doing an excellent job," Jack says. "How are you? Thirteen minutes, by the way."

"I'm shitty on all accounts," I answer. "You all might stop my heart, which didn't have a lot of beats left to begin with, and the one person in the world made to love me... doesn't. Fuck, did you put truth serum in this IV?"

"Twelve minutes, and the twinkle medicine, as we like to call it, can make you act a little drunk," Jack admits. "But it calms you. So, are you doing okay besides the life crisis?"

When I nod, Jack's face blurs and the lights from the ceiling burn brighter than before. I squint my eyes and turn my head away.

"I-I'm, um, as good, I think." My words jumble together. I'm thinking of what I want to say, but I can't force the words to leave my lips. Trying to see what's going on proves impossible. A sharp pain shoots into my brain when my eyes open and the bright white of the room burns into my retinas.

My lips move, but no sound escapes. All the thoughts I want to say remain buried somewhere inside, and I'm helpless, unable to utter a word.

"Theo," Jack says. "Theo, can you look at me?"

"Pulse down to..." someone's voice drifts off.

Hands turn my head, and someone pries open my eyelids. I want to fight them, keep them closed against the light, but I can't shut them. I can't... do anything. I've lost control of my head, and I try to wiggle my fingers, but it's just commands from my brain that go nowhere.

People run around the curtain, back and forth around the room. Beeping machines and Jack's voice are the last things I hear before it all fades into blurred darkness, and I'm alone.

I think of Emry, and I wish I had more memories of her smiling. She's always confused or sad, with a pensive look on her face. When she speaks about Sebastian, she smiles, but I never did that for her.

I never brought her happiness.

Maybe my death will?

My leaving cuts the tie between us, and I feel it fraying on the edges already, loosening its pull.

God, I wish I got to see her smile one more time.

"I'm sorry," I think to myself, and in our way, I'm saying it to her. I picture her in my head, and she's not smiling, but she's gorgeous nonetheless.

I talk to that memory of Emry.

She's the last person I'll speak to in my life.

"I'm sorry we didn't meet under different circumstances. I'm sorry I'm not Sebastian, and that our bond hurt you both so much. I'm sorry—" The words choke out, and I see her. She's sitting at the table in an empty room wearing scrubs, her eyes wild with panic.

"I'm mostly sorry I never found someone that loved me as much as you and Sebastian love each other. Never let go of that."

The last admission to her reminds me I can still give her something to smile about, even if I'm not alive to see it. I'm giving her what she chose all those years ago. She can honor her vow to her husband without this bond interfering.

"I'm sorry for all of that, but I'm glad for you, Emry. Happy you'll get your happily ever after that you chose for yourself. After everything you went through, no one is more deserving. This just proved how strong your marriage is, and it was going to end for me soon, anyway."

Her face drifts, and I think I can hear her voice, but it's a distant and soft sound in the back of my mind until all of my, *I'm sorrys,* drift away into nothing but darkness.

CHAPTER 30

EMRY

Sebastian left for work before I woke up, and considering his new commute, I understand. Last night I arrived back at our room later than expected, and I saw the worry in his eyes, but he didn't tell me.

I wish I had a picture of Sebastian's look of surprise when I told him about my day, the bulk of it talking with Theo about our marriage. It surprised me as well, but something about it felt right. There wasn't any jealousy or anguish, only good things, and I know Sebastian could tell how at ease it made me feel, knowing I didn't have to keep my relationship away from the bond.

I think about what Theo said again.

The three of us.

We'll make it work together.

It sounded ridiculous at first, but after the day of speaking with him, I decide maybe not. My goal is still to break the bond and let everyone live the lives they choose. Theo's heart is hopefully the better for this experience, but if that can't happen, I feel less morose about it.

What are you thinking, Em? Break this bond.

Someone knocks on my door, bringing my breakfast and letting me know the schedule for the day, and I'm grateful for the interruption. They're overly vague, but I can't find the energy to pry.

I eat in bed, hoping to catch up with Alison. She picks up on the first ring, her voice a steady constant that brings me back to earth. This place feels like a vacation from reality. A vacation I never wanted to have. At least there aren't hands running over my skin every chance someone gets. Even so, I miss my life and my job.

"Are you abandoning your cell phone forever?" she asks.

"No. Just for the time being," I say between chews.

She's breathing into the phone, the sound of the city in the background.

"Well then, you didn't get all the pictures I sent of me in your clothes," she says. "I'll spoil the ending. I look damn hot in your wardrobe."

I laugh at her and wipe away the crumbs I've left on the bedspread. Why do people like eating breakfast in bed? All this mess is going to agitate me when it's time to sleep.

"How's work?" I ask her. "Administration's having a blast with my leave, I'm sure."

"They postponed your class," she tells me. "I can't say I'm surprised."

"Right," I sigh. There aren't a lot of professors able to take more on their plate, especially without an end date. "I don't know how long this will take or when I can come back."

"You're coming back?" Alison questions. "To teach?"

I swallow the last bite, my stomach pleasantly full, and slip off the bed. "Why wouldn't I?" I look around the room for a coffee maker, but I can't even find instant. "Did these people not drink coffee? Oh, I'll die. Where is it?"

"But, why?" Alison asks.

"Why do I need coffee? Have we met? Are you new?" I scoff.

"No, no," she says. "I mean, why come back to work? I know you love teaching, but you could, I don't know, do anything? If you do the annual testing, your paycheck is fat with a capital F. Or is it P? I don't know. You'll have money, is my point."

"I don't get a check if I'm not bonded," I remind her.

There's a minute of silence while I rummage around the room, disappointed in myself for not finding the coffee maker days ago.

"Em, you can't possibly think..." Alison drifts off.

"Found it!" I shout, locating the machine hidden in a cabinet.

"What's that?" I ask her. "Think what?"

She doesn't say anything, and I struggle to hold the phone while hoisting the heavy device onto the counter.

It crashes on the wood, and I clear my throat. "Alison, are you still there?"

"Yeah, I'm here," she says. Her tone has changed, no longer bubbly and energetic.

"Okay, so think what?" I ask.

"Emry," she sighs. "You can't possibly think that at the end of all this, you'll be able to break this bond. I thought you were doing it to show support to Sebastian, give him time to break away slowly."

"No, Alison," I argue. "How could you think that?"

"I-I just. Emry, everyone—" she stops herself.

"Everyone what?" I bark, my pulse ripping through my body, making my skin hot. "I'm not everyone. We've established that years ago when I ran from students trying to touch me. Remember, I'm the weird settled professor."

She doesn't laugh, remaining eerily silent on the line, only the sounds of passers-by and the city coming through the phone.

"What is it, Alison?" I ask.

"I didn't want to upset you. Everyone thinks this is just a... temporary away because, well, because your mother, oh, fuck," she says and then apologizes to someone on the street that I imagine she's bumped into.

"My mother?" I question.

"Listen, you're away from your phone, and I didn't think about you not knowing it happened," Alison says. "Let me pop into a corner or something."

All the possibilities rush through my mind. Every single one ends with my mother hanging me out to dry and dollar signs for the lovely Blaire Crawford.

It's impossible to imagine how that woman could hurt me any more than she already has, but she never had this kind of ammunition. We didn't talk before I gave up my phone, the day the articles rushed in, identifying me and Theo, and she's been the last thing on my mind since. Sebastian's avoiding her at my request.

"She did an interview," Alison says.

The shock hits me like a hammer, even though I should have seen this coming. Fear and sadness, followed by anger, make my hands shake, and the rage comes through the phone at poor Alison.

"It's been less than a week!" I shout. I don't want to yell at her and take out all of my frustrations on my friend, but the fury pours out of me, unable to stay contained. "Interview about what? We haven't spoken."

"Okay, let me just get this out, and I'll call you when I get to work," Alison says. "I'm running a little late, and this is not your fault, and I mean that, but I'm playing dodge and run to get past all the reporters at the entrance of the university. All sorts of people try to flag me down to ask questions, so it's added another twenty minutes to my commute."

"I'm sorry," I bite out, and I am, even though my words are harsh. My lips tremble, and I bring my hand to my mouth so I won't interrupt her.

"She did an interview and said you were going away with Sebastian and Theo to have an amicable separation and then a union. That's a direct quote. She said you two talked and you're having your tattoo removed, and Theo and you are happier than ever."

I scream into my palm, and white spots appear in my vision.

That fucking bitch.

There's a crash followed by the sounds of breaking glass.

"Emry?" Alison worries. "Em, are you okay?"

I cry into the phone. My disappointment in my mother isn't new, but this cut of betrayal is fresh, and I'm bleeding out until I fall to a lump on the floor.

"Do you... want me to say something to the news? Refute it?" Alison asks.

"No," I cry.

"Emry, I'm so sorry. I've upset you and you have so much going on already," she apologizes.

"I'll let you go," I say. "C-call me later."

"Okay," she agrees, but she stays on the phone while I cry a minute longer until I get back to my feet and hang up.

I long for Sebastian and Theo to comfort me. I want them

to wrap their arms around me and tell me it's okay, and we never have to speak to her or see her again.

I want them both.

I've never wanted anyone except Sebastian, but at this moment, I can't imagine not having Theo by my side as well.

I need him.

I need *them*.

CHAPTER 31

EMRY

"I broke the coffeemaker," I tell Vera and motion for her to step inside my room. It's been an hour, and I found the energy to shower and get dressed, but the machine's remains are shards of broken pieces on the floor. It's almost as sad as my mother's betrayal, but at this moment, I think I love coffee more than her.

"I can see that," Vera says, glancing down at the carnage and then back at me.

Anyone else would ask if I'm alright or what happened, but Vera is smarter than most. She may not know the exact circumstances of my tantrum, but it's not a surprise to her, and she doesn't care to know the details.

"I need coffee," I say.

"Then you shouldn't have broken the machine," she retorts. A smile creeps up on her face, a first for Vera since I've met her. "We'll swing by the coffee cart on the way to testing."

It's the best news I've had today, but the bar wasn't exactly high.

We step over the rubble, and she calls for someone to take care of the mess. I insist I can handle the cleanup, but she waves me off. Taking her lead down the hallway, turning down corridors with ease, my mind drifts to Sebastian and Theo. I've kept Theo locked away and out of my head, and this morning I toy with the idea of reaching out. It feels too close to cheating, too illicit, and I decide against it.

We reach a coffee cart with a line of lab coats, and Vera steps in front of everyone, whispering something to the attendant who turns around and starts on our order.

A few employees intend to give me a snarky look, but when they recognize who I am, their faces turn to surprise and then curiosity.

Vera returns with two steaming cups of coffee, and I breathe in the caffeinated goodness while we walk.

"Could I get a lab coat?" I ask her. "I stand out."

"Your face is on ninety percent of the company memos this week," Vera confesses. "A white coat won't help."

I huff and sip on the best coffee I've had in years, and we walk in silence farther than yesterday, much farther. Her feet must hurt in those sky-high heels, but her posture never suffers, and she carries on at a decent pace.

"Could NeXus send a cease and desist?" I ask. "To my mother?"

Vera's eyebrows raise in surprise.

"If her actions were interfering with the testing. With me," I add.

She tilts her head in my direction and nods. "Yes, if needed."

"It's needed," I grumble. "At least, I think it's needed. She could cause unwanted attention."

"We don't pay attention to the gossip down here," Vera explains, but she looks me over, thinning her lips after a moment's thought. "But it's important to us that our test subjects can maintain their focus."

She looks back ahead, the *click click* of her shoes tap on the pristine floors.

"You'll need to provide a reason to appease the lawyers," she explains. "Whatever it is, I can doctor it up enough to pass it through the proper channels."

"She did an interview full of lies," I sigh. "Saying that I'm here to separate from Sebastian slowly and bond with Theo. I don't think it will be the last interview if they're paying."

"They're paying," Vera admits. "Well, that could be upsetting to you and add undue stress, which would not benefit the study. We also don't want lines of people outside or picketers."

"Who would picket?"

"There are a few settling communities," she sighs. "They come around every once in a while. The towns are drying up. Taxes on anything related to the bond give communities life, so they blame their poverty on the bond. In any case, I'll get it done for you."

"Whatever you need to do or say," I exhale.

"Consider it handled," she promises, and we stride through another set of glass doors and into a small lab. "This way."

I follow her, happy she's going to help me and that our walk is over. It's disorientating down here, and the further we go away from my room, the less confident I am that I'll get back on my own.

Taking a seat, I look around for something that will poke or prod me, but the room looks empty and unused.

"What's on the agenda today?" I ask.

"Please dress in this gown," she says, handing me a scrap of clothing barely large enough to cover a toddler and pointing to a partition I can change behind. "Opens in the front. You can keep your bra and panties on."

Why thank you.

I nod to her and change quickly, folding my clothes and carrying them out into the room. The crisp recycled air hits my legs, making them goosebump. A basket now sits on the table, and I set my things inside and wait.

"And now?" I ask, hating how I sound like an impatient child. The shift from commanding a room of hundreds to this hasn't been an easy transition. I should have been more focused on today's tests instead of the coffee, but I know myself. Coffee will always take priority.

Vera holds up a finger, stepping to the other side of the room with a phone to her ear. She doesn't give away anything about the conversation, clipping one-word answers in response to the person on the other line.

She opens a cabinet and pulls out a small box, and she holds it in her palm while I jitter in my seat from the caffeine, craning my neck to look. A red light blinks on the box, and she sets it on the table and says, "I understand," into the phone before she hangs up.

I don't understand.

More supplies appear from a cabinet, and all I recognize is the port. It attaches to my chest this time, as well as countless heart rate monitors that beep when they seal to my skin with thick glue. They're measuring my heart, maybe my lungs, definitely vitals, but I can't tell what else.

Vera takes my wrist, a large monitor sticker in one hand, and I jerk my arm away. She pinches her eyebrows together and sits back without a word, waiting for me to explain.

"Will you be attaching that to both wrists?" I ask.

"No," she answers. "Just one."

"Can we use this one?" I reach for her with my bare wrist,

and she eyes the Crowe tattoo on my other, biting the inside of her cheek at the sight.

"Of course," she answers, a hint of sadness in her voice.

She takes a seat at the table, empty except for the box sitting between us, its red light glowing and blinking.

I stare at her, hoping she'll say something, but I'm learning this place isn't forthcoming unless forced.

"What now?" I ask again, hating the pitiful question I repeat. This shouldn't be so difficult. I'm an agreeable subject, ready to do whatever is needed to break this bond.

A keyboard rises from the table, and a screen glows in front of Vera.

"Now, I send a request for your cease and desist," she answers. Her fingers fly over the keys, typing words that are blurred on my side of the projected screen. "Would you like us to press charges? Arrest her?"

I think about the possibility and consider the implications. On the way here, I worried Sebastian had seen her interview. How could he not? She hurt him, the one person in my life who defended her and encouraged me to keep our mother-daughter relationship intact. No one would think twice if I cut her off completely.

Even so, he wouldn't want her arrested, and I can't deny that she might believe the words she told the reporter. I disappeared without speaking to her and with both Theo and Sebastian. No one refuses the bond, so she drew her own conclusions and then had them printed for everyone else to agree. Her name was enough to get a paycheck for a dozen more receptions.

"No," I shake my head. "Just stop the articles, the interviews."

The light on the box keeps blinking, but the red has faded to dark orange.

I point to it. "Did the color change?"

"Yes," she answers. The screen disappears along with the keyboard, and she places her hands on the desk, her eyes meeting mine.

I hold back the urge to ask again what we're doing and stare at her instead.

"Theodore Lorwerth is going through a procedure this morning," she explains. "The duration of the procedure is under twenty minutes, and once complete, this will turn green. At that time, we will make our way to him in intervals."

"Procedure?" I question.

"We want to monitor the healing process the bond creates. The best way to do that is a device created by NeXus that connects to the tissues of his heart."

Her words swim in my mind, clicking in place. Vera's calm nature and assuredness make things sound less serious — perfunctory, but what she's describing is anything but.

"Open heart surgery?" I accuse. "That's the procedure? You're going to open his chest and do surgery so you can get data on the bond."

"It's not to the lengths you might be thinking. It's all done with a scope, and he's awake," she explains. "Also, you are close by in case—"

"That's a little extreme, don't you think?" I ask her. My rushed breaths burn my throat, and I feel sweat form on my temples, the nervousness making my skin tingle.

She swallows, fidgeting with her hands, the only tell that she feels the same worry as me. "It's not my place to question—"

"That's precisely your place," I cut her off. "You're a scientist. You ask questions."

The orange lights shift to the dusty color of a sunset, the light steadily blinking.

"My assignment is you, Emry," she continues. "Our team won't be privy to Theo's data just yet, and decisions about his medical care are therefore not something I can question."

"You're taking advantage," I accuse her. "You all saw a need and used it for something dangerous. Don't you see that?"

I cross my arms in front of my chest and fume, Vera averting her eyes to the blinking box. We asked for this testing to break the bond, and I'm a fool to think blood wouldn't spill in the process.

My bare legs grow cold against the seat until they're almost numb while both of us stare at the box. The orange blinks brighter than before, and I bring my hand to my chest, the bruise there healed leaving smooth skin that no longer hurts when I touch it. The port adhered to my body hums to life, spitting data to everyone in this building.

"Is that yellow?" I say, my pulse quickening in my veins. I'm dizzy and sway a bit in my chair.

"Are you feeling alright?" Vera says, not answering me.

I grab the box and stare at it, the light dimming before my eyes. When I look back up to Vera, her keyboard is back, and she's furiously typing away at the keys.

She's hazy, but it's not the cloud of the screen that creates her blurred appearance.

"Something's wrong, I—" As soon as the words come out, a piercing pain slices into my chest, and I scream, the words I meant to say lost in the strike of agony that pierces between my breasts and stretches down my abdomen.

Vera rushes over to me, and I stand, my hands running over my chest that's on fire, searing with pain. The tie to Theo pulls taut, almost yanking me toward him.

"You're killing him!" I accuse her.

Vera shines a light into my eyes as the phone in her pocket rings and rings, the sound reverberating inside the room. It's too loud, and I throw down the box I'm holding to cover my ears.

It's not blinking anymore.

"Can you hear me?" she asks. "Emry, tell me what you're feeling."

I push Vera away, the sound of her voice sending more sharp pains inside my skull.

"I'm sorry."

I hear Theo's voice.

It's soft and distant but soothing, a stark contrast to everything in this room. The slight reprieve is nothing compared to the onslaught of pain hitting me in waves, making me worry my heart might explode. I'm desperate to get to the source of the sound and away from Vera.

Pain changes a person. The way they think and act, and the decisions they make when they're of sound mind fade away. Physical pain, combined with knowing someone you care about is hurting, turns people into instinctual animals. You react with responses geared toward survival, and receptors of the brain focus only on fighting to save the life of your kin and yourself.

That's why I slam Vera against the table and take her badge.

"I'm sorry I'm not Sebastian."

"Shut up!" I say out loud. The last thing I need is Theo's apologies or his guilt.

"Emry, stop," Vera responds. There's a trickle of blood on her temple, and my twinge of regret quickly disappears as I make it to the door, scanning her badge to escape. Spots form in my vision and the world blurs at the edges.

"I'm mostly sorry I never found someone that loved me as much as you and Sebastian love each other. Never let go of that."

Vera's at my back, and I elbow her in the stomach, sending

her backward onto the table. I don't look back when I yank the door open and fly through.

My head pounds and the world spins, making it so I can't run straight, my shoulder bumping into the wall multiple times before I turn the first corner.

"Emry!" Vera calls behind me. The sound of her heels clicking on the floor is replaced by the soft stick of her bare feet running toward me, faster than I can get away from her.

Panic rises in my throat, and I choke it down, forcing myself to go faster, my body moving towards the feel of Theo.

When I skid around another corner, my heart goes into overdrive, the corners of my sight blurring almost to darkness, worsening my vision. I can feel him, almost seeing him in front of me. His body lays limp on a medical table, his eyes void of light, and a mist of sweat on his forehead.

"I'm glad for you, Emry. Happy you'll get your happily ever after that you chose for yourself."

"No!" I scream out, hot tears pouring down my cheeks.

An arm grabs mine, hooking into my elbow and pulling me up. I didn't realize I had hit my knees in the middle of an empty hallway. It's Vera. The trail of dark blood grew thicker on her face, sticking to her hair and neck. She's barefoot, and her lab coat stained with blood has a rip where I tore the badge free.

"Come on," she says. "Keep up with me."

I try, my feet faltering and refusing to work as they should, my vision all but black. She guides me down hallways I barely see. Reaching out for the wall to direct me, my hand can't feel the surface. Numbness spreads through my limbs, and I think I'm telling Vera, explaining the symptoms, but all that comes out are inaudible sounds.

"Lucas!" Vera screams. "Carry her."

Someone rushes over, another lab coat, another stranger, and I'm hoisted up. He doesn't ask questions, and Vera doesn't give a reason, but he's running behind her as I jostle in his arms.

It's complete blackness when I hear Theo's faint voice, and the pain leaves me completely, escaping my body with such force that I lose my breath, clutching at Lucas's lab coat and gasping for air.

"It was going to end for me soon, anyway."

"No," I say, but those words don't come.

It's just a gargled sound of my last breath until I lose consciousness.

CHAPTER 32

THEO

My eyes open, heavy and full of sleep, but they open.

Where am I?

I'm staring at a ceiling fan, its blades spinning and sending a steady flow of air across my bare skin. I expected to see medical lights or...

What happens after death? Pearly gates or the fires of hell, something like that.

If in death I'm trapped in purgatory to haunt NeXus, I'll kill myself all over again.

Am I dead?

Blinking a few times, my eyes darting from left to right, the room comes into focus.

My room.

I turn to see my nightstand. My water glass from this morning is still there, a ring of condensation around the bottom. The towel from my morning shower rests over the bathroom door, and my toothbrush hasn't moved from its spot on the edge of the sink.

I'm back in my room, and I don't think I'm dead.

Lifting my hand to rub my temple, there are wires and tubes attached to my skin. I twist my arm, staring at the devices, and follow them to a tower of medical equipment at the foot of my bed. Numbers blink across its face, but it doesn't make a sound.

No, I'm not dead.

Dead men don't have IVs.

I sigh, flopping my arm back down to my side. It feels too heavy, lethargic, and not working as it should. It's the worst hangover, head pounding and body aching, except I didn't enjoy what got me here like I would have an overindulgence in scotch.

A few deep breaths later, my limbs slowly come to life, tingling and itching under the sheets. I try to sit up, but something weighs down on my chest, heavy and solid, holding me against the mattress.

A deep groan leaves my body, and the rumble makes the object move, and it tickles my skin. When I look down, I rethink everything I believe about this moment.

I must be dead because death is the only reason I would find Emry Crowe sleeping in my bed, barely dressed, curled up against my skin.

And glowing.

Her skin. It's luminescent.

That's the only way my mind describes what lies before me. When I stare down at her, there's an emission of light or brightness, unlike anything I've seen before or could dare to describe. It emits from her, seeping around her edges, sending a ring of radiance where we touch.

Afraid to move, to breathe, I stare down at the fan of her

hair across my skin and her thin fingers that touch my ribs, the glimmer of them reaching out in five perfect arches.

I could stay like this for eternity, watching her beauty in amazement. Purgatory might not be so terrible after all.

Endless minutes tick by, but I don't look at the time or take my eyes off of her. Her back swells up and down with steady breaths that match mine, the thudding of my heart in cadence with her rhythm.

Once all of my senses spark back to life, I feel the essence that beams off of her. Warm and comforting, it creeps inside of me, fixing me, healing me, making me whole.

It's euphoric, and I bite my lip to prevent the moan that wants to escape. My cock tents the sheets, and I dare to wrap my arm around her back, pulling her closer to me.

She's in such a deep sleep, resting limply in my arms, that she doesn't stir. Part of me wants to wake her and see her smile that I already miss, but her peaceful slumber will do. It's enough to rest here with her, letting our souls entwine.

When I close my eyes, focusing on her and the energy between us, I think I can see her dreams. Flashes of a movie click through my mind's eye, beautiful things I can't place anywhere but Emry's memory.

She's walking around a university campus with a large cup of coffee, its steam billowing from the cup in the crisp morning air. The sound of her laughter and someone else... Sebastian. His boisterous laugh doesn't bother me, and I almost chuckle myself, as if I'm a part of some private joke between us three.

There's another woman at her side, giggling along with them. They're all so happy together, doing simple things on a beautiful day. It's companionship that brings her so much joy, not the bond. That's what fills her dreams.

There's a soft knock at the door, a tap-tap-tap that ruins my bliss, spiraling me back to reality. The visitor doesn't wait for me to answer before the door cracks open, and Jack's face peers inside.

His slow and calculated footsteps make their way to the monitors at the end of the bed, and I narrow my eyes at him, defensive on instinct.

He'll take her away, tell me there's been some terrible mistake and she should be with Sebastian.

Sebastian.

I look back down at the hand that rests on my stomach and see the curve of the black letters that reach around her wrist. Memories of him are turning into blissful dreams in that head of hers.

The pang of guilt sends a brick to my stomach. This isn't the man I want to be, but I can't force myself to push her away or let her go.

"Things did not go as planned," Jack says, tapping away onto his tablet. He sets it on the bed and walks over to my side.

"Whisper," I tell him. "You'll wake her up."

"No, we won't." He shakes his head. "She's in a type of self-induced coma. Her vitals show she's in a type of... hibernation. It will take several hours of a steady rise in vitals before she awakens. We'll know when she's coming out of it."

I run my hand along her back before I reach up to move the hair from her face, tucking it behind her ear. Her eyes move rapidly underneath the lids, but other than that, she doesn't move. Around the rim of her mouth and the slits of her eyes are concentrations of light. It's beautiful, and I drag a finger across her lips, mesmerized by how the brightness reaches out to me like a shimmering cloud of smoke.

Holding my hand up, I watch the vapor trickle inside the finger that touched her, illuminating the skin as it travels through my skin. It's drawn to me, connecting us with streams of white mist.

"It's magical, isn't it?" Jack says. His words convey awe, but not shock. He's been watching us for a while.

"That's not very scientific, doc," I say, still staring at my hand.

"No, that's my ordinary old human reaction," Jack answers. "I've never in all my years of study seen anything like this."

"How long have we been like this?" I ask.

Jack rocks back on his heels, his eyebrows raising. "Two days."

"Sebastian." The name slips from my lips without thought.

He's somewhere in NeXus, waiting while his half-naked and unconscious wife sleeps on the naked and very alert body of her bond. Her bond that is so alert, he can't help the erection that's painfully throbbing against Emry's thigh.

Sebastian doesn't deserve more worry or pain. I've caused the man enough for a lifetime. Now he's had to suffer for two days not knowing what's happening in this room, what I wish could happen.

Jack moves his lab coat back and shoves his hands in his pockets. "He knows," he says without giving away any emotion. "And he's being kept up to date on Emry's vitals."

"So you can take her back to him before she wakes up," I finish his sentence, or I think I am.

Jack's shaking his head before he responds. "Nothing of the sort. That's not something he's asked about. After he gets an update about his wife, he asks how you're doing."

I let out a long breath and close my eyes too tight, fighting back the regret and sorrow for everything. Sebastian is a decent man. More than that, he's a damn saint.

"What happened?" I ask. "And I don't need all the medical details. I won't understand it, anyway. Just tell me in your own words."

"That might be hard to do," Jack admits. "Do you want to watch the video?"

"Video?"

"Yes," Jack says. "We recorded the procedure, and what happened... after."

"Uh, yeah," I agree. "I think that would sum it up."

"It will show some disturbing elements, but it's better than I could ever describe," Jack admits. "We're still trying to make sense of all the data."

"Yeah, sure. Roll the tape," I joke.

"We'll need to turn it off if you get upset," Jack warns. "Emry was not in a good condition when they brought her to you."

Something inside me heats, a sense of rage spinning and growing, threatening to get out.

"Upset like that, Theo," Jack warns. "Don't get your pulse so high."

I squash the anger, forcing my heart rate to slow and the wicked thoughts in my head to cease. The spike on the monitor at the end of the bed rolls back down, and Jack nods in approval before he commands the screen in my room to flicker to life.

It's me lying on a table with Jack by my head just before the sheet comes down from the ceiling. Four squares pop up on the screen, all showing separate angles of the operating room, and I focus on the one that doesn't show the opening in my chest and a large scope being inserted.

A few minutes later, my head is lolling to the side, people scurrying around me, and Jack shining a light into my eyes.

"Before they attached the device to the tissues of your heart, you went into arrest," Jack explains. "It's one of the potential complications, and unfortunately, it happened."

I want to quip, "Obviously," but I keep my mouth shut,

watching the four pictures of panicked NeXus employees trying to save my life. The sight deflates my erection, but that's the only good thing about watching this. They shock me with paddles, my body jolting up on the bed. A tube gets shoved down my throat, someone pressing on a bag that moves air into my lungs.

Even with the thick masks that cover everyone's faces, I can see the shock in their eyes. No one expected this, especially not with a bonded. I sit up in bed, pulling Emry with me, wanting a closer look. The sheet falls down her back, exposing the skin, and Jack moves it back up to her shoulders.

I want to smack his hand away, hurt him for touching her, but I fight those urges and focus on the video.

Lights flicker in and out of the picture until the room drops into darkness for seconds.

"Wha—"

"Just wait," Jack says.

When the lights return, they shine so brightly that the screens are blankets of white. Thin grey outlines make out a few images, but it's no better than pencil sketches on paper. Jack pauses the footage.

"Over here," he points to the corners of a few images. There's movement from one side of the room. He lets the video roll in slow motion, each frame ticking through. "This is when they brought her in."

There's a glowing orb that floats across the screen. It's Emry, and it looks like she's flying.

"She's being carried by one of our scientists, Lucas," Jack explains. "It caught me off guard, too."

I can't blink, can't look away.

She's brought to my side, and the luminescence that burns inside Emry wafts off of her in curls of smoke. It grows like the wave of an ocean, rising and cresting until it crashes down.

It crashes into me.

Another wave ascends, brighter and higher than the first, and the glow of her existence, everything Emry is, pours onto me until the faintest light shimmers across my skin.

They place her on top of me, the shine of her enveloping me, wrapping its arms around my lifeless body.

"There," Jack pauses the frame and points. It's enough light to see us both. Emry is curled onto my bloody chest much like she is now, and my back arches from the table in the same way it did when they used the paddles.

"That's when you started breathing again," Jack announces. "That's when you came back to life."

CHAPTER 33

THEO

She saved my life.
And I'm ruining hers.

"Am I... hurting her?" I ask.

"No," Jack answers too fast. "In fact, you're helping her."

He brings up more images, and I need a moment to realize I'm looking at X-rays.

"She's suffered several fractures throughout her life, here and here," Jack says, pointing to the blurred lines of white that stand out from the seamless bone. "These images are from your first day."

I didn't remember getting X-rays, but considering the battery of tests we did when we arrived, it must have been in there somewhere.

Did Genome do this to her?

I fight to remain calm, knowing my rage could only upset her and somehow disrupt her beautiful dreams.

"This is a scan of her today." Jack waves a hand across the

image and flips it to a skeleton curled up on top of another. It's us resting in this bed. It's not surprising they're constantly watching and testing, but the picture gives me pause. I imagine an excavator finding two humans buried deep in the earth after hundreds of years. They're holding each other in their last embrace, arms and legs entwined in love.

"They're all healed. And these," " Jack says, eyes wide as he points to my collarbone, broken when I fell running as a child. It's still covered with a few lines of dense white.

"I'm still broken?" I ask.

"Because your heart needs repair before anything else," Jack says. "It's focusing on the parts of your body that need it the most first."

I don't bother asking what *it* is, this magical force that's wafting from Emry and transforms the bonded back to their youth. Jack doesn't know, and that's why we're here. This bond that we need to break and others want to discover still remains a mystery to us all.

"Did the Genome Enquiry do that to her?" I ask. "The fractures."

Jack steps away from the images and closer to us. He gazes down at Emry with a deep frown and swallows hard. "I was Emry's doctor for a long time. I can't discuss that with you."

"Fuck the confidentiality, Jack," I seethe. "Did they do that to her?"

Jack sighs, his eyes growing heavy. "I don't think we'll ever know all they put her through."

Deep sadness washes through me, the lump in my throat and rage in my heart making it hard to breathe. When I run my thumb along her cheek, she frowns, her face contorting in pain.

"Your emotions aren't just yours anymore, Theo," Jack warns. He sees the change in her comfort when I'm upset, and there's no denying this bond is stronger than any of us could imagine.

"Not until we break the bond," I remind him.

"If," Jack says. "If we can. If you both still want to."

Before I can argue, there's another knock on the door.

"Is it Sebastian?" I ask. He's on my mind, and I think I want to talk to him. A man-to-man, so to speak, but I can't decide if that's a good idea. My heart beats stronger, and I'm better than ever, but a punch is still a punch.

"No," Jack says, his eyes lighting up.

Moira strides through, and my heart leaps inside my chest, full and so glad to see a friendly face. The smell of whatever she carries in her basket wafts into the room, and my stomach growls in response.

"It's pesto pizza," she announces, holding up the package.

"Now, Moira, we talked about this," Jack mutters. "He hasn't eaten solid—"

"Oh, hush it," Moira brushes him off with a wave and a smile.

She stops short when she reaches his side, her mouth agape when she looks down at us.

"It's not as compromising a position as it seems, Moira," I tell her.

"It's not that. It's just the, wow, look at the light." Her eyes roam across our bodies, dancing where the light wisps off of Emry in small waves.

"You're right, Jack," Moira says to him. "It's magic."

"Not very scientific, though," Moira and I both say in unison, and she laughs.

"NeXus has approved Moira to work onsite. She was already your nurse." He raises an eyebrow, and I shrug. As long as I have a friend by my side, they can call her Queen of NeXus for all I care. "She'll be something of an assistant to you and me. As long as it's okay with you."

"Of course," I say. "That's really great. I could use some... guidance."

"Well, Jack and I have been working on this for a few days, and I'm glad we worked it out. It seems like I was asking too many questions around town that spurred NeXus's interest."

"Moira," Jack hisses, setting a hand on her shoulder.

"Well, that's why they finally agreed," Moira snaps back. They're acting like a settled couple, happily bickering back and forth between one another. Jack looks at her with a softness, and she can't help but smile when she meets his gaze.

Moira turns back to me, her hand still resting on top of Jack's. "I'm not just here for you," she says with her best attempt at a stern tone. "A woman named Alison found me, says she's Emry's best friend."

"She's on Emry and Sebastian's visitors' list, so we can confirm," Jack agrees. I think about the other woman in Emry's dream and wonder if that is the Alison they're speaking about. It must be.

"She made me promise to look after Emry," Moira says. "She said she'd check in on my shop from time to time. Seems like a nice girl."

Hearing about Emry's life in the real world makes me more aware of our current position lying in bed together. We're cocooned here, stuffed away from the reality of our lives. I imagine Sebastian walking in, and somehow he wouldn't be upset. Fuck, according to Jack, he knows what's happening, but if this was outside NeXus's walls and in his bed, he'd skin me alive.

Emry tightens against me, her body going rigid for a moment too long. She feels what I do, the discomfort, the worry, and I try to push it away, pretending everything is normal and as it should be.

"Emry wouldn't have friends that aren't good people," I tell Moira. "Please keep her in the loop."

She nods with a close-lipped smile.

"Would you hand me that water?" I point to the side table, and Moira fills the glass before handing it to me.

The first refreshing sip eases the throbbing in my head and Emry lets out a long breath of air, mirroring my relief.

Jack and Moira see this, both of them exchanging worried looks they fail to hide.

"I'll report that you're up," Jack says, heading toward the door. "We'll run a few more tests, and then..." He looks to Moira, unable to finish his thought.

"And then?" My question hangs in the air unanswered as Jack turns to leave, the door closing with a soft click.

Moira takes a seat at the end of the bed, moving some tubes to the side to make enough room. Her eyes trail down the wires and then to the machine, and she laughs to herself. "I can't believe your company thinks to pay me as a bedside nurse, and now I'm an assistant. Meeting you really changed my life."

I laugh with her. "Seems to be all I'm doing in this city. Walking around and turning people's lives upside down."

"And that," she points to Emry, or more the place where Emry's hand touches my skin, "Looks like magic."

There's a thin line underneath Emry's tattooed wrist where they cut my skin, and I run my finger over the spot. Perfectly sealed, as if they sliced into me months ago.

Two days, I think to myself.

It's fading by the second, and tomorrow I doubt there will be anything to show of the botched surgery that brought her to me. Moira's right. Even if there's a scientific reason behind all of this, it's magic.

"Jack left me to do his dirty work," Moira admits. She places her hands on her lap and looks down at them. "There's a genuine fear you'll shoot the messenger."

This can't be good.

"You can do no wrong if you give me what's in that basket," I tell her, pointing to the food she set on the dresser.

She rises and unpacks a few things, making a plate full of Italian favorites. My mouth is watering by the time she brings it to the bed, dragging a chair behind her to sit down.

"She won't remember this," Moira announces, the chair halting and her sitting down in a huff. "The part of the brain that holds memory. I don't know what it's called."

"You're right. You aren't good at the medical part of this job," I joke.

"What even is this job?" she quips back.

I shrug my shoulders at her point and take a bite of food. The flavors explode in my mouth, and I let my head fall back and savor the taste.

"Anyway, that part of her brain is in some kind of dormant state." Moira waves her hand at us. "She'll wake up none the wiser to all of this."

"That's probably a good thing," I point out, going in for another bite. "She's had enough trauma in her life already. Remembering this just adds to that pile."

"Exactly," Moira agrees and stares at us. Her eyes shift from the beautiful woman sprawled across my chest, back to me, and then down and back again. "Exactly, Theo."

"Oh, fuck," I say. "How much longer do we have together before she wakes up?"

"Jack told me her vitals were rising right before he left," she admits. "He's going to get some woman named Vera and a few others to get her... if you agree."

I look down at her and notice how the glow isn't as pronounced as before. The illumination from her fingertips fades more and more. Her job is complete, and her body doesn't need to remain in this stasis here with me. When she wakes up, she'll be horrified — filled with guilt.

"And Sebastian won't tell her?" I ask.

"That I don't know," Moira says. She leans back in her chair and takes out a roll, breaking it apart down the middle. "But I think that's a conversation husband and wife should have, don't you?"

"Yes," I agree. There's a chance she won't know about any of this. How she saved my life, how we connected in some magical way, will never cross her mind. "I don't want her to wake up confused and scared, even though it kills me to let her go."

"No, Theo," Moira corrects me. "It won't kill you. Quite the opposite from what those scientists are seeing out there. You're far from death."

She's right, and now that I've had some time, I see it. It's not just the healed scar or the way my heart beats with a strong rhythm inside my chest. The hand that rubs Emry's back looks different, youthful somehow. Veins protrude from my muscles, pumping the blood through a refreshed body, one that doesn't have shortness of breath.

"There's something else before they get here," Moira adds.

I nod, ready for what she needs to tell me.

"Your bond will be... stronger... by a lot," she says. "Jack is bringing men to hold you down when they take her. Once she's fully conscious, you may not be able to control yourself."

"You make me sound like a wild animal."

"Because that's a real possibility," she warns. "And I don't want you to blame yourself for what happens next in this experiment. You won't be yourself, and this whole thing may not end the way you expect."

Emry shifts against my chest, her body growing warmer and coming to life.

"I don't know what to expect anymore," I admit. "All I know is in this exact moment, everything feels right."

CHAPTER 34

Vera comes into view when I open my eyes and then Sebastian. They're staring at me like an animal in a cage, but I'm not in a lab enclosure. This is my room — my bed. I grip the soft sheets around my body and try to sit up.

My head has a faded ache, as if I've taken enough medicine to dull something just below the surface. The draw to Theo almost yanks me to standing, ripping at my insides, telling me he's near.

He's alive.

I want to ask about him, desperate to know what happened. A part of me begs to run in his direction, see it for my own eyes, but then I look at Sebastian. His face lit up at the sight of me, and questions about Theo will wipe away his handsome smile, so I press the urges down and ignore them.

"Sorry about your face," I tell Vera. She has a white bandage on the side of her temple that peeks out from her dark hair. There's a faint memory of me slamming her down on the table, tearing myself from her, and then running.

"How are you feeling?" she asks, avoiding my apology.

I swing my legs around the bed, taking the sheets with me. Electrodes scatter across my chest, a few wires still attached to an ominous machine at the foot of the bed.

"I-I don't know," I admit, looking at the readouts. I'm fine, and I want for one moment for everyone to stop tracking my every heartbeat and breath. I asked for this, and I should have known what that meant more than anyone. There's no privacy when you're the test subject.

Vera stands, grabbing a bag at her side. She sets it on the bed and gets to work, logging my responses to her questions on a tablet, taking measurements of everything from my pupils to my pulse.

Sebastian waits patiently with a book in his hand, some thriller he's read a thousand times before. Vera's cold fingertips feel around my neck, and I blow out a breath of air, watching him turn the page.

"Is that from home?" I ask.

He looks up. "I sent for a few things, and Alison was kind enough to bring them over."

My face falls with the sound of my friend's name, wishing I could talk to her now, hating that I missed the chance.

"She visited," Sebastian tells me. "But you were still resting. I promised to tell her when you woke up, and she'll stop by."

"How long was I..." I trail off, looking up at Vera.

"Close to three days," she answers.

I jerk back, shocked at how much time has passed.

"And you're as good as new. Better than ever, in fact." She unclips a few cords from my chest, and wraps them up, placing them in her bag. "And so is Theo."

"I didn't ask about Theo," I rush out.

"I know," Vera says with no infliction in her voice.

"You can ask about him, Em," Sebastian says. He sets the book down and leans forward. "He almost died."

"Well, um, it's good that he's okay," I say, wanting to know more, but afraid of the longing that builds up inside of me. The mention of his name sends my desire into overdrive, sparking something to life, and I worry I've lost control in these three days.

Something has happened.

Something big.

"I'll leave you to chat," Vera says. "It's late in the evening. If you're up to it, we'd like to hold a session tomorrow."

Sebastian opens his mouth to reject the idea, but "I'm fine," rushes from my lips. The part of my brain that can't resist the bond answers before I can stop myself, and Sebastian nods instead of fighting the idea.

"Wonderful," Vera says. "We'll send some food. Eat and get some rest."

"I am sorry about your face," I tell her again, but she doesn't respond, stepping through the door without a word.

"She's not mad about it," Sebastian says. "I think she doesn't like to feel weak, so she doesn't want to acknowledge anything happened."

"Do you know what happened?" I ask.

Sebastian nods and sets his book down, coming to sit beside me on the bed. He kisses my forehead, and I sink into his embrace, breathing in his scent. The smell of the outside is more enticing now that I'm living in a concrete cell, and I wrap my arms around his middle while he holds me tight.

He goes through the basics, things I already know and remember, before he asks if I want to see the video. I agree, and after the food arrives, and we set up the meal in bed, we watch it together.

It's clear a few minutes in that he's seen this before. Sebastian eats calmly, watching the show before us, while I gape in shock and awe. I see my body turn into something else, something almost inhuman before my eyes. Then I listen as Sebastian explains in his best medical terms what occurred between us, and how I went catatonic, my body healing Theo's before I could wake up.

"That doesn't make sense," I argue. "Bonds don't do that. There's never been any record of anything like this before."

"There's never been a bond in duress like this before," Sebastian explains. "Never has one been in danger, near death. This is uncharted territory."

He's right.

Bonds, after finding each other, make each other younger and stronger. There's never a trace of cancer in their body or an illness they suffer after bonding. It's luck that one never suffered a horrific injury, but when I think back, there was one instance.

An attempted kidnapping of a bonded, before I was born.

It happened when the government was just dipping its toe in the bonding obsession, when the people were crying out for the magic recipe of youth. Today they have security in exchange for science, but that wasn't always the case.

The story had a lot of coverage, but no one knows much of what happened that day, only that the kidnapping was unsuccessful, and the kidnapper said he couldn't see. A cloud of smoke blocked his vision.

No one cared much about his story. They cared that he almost took someone precious to society. Bonded pairs hold the key to living longer, and he was a villain and criminal who tried to hurt them. Shortly after, bonds had more rights than the rest of us and a salary simply for existing.

They're granted round-the-clock security and protection, and an endless stream of money, and all they have to do is to give some blood and answer questions once or twice a year.

I wonder what happened to that pair of bonded that day, and it strikes me I could ask. They're alive, probably looking no older than I do today.

"In the days following, you stayed with Theo," Sebastian says, his arms tightening around me, almost pinching the skin.

"Okay," I answer, unsure what he means. "In the hospital?"

I feel him shake his head, but he doesn't answer right away.

"You responded better, and so did he, in a more private environment," he explains. "In his room. In his bed."

I pull back, my thoughts jumbled, searching for any memory of that. There's nothing. It's void of everything before I passed out in the arms of a NeXus employee, sure that I was dead and that Theo was dead.

"N-no," I shake my head. "I don't remember that."

Sebastian doesn't argue, just looks over at me, waiting for my denial to pass.

"Three days," I whisper.

"In a coma," Sebastian adds. "Of sorts. No one really knows what to call your Tinker Bell trick."

His words make me sputter a laugh, and he does as well, giggling over his wife in bed with another man. That thought sticks somewhere in my mind, and an image of us comes into focus. Theo was in a memory, something unreal but set in real life. I remember him standing with Sebastian, Alison, and me on the lawn of the university.

Was he in my dreams?

I felt his essence pouring into me, and I was giving mine to him. It swirled through us, spreading waves of comfort in my sleep.

"I-I'm sorry," I say, my face flushing red from the memories. Sebastian can't read my thoughts, but the guilt from those moments and how they made me feel makes me sick with worry.

"Nothing happened," Sebastian says. "Between you two. And Theo wanted you to wake up here. With me."

I gasp a little, surprised he did something so kind, and knowing from the feeling of need ripping through my veins, it must have hurt him. The knowledge that Theo is somewhere close by, his yearning as strong as mine, physically rips at me.

Theo and me in bed, holding each other for days. It makes my skin tingle and my pulse quicken. I stretch my neck and listen to the bones pop.

"He didn't let you go easily," Sebastian smirks.

"What?"

"He almost broke someone's arm when they took you from his room," he explains. "From what I understand, the bond made him crazed. He didn't want to – apologized all over himself after."

"Oh." That's all I can manage to say while I stare at Sebastian, who acts like this is some big joke.

"Are you sure you're okay with more tests tomorrow?" Sebastian asks. He traces his fingertips along my jawline and brings his lips to mine.

Something inside me stirs with his kiss. The knowledge that I was in bed with my bonded for days, and now Sebastian sits next to me when I didn't touch him all that time, it sparks a longing that I can't ignore.

I nod and stand up, feeling the pool of slickness between my legs. I'm suddenly insatiable, wanting nothing more than to have my husband inside me. My mind flashes between memories of him and my desire for Theo, unable to decide what it wants.

I'll decide for myself.

"I need to take a shower." My fingers work at the buttons of his shirt, almost popping them as I expose his chest. "Let's take a shower."

"You... you just woke up, and I know this is shocking news..." Sebastian says one thing, but he doesn't stop my attack on his clothing. I'm working at the buckle of his pants, ripping the belt from the loops.

"Bonding on the street and getting a broken nose is shocking," I mock. "Being stolen as a child while your mom parties is shocking. I don't know, Seb. Not a lot throws me off anymore. Get in the damn shower."

I pull at the electrodes on my chest, enjoying the sting as they rip from the skin. Sebastian helps, removing them and tossing them to the side. They don't need to measure the moments between a husband and wife. Some things are just for us, free of this place.

He's focused, and when I'm cut loose from all the wires, I'm pulled up into his arms, my legs wrapping around his waist.

Stepping inside the bathroom with his wife in tow, Sebastian turns on the water. I catch a glimpse of us in the mirror, and I smile at our reflection. My husband, broad and strong, holding his wife who can't wait to have him inside her, to make her moan and come, taking her body because it is his. I belong to Sebastian.

His mouth is on mine, hungry and desperate. Rough hands grip my skin, almost bruising me in places. His erection pushes between us both, begging for my attention. Steam billows out from the shower, and he brings us inside, never setting me down or letting me go.

My back hits the wall, cold at first, but slick from the streams of water that rain down on us. His hands hook under my knees, and in one solid thrust, he's sheathed within me, his cock filling me up.

His growl in my ear makes me wild, my heels digging into his ass, begging him to continue. Sebastian always feels good and right, our bodies coming together in a familiar comfort of love and pleasure.

I need this.

We need this.

"I love you," he hisses into my neck. "Forever."

CHAPTER 35

THEO

I'm not upset she had sex with her husband earlier.

I'm not.

I'm upset that I'm forced to feel it. Every ripple of sensation and spark of ecstasy doesn't just flow through her. It fills my senses, making me crazed for my bonded and all that she's feeling. My body longs for it, in dire need of just one taste.

Does she know I was... there? Not physically, but in the way the bond keeps us together, all our emotions flowing in a river back and forth.

I doubt it.

I can't imagine telling her, hurting her like that, betraying her trust. How would she know? The pendulum doesn't swing both ways because there's no one I'm fucking to return the favor.

Not that I ever would.

There's no one but Emry.

My chest burns with my intrusive thoughts. The only

person I want is her, and she doesn't understand how joined our lives are with one another already. She felt me dying, but could she imagine how her orgasm sent me to my knees without warning?

What's worse is it wasn't just the physical sensation that overwhelmed me, taking the breath from my lungs when I came in tandem with her.

I felt how much he loves her.

That love — that admiration — it's not something I've experienced and likely never will again.

I shake my head, reminding myself it's a love solely for Emry. Its strength perseveres even though I'm a force threatening to tear them apart. I'm not meant to feel that adoration. Sebastian gives love to her alone, and everything I experience is a mirror image of his gift. I'm an echo chamber of their emotions.

The realization leaves me horribly empty, longing for something more. Not just Emry, but that feeling they both share.

Sebastian loves Emry completely, for better or for worse. What could be worse than our situation for a marriage? Yet he's still here and utterly obsessed with his wife.

"I'll never feel love like that," I say out loud. My words die in an empty hallway, and no one responds.

Hallway?

My eyes dart around in a flash of panic. I find myself in a random corridor inside NeXus, the white walls and dim lighting unrecognizable to me. I spin in place, taking in my surroundings. My hands run down my chest and stomach, feeling the soft cotton of the clothes I wore to bed.

"What the fuck?" I whisper to myself.

Was I sleepwalking? I've never done that before, but my life is a series of firsts.

I'm not wearing any shoes, and I huff to myself at the thought. This sterile facility sullied by my bare feet, wandering down a hallway in the middle of the night. It must be late, because no one else is around, and the overhead lights barely illuminate the hall.

I look for a camera or some way to wave someone down. It's eerily quiet, and it strikes me I don't know where I am or where I was going.

They never gave me a map, and I never got around to ask for one. Someone must be watching me, making sure I'm not wandering too far, but I'm alone, unable to reach them.

The pull to Emry overrides my confusion, tightening around my center, almost forcing my feet forward. I shiver from the cold floor I'm now aware I walk upon and take a step. To where, I'm not sure, but it's closer to her.

My head takes over, telling me to stop. I can't simply walk up to her door and knock. She doesn't want to see me, and what's the point? What do I hope will happen?

It doesn't stop my body from walking further.

There are other senses, now, stronger ones. Parts of me that tell me to take a right at the end of the hall, then left before the elevator. I'm almost jogging when that feeling deep inside that pulls me, telling me where to go, sets me in front of a steel door.

Her door.

I'm fighting the urge to turn the handle.

"Don't."

Her voice whispers in my mind, but it struggles. She feels it too, pulling at her, begging her to join her bonded.

This is torture, a purgatory for us both. Why this bond was given to the most unwilling people, I'll never know, but we're both stuck in its hold.

"I'm sorry." My apology is all I offer, unable to move from

her door. I can't back away — can't leave. *"I don't know... I don't know how I got here."*

She's just on the other side of this steel, the heat of her body coming at me in waves and pouring into me. Her essence flows through the shut door, and the groan that escapes me would wake the dead.

It would wake Sebastian.

I smell her, taste her, and it's the sweetest flavor, one I've never tried before. My mouth waters for her, desperate to lick and kiss every inch of my bonded. Something inside me knows she feels the same way, but her voice in my head urges me to go.

"Please leave."

I know I should listen to her, and the man I want to be screams somewhere in the back of my mind, telling me to step back. The sensible man, the voice of my father, begs me to get away from her, but I... can't.

It's still a mystery how I ended up at her door when I should be asleep in my bed. Wrapping my arms across my stomach, I fight the scream that threatens to escape.

All the anger and frustration I've hidden away for my entire life bubbles to the surface, forcing me to feel everything. She does this to me, cutting me open, begging me to bear myself completely to her.

I can't stop how vulnerable I am with her, and especially at this moment. It's the bond trying to split us open and shake up our souls, then put us back together as one. I repeat the facts in my head, reminding myself she doesn't want me. She doesn't need me.

"I do."

Her words make me jolt upright, my palms slapping against the steel door.

"You do?"

My question is so pathetic, needing the reassurance that she heard my innermost thoughts even though I didn't want them revealed to her. Her emotions rush through me, a mix of guilt and longing.

"I do want you. That's why you have to leave. I — I can't... stop myself."

The door clicks, a lock opened between us.

Both of my hands clamp on the door handle, and I'm at war with the idea of swinging it open, grabbing her, and wrapping her in my arms.

My heart spikes its rhythm, and for a moment, it scares me. That's before I remember this heart is strong, beating with a newfound force that I shouldn't fear. I won't ever have to worry about the unsteady thud sending me to an early grave.

My hands push down on the handle, shaking as it turns.

A crack appears when the door comes ajar, letting me see into the dark room she shares with Sebastian. His form appears on the bed, and I notice him move, the sheets rustling from the sound of the open door. I know his type, trained in a militaristic style. There's not a chance he's asleep through all of this commotion.

He doesn't stop us, deciding instead to fake sleep, letting her do what she must.

I can't do this.

"Sebastian!" I scream out his name, a final act from the part of me that knows this is wrong. The man I want to be, fighting to break through and save me from myself. I release the handle, resting my face in my hands.

There's a rustling on the other side of the door, and I can't stand to look. Two feet hit the floor, and I hear his muffled response. If there was ever a moment to back away and run, it would be now, but still, my feet refuse to move.

I've just awoken the husband of my bonded after trying to

take his wife from the bed they share, wanting to do unspeakable acts with her.

"Emry?" Sebastian says her name with care, soft and low. She whimpers in response. The door slowly clicks closed, cutting off their words. My hands slap down at my sides, and I close my eyes, straining to hear them, but it's only emotions. The guilt from Emry is stronger, and a lump forms in my throat. I find the will to take one step backward and then another before the door opens again.

"Don't leave."

My eyes fly open with Emry's thoughts.

"Theo," Sebastian says, his large form standing before me. I expect him to lunge forward, grab me by my collar, and drag me down the hallway. It's what he should do and what I deserve.

One wide hand rests on my shoulder with a few strong taps, and it takes all of my nerve not to flinch.

"I don't know how I got here," I say to him. "Fuck, I..."

"I can see that," Sebastian says, looking me over. It's clear I stepped out of bed and landed at his door. His hair is unkempt from their lovemaking, and I can smell her on him. If it should bother me, it doesn't.

I have the oddest urge to hug the man, but I resist. I gather Sebastian has that way about him. He's a person who brings comfort wherever he goes, even when it's undeserved.

"You hungry?" he asks.

We're walking away from his door, but he isn't pulling me along with him. I'm following willingly in step with him when I hear Emry's door shut and lock behind us.

"It's early, but the kitchen opens at five," he says. "I promised Emry I'd bring her back some bacon. She loves bacon."

His arm rests heavily around my shoulders, one hand

pulling me against his side in a walking hug. It might be to ensure I don't turn back and run toward her, but I'm in control again. My excitement about seeing Emry calms, and the heart that almost beat out of my chest a moment ago slows.

"I haven't... had a lot of bacon," I say, unsure why we're talking about pig fat and why he isn't beating me to a bloody pulp. "What time is it?"

"Because of your heart, right?" Sebastian asks.

I nod and he pulls us around a corner, the smell of food hitting my nostrils making my stomach cramp with hunger.

"And it's ten till five," Sebastian adds. "Quite the alarm clock you are."

We step inside the kitchen, which is empty except for some workers milling about behind the buffet. I take a seat at one of the empty tables in my pajamas while Sebastian talks to someone behind the counter. He slips behind a register, and I think this is my chance to get away. Any moment, he'll snap and break my jaw, and I'm sitting here waiting for the hit.

"He won't. He's not like that."

Emry's voice speaks to me in a sleepy tone. She's back in bed, listening in somehow. She's thinking of me with her husband, I'm sure. Maybe that's all it takes. The thought of one another turns on the right frequency and then we're with each other.

I imagine myself speaking through an open door, as she likes to call it.

"Go to sleep."

I sense her relax, drifting away from me somehow, hopefully, to rest. We're both exhausted from resisting the pull to one another, but she's in a dark room with a comfortable bed. She'll be out in no time.

Sebastian returns with two trays overflowing with food, one stacked high with bacon. He sets that plate in front of me.

"Why are you doing this?" I ask. "Having breakfast with me. You should have just... kicked me to the curb. Wherever a curb is in this place."

"You do seem a little lost," Sebastian says, taking a large bite of bacon before he opens a biscuit in half. I can't imagine how many calories this man eats to feed all the muscles stacked on him.

"Why?" I ask again.

Sebastian opens a packet of butter and spreads a liberal amount on the biscuit, offering me a half. I stare at him, unmoving, waiting for him to respond.

"Is everything okay here?" A woman's voice startles me from behind. I turn to see her standing with three other scientists, people that I've met before, with names I can't remember.

"Just fine," Sebastian says. "Biscuit?" He holds up one half, offering it to her.

"We don't think it's advisable for you two to commingle. It's most definitely a conflict of interest in the—"

"Calm down, Deidre," Sebastian cuts her off.

"It's Dr. Michaels," she corrects him. Her eyes go to slits, and she types something into the tablet she's holding. "It could alter—"

"Alter what?" Sebastian interrupts her again. He doesn't strike me as rude, but it's obvious there is a firm divide between whatever Sebastian does at NeXus and the scientists. She speaks down to him, her voice condescending and dripping with annoyance.

"Do you think anything we will talk about at breakfast will interfere with the bond? If you do, you should go back to scientist school," Sebastian mocks, dropping the biscuit on his plate.

"Scientist school?" she hisses.

"We're fine," I tell her. "I got lost and ran into Sebastian. I'd like to have breakfast with him."

She raises a hand to her hip and looks me over. "Your bond pulled you to Emry Crawford, and Sebastian interfered."

"And now we're eating bacon," Sebastian says.

She doesn't look at Sebastian, her foot now tapping with annoyance.

"Really," I continue. "You can't stop us from eating together."

"You're an asset to NeXus, and..." She trails off.

I raise my eyebrows and lean back, knowing what she's holding back.

"You need us just as much as we need you," I remind her. "I've already seen the influx of NeXus's stock price, no doubt from sponsors' contributions to this charade, and it's no coincidence the cash flow started the day we arrived."

She juts her chin up, unable to argue the point, but aghast that I've called her out.

"We won't turn this into a barroom brawl, and I'm sure you'll be watching from somewhere. Have a good morning. We're okay." I turn away from the group and scoot my chair back into the table, taking a piece of bacon and allowing myself a bite. It's salty and fatty and so delicious, allowing me to ignore the group still hovering behind me.

Her heels click away as Sebastian calls out, "Bye, Deidre." He shakes his head before eating more of his breakfast.

"How's the bacon?" Sebastian asks me.

I lean forward, risking closer proximity to someone who could take me out with a single punch.

"Do you really want to talk about bacon?" I ask. "Really?"

"No," Sebastian says, kicking a heel over one knee and picking up his coffee. "I want to get to know you."

"Why?"

He sighs, rolling the coffee cup in his hands. "Because I think... at some point, she'll be unable to resist this. And this place—" He waves a hand around the room. "—won't stop you from being together."

"But you will," I say.

"No," he answers too quickly. "No, I won't. And I want to get to know the man that will be sleeping with my wife."

"You can't be serious," I argue.

He looks down at the floor, picking at an invisible piece of lint on his pants. "I think I knew before we got here. I haven't said it out loud. Feels kind of good to let it out, especially because everyone knows. There's no way to break the bond. This ends with you and her together in some way."

"I won't," I promise, but as soon as the words are out, I know I'm lying. I can't promise him this, and I don't want to hurt him any more than I already have.

"I don't want to," I correct myself.

"Yeah," he nods. "I know. I think that's why we'll be friends despite all this shit. But as much as you don't want to—" He pauses, taking another sip of his coffee. The vein in his forehead pulses, a subtle tell that he's struggling, keeping his anger hidden beneath the surface.

"As much as you don't want this, you want her. And as much as she doesn't want a bond, she has it," he sighs. "So, I'd like to know the man fucking my wife isn't a complete asshole. I have the right to know you if you're going to be a part of our marriage."

CHAPTER 36

EMRY

I smell bacon before I open my eyes while I stretch under the warm covers. It takes a moment before I realize it wasn't a dream.

Theo was here last night — this morning. I'm not sure when, but I fell back asleep after exhausting myself from resisting our bond. It took all my strength to keep from ripping open the door and jumping into Theo's arms.

Theo resisted, too, and for some reason, called for Sebastian's help before I made a huge mistake, one that would break my husband's heart.

"I brought you breakfast," Sebastian says, sitting on the edge of the bed. His weight creates a dip in the mattress, and I scoot back, sitting up and facing him.

He doesn't look at me, pensive with his thoughts this morning. Reaching out for the food, he places the container in my hand without his eyes lifting to meet mine.

"Is that where you went? To get breakfast?" The clock by the bed reads half-past eight in the morning.

"With Theo," he adds.

I freeze and drop the food, bacon and biscuits falling onto the bed when the container breaks open.

"W-what? Why would you... I know you walked him to breakfast, but I didn't think you'd stay and eat with him."

Sebastian stands, picking up the spilled food and scooping it back into the container.

"Why did you both have breakfast? Are you okay? Is he okay?" My questions fly out one after the other, not giving him a chance to answer. It's just bacon and coffee, but panic rises in my chest thinking about Sebastian and Theo spending that much time together.

Sebastian takes off the top blanket, soiled with food and grease, and shoves it into the laundry chute.

"Sebastian!" I bark. "We said we wouldn't keep things from each other. Why aren't you talking?"

"I'm collecting my thoughts," he admits, walking back and sitting next to me. His phone buzzes in his pocket, the only sound filling the space between us.

A long minute later, he sighs and smiles. "I kind of like the guy," he admits.

"You like everyone," I say.

"Not true," he corrects me. "I don't like Deidre. She thinks she's better than everyone."

"Who's Deidre?" I ask, slapping my hands on the bed. "What?"

"She showed up as soon as we sat down to breakfast. You've met her, but may not remember."

It's impossible to know with all the people in white coats that they've introduced to me.

He continues, "They were, uh, watching Theo wander the

halls sleepwalking. She knew he would come here, and she didn't do anything to stop him."

"Oh. Should they have? I mean medically. Do you even do anything when someone is sleepwalking?" I rush to correct myself, afraid Sebastian will think that I wanted Theo to show up here.

"I know what you mean, and I'm sure seeing him find you without knowing where your room was gives them another point of research for this whole charade," Sebastian says. "My point is I don't like everybody."

"But you like Theo?" I ask again, unsure why I'm not believing what he's clearly telling me.

He nods, leaning back and resting his hands behind his head.

"You shouldn't," I whisper, picking at what's left of the food.

Sebastian sighs, letting a deep breath fill his chest. "I don't get a lot of choices lately. Who my wife bonds with, for example."

I stiffen, unsure of what to say.

"But I decide who is a decent person in this world and who I might, in other circumstances, be friends with. I decide who I give energy to, and hating someone... that takes a lot out of a person."

He's right, and I feel shallow and selfish. This isn't the woman I want to be, the one who would lead classrooms toward the greater good. There's no reason to dislike Theo. He's done nothing wrong.

"So, what did you talk about?" I ask.

"A lot of things," he answers.

I resist the urge to roll my eyes at his apparent lack of detail.

"Could you be less of a man right now and more of a

gossiping girl?" I mock. "Feel the spirit of Alison, and tell me what you two talked about."

"We talked about his father, his friends, or lack thereof," Sebastian says. "He's still in shock that he'll live longer than he thought. He expected to be dead in a few years. We talked about you. He asked me how we met, our wedding."

"He wanted to hear about that?" I ask with a bite of food still shoved in my cheek while I talk. "Why?"

"We just got to talking," Sebastian says with a shrug. "We would still be talking if I didn't have to get to work. I need to log in and see where they want me today."

I swallow my food and set it down, reaching for his hand. "I'm sure that was hard for you. I'm sorry."

He takes my hand, squeezing it and kissing the back of my palm. "It would have been harder not to and now we have an understanding."

I tilt my head and squint my eyes, unsure what he means.

"An understanding between two men that love the same woman," he adds.

"We're here to break the bond, Seb," I remind him.

"You won't make it until then," Sebastian argues. His phone buzzes again, and he rips it from his pocket, frowning at the screen.

"Make it?" I ask.

"Like we talked about, I'll stay in your room at night when you ask, but at some point—"

I stop him. "No! I won't do that to you." I rip my hand from his grip and point a finger in his face. "You're staying in my room, and we're married. I love you. This morning, he just showed up here, and he's not supposed to know where my room is. We need to change rooms."

Sebastian shakes his head and places a hand on my cheek, stopping my rambling thoughts.

"At some point, you will find yourself unable to resist the bond with Theo. We can still try to break the bond if you want, even if you two find yourselves... coming together in some way."

"In some way?" I spit at him. "You think I'll slip and fall on his dick?"

"I think some sort of slip might happen, yes," Sebastian says, running a thumb along my cheek. He's calm, smiling at me with kindness despite this awful topic. "And I wanted to get to know the person who may be intimate with my wife."

"N-no," I protest. "That's not what's happening here."

His phone buzzes once more, and Sebastian groans, picking it up, and I catch the name on the screen. *Blaire Crawford.*

"Has she been calling this whole time?" I seethe.

Sebastian declines the call, dropping his hand from my cheek and leaning back against the headboard. "She's been calling nonstop since we got here," he admits.

"Is that before or after she started talking to reporters about me?" I snip.

"You knew that would happen," Sebastian says. "She's greedy like that."

My eyes widen at his words. He's never been one to speak negatively about my mother, mostly because I'll take any small window to cut her out and run with the opportunity. Sebastian always thought I would never forgive myself if I removed her from my life, but from the sounds of it, he read that article.

"Did you see the interview?" I ask.

"Not much of it," he admits. "But she's been trying to get a hold of you. I wasn't keeping that from you. I promise. I think I blocked it out because I keep declining the calls. I meant to block her, but I thought that might make it worse. You'll have a thousand missed calls when you get your phone back."

"I get it," I tell him. "But I'm not calling her, so please block her. Save yourself the heartache if you accidentally answer one time."

"Heartache," he says under his breath with a frown.

"Sorry," I murmur. "Poor choice of words."

"It's okay," he says, closing his eyes and sinking lower into the bed. "Eat some breakfast. I don't think our early morning visitor will save you from another day of testing."

I move closer to Sebastian, curling into the crook of his arm and resting my head on his chest, letting myself sink into the comfort. In his arms, I know everything will work out and he'll keep me safe.

"Hey, babe," I say, my eyes running over the tattoo on my wrist.

"Don't say you're sorry for all this. We're here and taking things day by day. This isn't your fault."

"I wasn't going to say that," I tell him.

Sebastian grunts a laugh, tightening the arm around my waist and pulling me closer to him.

"I was going to ask you to sleep here tonight."

His eyes drift to my tattoo, and he pulls my wrist up to his lips, planting a soft kiss there. "Okay," he says, a smile creeping up on his face. He turns my wrist in his hand, his eyes moving back and forth over the letters.

"What is it?" I ask.

"Nothing."

"No, no," I say. "We agreed. Don't keep anything from me."

"Okay," he sighs. "It's just that, Lorwerth... It's already in Crowe."

"What?" I ask, confused.

"Look at the letters," he says.

I do as he asks, noticing how many of Theo's letters fit in the combined name Sebastian and I chose for ourselves.

"It's a coincidence," I shrug, curling myself closer to Seb.

"Is it?"

I say nothing, too afraid to answer. The last thing I want to do after this morning is lie.

CHAPTER 37

"Jack's waiting," Moira says.

She walks into my bathroom, catching me staring at my reflection, hands gripping the counter for dear life. The breakfast with Sebastian sent me into a million directions.

After the awkward start and then more bacon talk, we had a genuine conversation. Sebastian was right about the bacon. It's not something I allowed myself before, and that topic spurred us into talking about our childhoods and life decisions. Hours went by in a blink. Sebastian left when he had to get ready for work, promising we would talk again.

And I want to talk again.

I like the guy.

"But he can wait," Moira adds with a smile. "What are they gonna do, fire ya?"

That reminds me of the blinking email sitting in my inbox, waiting to be answered. An offer no one in their right mind would refuse from NeXus, but the sign-on bonus and massive income don't spark a flicker of joy. All that money, and I can't buy my way out of this hell.

"Speaking of getting fired, is Robin all set for tonight's reception?" I ask Moira. "She didn't email me once, which is out of character."

"Well, she emailed me seven times," Moira huffs. "But it was all redundancies. Re-checking everything you'd already taken care of."

"And Alison?" I hate to ask, but after learning about Emry's best friend who's obsessed with the bond, I can't help but feel protective of her. Caring for my bonded isn't just about Emry. She has friends she loves, one in particular, making questionable decisions, and I need to give her some protection. Sebastian regards her as sweet, but naïve. A combination for disaster.

"She's on the VIP list with a guard," Moira confirms.

A little research shows me that Alison insists on attending every reception she can get her hands on, even the underground ones, and it's dangerous. I'm still toying around with the idea of telling Sebastian those details, but for now, I've decided against it. We aren't friends, him and I, but in a way we're alliances.

Are we friends?

I think I'd like to be, but that may not be possible in this lifetime.

Shaking my head with the thought, I return my focus to Alison. She's a grown woman, and giving away private event information would get me fired. I'll keep this to myself unless I need Sebastian to step in. I don't want to be out of options and working for NeXus out of desperation.

"There's something else that's come up," Moira adds. She's shifting her weight from side to side, avoiding my eyes in the mirror's reflection.

"Spit it out, Moira," I order. Realizing I'm being harsher than I have any right, especially since this brand new friend dropped her life to help me, I add, "Please. Sorry — please. I had a very early morning, and I'm not myself. What's the thing?"

Moira brushes my sharpness off and continues. "Emry's mother is a woman named Blaire. She did an interview with The City Central. Someone mentioned the company you worked for in the comments. Not in the interview, but it still ended up there somewhere, so Robin flagged it," Moira explains.

"No surprise. She's trying to sell the company and doesn't want any bad press surrounding the name," I reply.

Robin's a bloodhound, even more so now that her business is lucrative. She wants to keep it that way and sell when the iron's hot and the old man doesn't have a choice. If he enjoys being reconnected with his daughter and sees dollar signs, he might even agree.

"Robin had Blaire... somehow, followed in a sense. Or her activities," Moira adds. "You know I could tell when I read the article she'd made the whole thing up. Probably for money, which is terrible. What kind of mother is she? Well, terrible, but I don't know if she needs to be tracked."

"Robin's protecting her investment," I say. "If they loop my name in with her investment, she'll sink her teeth in."

I shake my head at the whole thing. How right I am in my presumptions about Robin, and how innocent Moira sounds. In this instance, Robin and I agree. This Blaire woman needs a bell on her if she's going to be pulling shit like this.

Moira frowns, not sold on my explanation. All the worlds are colliding, business and personal mixing together, but there's nothing that can be done. Emry and I are a spectacle to everyone who will listen, and they're all sitting back with their ears open.

"It's not illegal to track Blaire," I assure Moira. "You can trace someone's online profile and calls if they've taken any money from the government, and most everyone in this city, and everywhere for that matter, has."

"Right," Moira lets out a sigh of relief. She's not one to break the rules.

"Well, this Blaire character is hunting for another interview, planned on doing something on air, but it seems she's been blackmailed." Moira contorts her face in confusion. "Wait, that's not right. What's the word? When no one will work with you?"

"Black-balled?" I smile at Moira, loving that she's so innocent.

"Yes!" Moira exclaims. "Anyway, Blaire's upset about it. Went on some forums to complain, saying she's already spent the money promised to her. Soon as each article is posted, the threads are deleted. Started a few days ago, and today... she was making threats against you and Emry."

"How kind of Robin to let us know," I say sarcastically.

Moira shrugs. "She's not terrible, just business-minded."

"I can't believe Blaire wouldn't be able to get an interview, and they would pay a lot..." I trail off, answering the query in my head. "NeXus killed the story?"

"Or Adherence is Robin's guess," Moira says. "No bad press around bonds. That's bad business."

I grumble to myself, making a mental note that I need to set some things in motion to take care of Emry's mother and respond to the NeXus job offer. What I know about this Blaire woman isn't good. Damn, it's terrible. Letting your daughter get kidnapped by Genome Theory. Larger forces were at play, I understand, but years went by, and my guess is Blaire was having too much fun to worry about Emry while she cashed her checks.

"I'll take care of it," I tell Moira. "Blaire just wants money. That's easy to come by."

Moira's shoulders lower from her ears, the tension drawing out of her body. These threats scared her, but I've had my fair share from restructuring companies. It doesn't phase me anymore. After everything she put Emry through, her mother is still hurting her. It's disgusting, and I'll protect Emry from her with every weapon in my arsenal.

"Email Robin," I tell Moira. "Tell her to get more than a digital trace on her. She'll know what I mean."

"Oh-kay." Moira draws out the acknowledgment, making herself a note.

"Let's go," I say, releasing my grip on the countertop. There's a crack on the right side, and I wonder if I caused the damage. My strength is unlike ever before, and I can't deny the transformation of my body.

My muscles cut from my skin in ripples, bulging larger, and the strength of my steady heartbeat could take me anywhere. I could run for miles without getting out of breath. Even my eyes are clearer, and my vision's improved. Everything is different — better somehow.

Moira grabs a laptop as we head out the door and greet Jack. She carries on about her daughter, who calls her twice a day. I'm happy for her, but I can't tell her because I'm using every bit of strength to remain in control. Each step tightens the pull to Emry, the invisible rope between us twisting and ripping apart my insides. We're walking straight for her, and if I didn't resist, I'd run, steal her, and take her far away.

My feet stop, and I use the wall for balance, the gnawing in my gut almost unbearable. The need inside me draws a clear path to my bonded, and we're heading that way. "Jack, where are we going? What's today's torture?"

He sighs, coming to my side and resting a hand on my shoulder. "It's simple, really. We're putting you in rooms next to each other, measuring everything that comes out of that."

"Great," I growl, knowing the pain I'm about to endure.

"You okay?" Jack asks. "I have... something you can take. Something that may help?"

I push him away gently and straighten my back. "No," I grumble. "I'm fine."

"You may not be yourself, and that's okay," Jack says. "We all know that. Emry knows that."

Just the sound of her name makes me want to throw Jack to the ground, grab his badge, and make my way to Emry. It startles me how I never feel this way toward Sebastian. He described their wedding in great detail, and all I did was smile at the bastard.

Why didn't it bother me?

We make it to another lab, and I'm sweating, out of breath from the effort. Odd how I was sure I could run a marathon earlier, but restraining myself from my bonded steals everything from me, making me weak, barely able to stand.

"Where is she?" I ask as we step inside a room full of doctors. They're chomping at the bit to attack me with their tests, and I close my fists at my sides, forcing a close-lipped smile. They're here to help do what we asked, and I need to be a good patient.

"Emry's in the next room," Jack explains. "We need to prep you both."

Scientists put electrodes on my skin and around the crown of my temple, then lead me to an empty room with a single chair in the center. Jack offers me some magic medication once more, and I refuse. I've made it this far, and anything that numbs the bond might delay their research. When I bring this up to Jack, he confirms my suspicions, so I grit my teeth and sit down.

"Wrists facing up," someone in a white lab coat tells me. I look up at Jack, who nods before I comply. They tighten the straps around my wrists, doing the same to my ankles.

"Your heart rate is one-eighty," Jack says. "Can you take some deep breaths for me? Try to calm yourself."

I pull at the straps, tightening the muscles in my arms, the veins protruding and my pulse doing the opposite of what Jack requests.

"This isn't exactly calming, Jack."

"It's for the test," he explains. "If you ever feel that it's too much, we can stop."

"We shouldn't stop in the middle of testing," a man at his side says. I can't read all the letters after his name tag that make up his doctorates. "It would create inconclusive results and negate the purpose."

"We can stop at any time," Jack repeats to me, ignoring the man.

A blanket of warmth drapes over my skin, and I pull up at the straps, the chair straining from the effort.

She's close.

Closer than before.

"Where?" I ask, my head whipping from side to side. "Where is she?" The scientist next to Jack backs away. There must be something in my mannerisms, the way I strain the metal of the chair, that worries him.

Jack points to the black mirror at my right, and I growl at it, still pulling at the ties.

The man who strapped me down stands before me with a basket of medical supplies, hesitant to come any closer.

"Will you let Miller put in an IV?" Jack asks. His eyes move between us, noticing the tension. "If we need to sedate you... ease the discomfort, it needs to already be in."

We haven't started yet, and I'm already hanging on by a thread.

"Calm down."

Her voice catches me by surprise, soaking into my thoughts and sending a wave of calm over my limbs. I relax my forearms, and they rest on the arms of the chair. Red streaks line my wrists from the restraints.

"Are you okay?" I ask her without words.

The man kneels before me, strapping a piece of plastic around my bicep and looking for the vein. My head turns to the mirror, and I think I can make out her outline. She's sitting in a chair like mine, tied down and kept from her bonded, unable to reach me.

I think I hear her chuckle, or I feel it, the laughter that bubbles up from her heart that beats slower than mine.

"None of this is okay."

There's nothing to say to that, so I stare at the black pane of glass between us, hoping whatever we do here today helps her. The IV is complete, and Jack is the last one in the room with me.

"I'll just be over there," he says, pointing to a clear pane of glass.

I'm in a fishbowl. A true test subject for everyone to study. There's someone on the other side of the glass standing toward the back and wearing different clothes than the scientists. I squint to make him out, and then I recognize him.

"Sebastian?" I mouth in his direction.

He waves, stepping to the front of the crowd so I can see him more clearly.

"He can leave if that would make you more comfortable,"

Jack says. "They gave him a day off, and Emry asked him to be here."

"No," I answer. "He should be here."

Sebastian offers a half smile, and motions his thumb to the door, asking without words if he should go.

"Stay!" I yell at the glass, motioning for him to come in.

Sebastian takes in a breath before crossing the threshold. Everyone freezes as he walks up to me except Jack, who offers him a half hug when he comes over.

They greet each other before Sebastian kneels down, bringing himself to my sitting height. He's absolutely massive, as if he grew from this morning. Broad shoulders and muscles bulge from his uniform. He's a few inches taller than me, but I would guess fifty pounds more in weight.

Behind all that, his face is disarming, and he meets my eyes with kindness. It's calming and even though I don't understand why, I'm glad he's here.

"How are you feeling?" he asks.

"Right this second?" I quip. "Not great, but I'm alive. That's better than..."

"I'm glad to hear it," Sebastian saves me from my thought. "Emry's health is the most important thing to me, but you aren't far behind, man. As I said – this thing happened to both of you, okay? It's not your fault."

I'm speechless, except for a huff and a smile.

"Did you think I was gonna come over here just to hit you?" Sebastian jokes.

I shake my head, my smile broadening. "I keep waiting for it. Wouldn't blame you. I would if I were you."

"No, you wouldn't," Sebastian says.

It would be easier to hate Sebastian, and maybe he's keeping his enemies closer, but I push that thought away. He checked in on me, knowing his wife was in my bed for days.

He's here when he could steal Emry and run to the farthest corners of the earth. This man's job since before he met Emry was to help people, risking his own life to do so.

He's not someone to hate, and Jack's right. I'm not his enemy. We're brothers in arms, somehow.

Fuck, I like this guy.

"He's easy to like."

Emry's voice runs through me again, and I jerk my head to the window. There's no privacy this close in proximity, every thought heard between each other. In the time I've been sitting here, I've felt the prick of the IV in her arm, the wariness she feels toward one of the scientists. It's a constant flow of information between us, a faucet you can't turn off.

"So, do you know what they're doing?" I ask Sebastian. Jack frowns at both of us while Sebastian shrugs.

"I don't even know why they're allowing me in here," Sebastian admits. "First, they sent me as far away as possible, and now I'm in between you both. Kind of my place, I guess."

We both let out an uneasy laugh.

I glare at Jack. "Is he part of the test or something?"

"He's..." Jack sighs, tapping his thumb on the tablet. "A control of sorts as long as he's here."

I don't like the sound of that, but for an unexplained reason, I like that Sebastian's here.

He's a part of this.

A part of us.

CHAPTER 38

EMRY

Talking to Theo helps, especially because he's with Sebastian. Two people I care about are laughing together when they should hate each other.

That's not Sebastian's way, and I'm realizing it's not Theo's either.

"What's next?" I ask Vera. It's my favorite question for that woman, but I'm a toddler again, awaiting my mother's direction. Except I'm strapped to a chair, my body covered in electrodes and an IV of blue liquid pumping into my arm.

"That's helping with images," Vera says, noticing my lip curl at the sight of the fluid. "On a scale of one to ten, one being no acknowledgment and ten being a distinct awareness, how much do you feel Theodore Lorwerth's presence in the next room?"

"Ten," I say.

She taps a few things on her tablet.

"One to ten," she continues. "One being weak and sickly, and ten being superior health. How are you feeling physically?"

"Ten." I notice a theme with my answers, and maybe we can leave early. They can put all this nonsense in a test tube, and offer me a cure.

Vera pushes her hair back behind her ear, and a small bandage appears where I cut her skin. I avert my eyes and bite my lip, trying not to apologize again.

"I'm going back to observation." She points to the window of scientists watching. "You'll see me in and out as I walk back and forth to view both rooms."

I nod, understanding that there is an area where the scientists can walk back and forth between the rooms, but even though I can see them, I can't see Theo. They keep that pane of glass black, and I'm blind to what's happening to him, even though he's sitting a few feet away.

"Also, that will be the composition of questions going forward. One to ten answers," Vera adds. "Do you understand?"

"Yes," I tell her. She leaves, her heels clicking on the floor before the door she walks through hisses shut.

I can feel Theo even though he's behind that wall. Like me, he's uncomfortable, strapped to a chair and being watched by a wall of doctors. Thankfully, Sebastian's looking over us both from the observation area with the other scientists.

They ask more questions before the real tests begin. They carry little meaning, making me wonder if I'm at a ten-year-old checkup or at the leading research facility in the world.

"I will administer a small shock to Theo." A man's voice comes through the speaker. "It won't be more than a pinch, but we need to know your level of pain. One being nothing of note and ten, unbearable."

The change of pace sends prickles through my body, making me sit up at attention.

"Unbearable?" Both Theo and I have the same thought in tandem.

How could something jump from a pinch to feeling unbearable? They're playing games with us, testing to see if one person's pain affects the other just as much.

"Give me the sho—" Before I finish my words, I feel the zing. It zaps my biceps and thighs, making me lift my bottom from the chair.

"Fuck! Four. No, five!" I bark at the crowd of onlookers.

"Were they shocking you or me?" I ask Theo.

"That hurt like a bitch. I honestly don't know."

Vera comes into focus, taking the microphone from her coworker, and glaring at him. I can't make out what she's saying, but he moves away from her with a frown. Her voice muffles through the speaker. "Okay, it won't be as intense this time. Are you ready?"

"Who is she asking?" Theo asks.

Before I can answer him, there's another zap to the same spots, less intense, but just as present. "Three," I yell to her.

"Again," a male voice comes through, Vera's head whipping around to figure out who's talking.

This shock is stronger than the first, and I squeal. "Vera, that's a little more than a pinch!" I accuse.

I'm sweating, my heart pounding in my chest with antici-pation of the pain. Theo's reaction is the same, and I worry about his heart, closing my eyes and trying to hear the beat. I don't know who is getting shocked. It feels as if I'm sitting on electricity, but it could be runoff from Theo. It doesn't matter, considering it's awful either way.

"Okay, one more," the man says, and I focus on Theo. His blood rushes through his veins, but his heart doesn't falter.

There's a moment of relief when I hear him tell me to get ready before I see stars.

The pain sears into my bones, making my body rigid. It's not just Theo I hear anymore. Sebastian's voice yells from somewhere close, screaming at Jack to stop.

"I-I'm sorry," Vera rushes to the microphone. "That wasn't supposed to happen. Emry, are you okay?"

My vision returns, and I see Vera pounding on the door of the observation area, trying to get to me. The lab coats behind the glass are arguing amongst each other, and she's waving her hands at a familiar man, chastising him while she tries to get the door open.

That's when I notice I'm glowing, and when I look up, I see the faces of the scientists. They're frozen in time, jaws slack at the sight of me.

"What the fuck is in this IV?" I yell, my voice louder in my head than it comes out. There's a chance they struck me and Theo with a lightning bolt to see if we'd die.

"I'm giving the test subjects a visual of each other," the speaker says.

"Open the door," Vera yells.

The wall between me and my bonded goes clear, revealing Theo, who sits ten feet away, his head hanging low and chest heaving in breaths of air. The glow mists off of him as well. We're still separated by a thick pane of glass, but I see him clearly.

"You okay?" he asks me without words.

"No," I say back to him.

His head turns to his observation area, and so does mine. Both of us see Sebastian being held back by several men, his body jerking and fighting. Jack is trying to pull them off of Sebastian, but he's no match for the group. Someone swings, and Sebastian's jaw snaps with the sharp hit.

"Stop them."

It's not a command or request, but something echoing between Theo and me, an order to be carried out, even though I'm not sure how we could.

The glass between us shakes, vibrating and sending a thunderous noise throughout the room. There's no earthquake, no great object that's been tossed between our chairs, but it rattles uncontrollably until a large crack appears at its center.

It's the same for the window that separates the test subjects from the testers. It's violently quaking until snowflakes of broken glass appear in the pane. A full-grown man throwing baseballs at the window couldn't cause this much damage.

We don't stop, but in truth, I don't know how we started. They're still holding Sebastian, and when I think we're about to break through, take down the barrier between us all, another wave of pain hits, electrocuting me where I sit.

One arm breaks free during the agony, shredding the strap that tied me down. Theo screams at my side, the glass still shaking with such noise that several of the scientists cover their ears.

Theo's free from both straps, and he stands just before the glass shatters all around us, shards flying out in all directions. The glow we're both emitting stretches out to Sebastian, surrounding him in our energy.

The moment it reaches his skin, he throws the four men across the room.

CHAPTER 39

EMRY

"It's more difficult to punish them when the board knows their theory is correct," Vera explains. "They are on leave. And Bob got a spike of glass to the testicular region, so that's something."

That's not enough after the stunt the over-excited scientist and a few of his friends pulled on us all.

Now that the dust has settled on the debacle, Vera and Jack explained to us that Bob, the one with a theory of a spectrum that creates its own dimension for the bonded, went rogue. He took the experiment into his own hands, wanting to be the lead researcher and using our responses to prove his point.

The problem is, he did. Theo and I created something that reached out to Sebastian. The after effects of it, no one can explain, and he rests in bed beside me while Vera and I talk. He was sleeping so hard that I worried he was dead, and I only stopped panicking when they gave me access to his vitals on the monitor. Sticky patches cover him from head to toe, reading his every breath.

Vera hasn't left my side, keeping watch over me after all that's happened. I gave her a blow to her head, but then her co-worker electrocuted us, so we're even.

"This isn't going well," I say. "This entire thing."

"Did you expect a smooth case study?" she asks.

I sigh, looking at the screen with Sebastian's vitals once more. Everything's evening out, almost back to normal, and I hope he will wake up soon. He's been asleep for almost eighteen hours.

"I expected discomfort," I admit. "But your group likes to pour salt on slugs."

Her eyes squint in confusion.

"You know, pull the wings off of a fly, legs from a cricket." I realize how sadistic I sound. "Kids do it. It's terrible but..."

"Oh, the ritualistic test of power in youngsters," Vera says. "When youth exert their will on others, learning how their actions can be independent of their parents' direction."

"Right," I respond. "For the record, I never did any of that."

"Given your history, I wouldn't think so," she says.

I stiffen, realizing she knows everything about me. Jack's files were open to them all, and I allowed it, hoping it would help break the bond. She's right. I never fought against my mother, and it almost killed me.

"You found your power by other means then," Vera says.

I shrug, not feeling powerful even though I sent shattered glass into Bob's balls.

Sometimes conversations with Vera are like talking to a robot, and I wonder if I had hit her harder in the temple, would wires poke through her skin?

"Anyway, does administrative leave mean Bob and his

horrible friends are sitting at a desk somewhere in this building?" I say to Vera.

"It does," she admits. "I wish I could do more, but the read-outs are unmistakable, and the board feels real progress has been made in such a short period of time. Even though Bob was out of line, he's arguing that it was for the greater good and to serve your wishes."

I've heard that before.

My tablet dings with an email, and I lean back against my pillow to open it and distract myself. I still haven't asked for my phone, not that Sebastian is conscious to tell me where to get it. Vera crosses her legs and gets back to her work, typing away while her eyes scan over my husband's readouts.

It's from Moira, Theodore's assistant of sorts, and he's copied on the email as well as Jack.

I'm on my way to NeXus, and I don't have good news. Robin contacted me this morning. Alison Smithson attended a reception last night for a new company, Synergy, after she left the Adherence event. One guard reported in with several injuries and has been taken to the hospital. They can't find the other assigned to her protection. They were attacked, and Alison is on the registry for riders who are unaccounted for. There were seven, and five have been located, but she's not among them.

Theo's response chimes in before I finish reading.

He's added a woman named Robin to the email.

What the fuck, Robin? I gave you one job while I was away. Find her now. Utilize all resources. Call Andrew at Seeker Solutions and tell him to put his best on the case. Now.

My hands shake, and I'm standing, my feet walking to the door.

"Emry, what's wrong?" Vera asks. "Get back in bed. What's happened?"

Jack rushes inside, almost knocking me backward when I try to open the door.

"Where's my phone?" I ask. "I told Sebastian to keep it from me, but she could have called."

Jack doesn't answer, gaping at me without words.

"Where the fuck is it, Jack?" I bark at him.

Jack shakes his head. "I don't know where your phone is, Emry. Sebastian didn't have it stored that I know of. Listen, I'm so sorry about Alison."

"Don't say that like she's gone, left in a ditch somewhere!" I scream at him.

My mind flicks through news articles we all try to ignore. The reception companies make that easier because as soon as an article pops up depicting the receptions in a negative light, they're wiped, gone forever. There have been countless reports, but they never stick around.

People stolen from receptions.

Women assaulted.

Children missing.

I was one of those children. They erased my story.

Last year, a story ran for almost an entire day, gripping the city in a chokehold. I can recite it almost word for word, having read it fifty times.

Megan Adler, thirty years old, attended an adherence reception. Five men kidnapped her, taking her to an apartment they rented together. Megan was raped and brutalized for over forty-eight hours.

When she reported the incident, the reception company

offered her a lifetime salary in one lump sum. She accepted and spent the money in less than a year.

Megan visited every news outlet, desperate to tell them what happened. Most couldn't get the article to post. The reception companies have deep ties, but someone with a grudge broke through every roadblock, and the story ran for hours.

I wasn't surprised reading the article, but when I brought it up to Alison, she avoided the subject or brushed it off, not wanting any ill words spoken about her precious receptions that would bring her a bonded.

"Jack, I need my phone. I need it now," I insist. It's my only tie to Alison, and I can't help but think she would reach out to me. I picture her somewhere hidden away, calling me from an alley or hiding in the grasses of a field.

"Did you come to NeXus with the device?" Vera asks. "Give me the number and I'll run a trace."

I shout out the digits, my words shaking, and close my eyes to prevent the tears from falling.

"We'll figure this out."

Theo's voice comes through, and I want to believe him and let the words comfort me, but they don't. I close my eyes and feel him drawing closer, running toward me.

"She's my best friend. I need my phone. She might have called."

"Are you speaking with Theo?" Jack asks. Opening my eyes, I see his are wild, searching mine for the answer.

I nod. "He's on his way."

"It's at this address." Vera hands me her tablet, and there's a picture of our home, a red dot blinking on the bird's-eye view of the roof.

"I have to get this," I tell Jack.

"I'll send a courier, no, I'll go myself," he says, but I'm shaking my head at his solution.

The pull to Theo mixes with my fear, making my head spin.

"Let Jack send someone."

"I'm going," I announce, partially to Theo, who invades my thoughts and to Jack who stares at me quizzically. I yank on pants instead of the hospital garb they provide, grabbing only what's necessary before I go. "Call Moira and tell her to pick me up."

"I don't think that's advisable," Vera says.

"Did I sign a contract? Am I bound to this place? Locked in?" I shoot off the questions when I know the answers and yank a sweater over my head. Theo hasn't argued further, but I feel his displeasure with my decision. He's getting closer, finding me to keep me from leaving.

"Stay with Sebastian. Let's make a plan together."

Worry trickles down my spine, but it's not my own. Theo doesn't want me outside looking for my phone, much less for Alison. That's too bad, because now that his heart is fixed, he doesn't need me anymore. We can break this bond later, but my best friend is lost somewhere and if the reception companies have anything to do with it, no one will ever know.

"Jack, tell Seb when he wakes up," I order, pushing myself through the door.

Vera's heels click after me, but she doesn't keep up, giving up when I break into a jog. Theo's too far away to stop me, and I do my best to shut the door between our minds, blocking him out for the next ten minutes of running through twisting hallways.

Somehow I make it to the surface of NeXus, the curious eyes of security running over me when I head to the doors. People try to break in, not escape, so I lift my chin and move past them.

Stepping outside into the same area where Sebastian and I

arrived only weeks ago, I take in a deep breath of fresh air. Theo pounds at the door of my mind and breaks through, his warning slamming into my skull.

"Wait for me!"

I cross my arms in front of my chest and realize I might not have a choice. Moira was on her way, but from where? Also, I don't know what the woman looks like, but she must know my face. It's plastered all over every news outlet.

I crane my neck, searching the empty area and finding no one except NeXus security personnel.

"I will be back once I find my friend. Divide and conquer if you want to help." I tell Theo.

A guard by the front of the garage walks towards me and radios something into his shoulder, but I can't make out much. There's a vague sense he said something like, "She's here."

There's another way to get to my house and look for Alison. Our car is still here, and I race up to the guard.

"Can you help me find my car?" I ask him. "I'm a... patient of sorts."

"I know who you are," he tells me. "You want your car?"

"Yes. I had someone coming to pick me up, but I can't wait."

This is not a grand escape plan, but I shouldn't have to escape. Everyone should rush to Alison's aid, but I know that's not happening. She'll end up one of the forgotten women swallowed up by the receptions that no one speaks about.

The guard takes me by my elbow, and I search his uniform for a name but find nothing. We walk through the entry gates and around the side of the outer garage. There's a pebble stone path lined with bushes in the landscaping. I have to high-step over some of the overgrowth.

"Where are we going?"

"It's a shortcut to where we keep cars for residents," he says, sensing my frustration.

"Emry run."

Theo voices the feeling I'm pushing away, something brewing in my gut that I'm ignoring but shouldn't. It's not agitation as we walk further away from the other guards and the front doors. It's unease. There's a wariness that creeps in, telling me to get away, that this man isn't helping.

"Emry, get away from him. Don't you feel it?"

I do, but I'm torn, wanting so badly to talk to Alison, to help her. I slow my steps, but he pulls me forward, and I stumble over the rocks.

"Where are we going?" I ask again.

"To your car," he answers, his grip on my elbow tightening.

I stop, yanking it back to my side. I look around and see nothing but the trees that surround the building and a large cement wall of the garage, my feet backing up.

"It's right there," the guard points.

I squint and see a few cars in the distance, parked in a grassy field.

"That's not my car," I say. I'm unsure, wondering if I'm overreacting. This is an employee of NeXus — a guard. What am I worth to him, anyway? Everyone knows my face.

"Emry run!"

Theo's voice is louder, making me cover my ears and jolt.

"What's wrong with you?" the guard argues. "You say you want your car, and I'm taking you. Go back if you want. I don't need this shit."

He strides past me, checking my shoulder on the way, and knocking me into the side of the building.

"He's gone." My words to Theo don't ease his nerves.

"You need to come back. Wait for me."

I shake my head to no one and walk forward, just to get close enough to see if it is my car and if I'm being foolish.

"Emry, baby!"

The words stop me in my tracks, throwing my world off kilter.

"It can't be," I whisper in disbelief.

Theo's panic rises, and there's a flash from his sight that blinks in my mind. He's at the doors, about to come above ground.

Staring at the figure in the distance, I walk toward the woman, knowing Theo is only minutes away.

"Emry, come here. I've been trying to call you for days."

My mother's form comes into view, standing in between the cars.

"Alison's missing," I yell to her. "I need to find her."

"Okay, well let's go," she offers, opening the door to one of the black cars.

None of them are mine.

"Emry, get the fuck out of there now. You can't trust your mother. She's dangerous."

I stop ten feet from the cars, confused and curious, but also a little unnerved. Theo doesn't know my mom. She's not perfect, but she's still my mom.

"Mom, what are you doing here?" I call out.

Theo's in the field behind me, yelling now with his words for me to come back, but I can't bring myself to turn to him.

"I've been trying to find you." My mother doesn't meet my eyes, and even though her words are clear, they're distant somehow. She's talking through me, avoiding looking at her daughter.

"What's wrong with you?" I ask her. Something's off, but I can't figure it out. Everything feels wrong since I bonded, so the feeling isn't too unfamiliar, but my mother's usually a force to be reckoned with. Here she seems... sad.

"Mom?" I walk towards her, and she stretches out one hand but then drops it to her side.

"I'm really sorry," she answers.

"About the article?" I ask. "I just need a ride right now. We can deal with that later."

"No," she shakes her head and looks to her feet. I'm standing in front of her, looking at how much older she looks. It hasn't been that long since I last saw her, but she's different today. There's no makeup on her face, and her hair hasn't been retouched in months. Thick wrinkles surround her mouth and eyes, and she pales, turning almost green before me. I touch her arm that rests on the open car door, but she jerks it away.

"Are you sick?" I ask her.

"They said they can help," she mutters to her feet.

I hear Theo yell out, his fear evident in his tone. He's sprinting towards me, but it's too late. Someone puts a black sack over my head as two men pick me up and throw me into the back of the car.

We speed away as Theo rages and screams. His fury courses through me, but an unfamiliar scent fills my nostrils, making me hazy. I can't force myself awake or fight my way out of the car, my body limp in seconds.

His voice is the last thing I hear before I drift off.

"We'll find you."

CHAPTER 40

It's been four days since Theodore Lorwerth and Sebastian Owens (Crowe) reported the kidnapping of Emry Crawford (Crowe) from the NeXus facility.

Marcus Lake has been arrested and held for questioning in relation to the abduction. Upon Emry and Theo's arrival at NeXus, Marcus was paid a half-million dollars from an offshore bank account. Authorities theorize his payment was in exchange for information, and upon further review, he wasn't alone. Four other members of security received similar payouts, keeping Emry and Theo under close watch.

But from whom?

External cameras from NeXus could not reach the abduction location, but there are rumors that both parties close to the couple personally as well as NeXus employees took part in the kidnapping. Theodore Lorwerth states abductors tied Emry up, placing a cloth bag over her head before tossing her into a vehicle. His report is not under question, considering his bond with Emry, but the world is in shock at the accusation.

Who would hurt a bonded that is so willing to partake in research this soon after a bond?

The most likely culprit?

Authorities have denied this, but The Genome Theory continues to arise in conversation.

Those responsible for the Genome Theory's inception and funding have been held accountable, but rumors never ceased that some members of the collective still believe in its cause. If the Genome Theory exists, someone is footing the bill. In a world filled with people obsessed with finding the bond, this is entirely possible, if not probable.

Certainly... it's profitable.

It's suspected that hundreds of employees made up the Genome Theory, and only thirty-seven served time for the crimes against children. With the victims dwindling from view, either making themselves unknown or succumbing to rampant suicides, who will put the others to justice?

NeXus offered a formal comment:

THE ABDUCTION OF EMRY CRAWFORD (CROWE) ON OUR WATCH IS INEXCUSABLE. WE ARE COOPERATING WITH THE JUDICIAL BOARD AND LAUNCHING OUR OWN INVESTIGATION AND SEARCH. NEXUS WILL NOT ALLOW EMRY TO REMAIN UNFOUND.

Strong words with lots of promises.

Those close to the case say they believe Emry's husband Sebastian Owens is leading the task force to find her. It would only make sense that Theodore Lorwerth would also be heavily involved in the search, having bonded with the victim.

Experts believe this bond will lead them to Emry, and soon, but under what circumstances and conditions will she be returned?

Do the abductors want money or something else?

Various reports of Theodore and Sebastian spotted together have yet to be substantiated, but would they work together in a search for Emry? The scorned lover and fated mate may create their own bond to save her.

Now that's a story this news outlet can't wait to cover.

TO CONTINUE READING...

The completion of the Fate and Flame duet can be found on Amazon. It is titled, Twin Flame.

For other works and signed paperback copies visit www.lizhambletonbooks.com and read below.

The Storm Series is a completed trilogy. It follows Rowan as she navigates a post-apocalyptic future with her twin nephews. She stumbles across an unconscious man, and they create a family together in the chaos of this new world.

The first book in the series is The Third Storm.

The Center Duet is a romance set in a dystopian future where marriage is only promised for ten years at a time before you are forced to renew or find a new partner.

The first book in the Duet is The Discovery Center.

Affluence is a dark romance standalone about a woman who comes back to her island job ten years later to seek revenge and come face to face with the man she still loves.

Keep in Touch is a contemporary second-chance romance standalone about a woman who moves to another country. She wants to connect with a pen pal she's kept since childhood, but an unexpected romance blossoms along the way.